KISSING THE MARQUIS

"Come here, lass." Ross grabbed her hand and led her behind the trees lining the path. He smiled into her questioning gaze and gently drew her closer.

Blaze knew he was going to kiss her. And she was going to allow it.

His head dipped lower, his mouth inched closer, his breath mingled with hers. His lips were warm and firm, his kiss gently persuasive, his invitation subtle.

Accepting his invitation, Blaze pressed herself against him. Ross wrapped his arms around her body, and her hands slid up his chest to entwine his neck.

His mouth on hers sent delicious shivers down her spine. She sighed, surrendering to these new sensations.

The kiss deepened, demanding her response. She met his growing passion with equal fervor. The world faded away, leaving her alone in the universe with only this man . . .

Books by Patricia Grasso

TO TAME A DUKE

TO TEMPT AN ANGEL

TO CHARM A PRINCE

TO CATCH A COUNTESS

TO LOVE A PRINCESS

SEDUCING THE PRINCE

PLEASURING THE PRINCE

TEMPTING THE PRINCE

ENTICING THE PRINCE

MARRYING THE MARQUIS

Published by Zebra Books

MARRYING The MARQUIS

PATRICIA GRASSO

ZEBRA BOOKS
KENSINGTON PUBLISHING CORP.
http://www.kensingtonbooks.com

ZEBRA BOOKS are published by

Kensington Publishing Corp.
119 West 40th Street
New York, NY 10018

All Kensington titles, imprints, and distributed lines are available at special quantity discounts for bulk purchases for sales
promotion, premiums, fund-raising, educational, or institu-
tional use.

Special book excerpts or customized printings can also be created to fit specific needs. For details, write or phone the office
of the Kensington Special Sales Manager: Attn. Special Sales
Department. Kensington Publishing Corp., 119 West 40th
Street, New York, NY 10018. Phone: 1-800-221-2647.

Zebra and the Z logo Reg. U.S. Pat. & TM Off.

ISBN-13: 978-0-8217-8074-9
ISBN-10: 0-8217-8074-3

First Printing: December 2009
10 9 8 7 6 5 4 3 2 1

Printed in the United States of America

Chapter One

Newmarket, England

The duchess was giving her grief.
Blaze Flambeau crossed the bedchamber to the window overlooking the gardens. Her lips quirked in grudging admiration for her stepmother, a woman determined to reach her goals, not unlike herself.

Her Grace refused to accept that she planned never to marry, and discussing the situation with her father had not helped. He had shrugged at her complaint and explained that his dearest Roxie wanted everyone to marry and live as happily as she. Of course, as the duke's second wife, his dearest Roxie had not been abandoned at home while her husband sired seven daughters on Gabrielle Flambeau, his long-time lover.

Blaze knew she would not feel differently once she had met—as her father insisted—the right man, her true love. What had love given her mother except heartache and seven daughters?

Scanning the world outside her window, Blaze

spotted the gardeners performing their daily chores. She would need to wait before slipping outside to complete her task.

Blaze leaned against the windowsill, willing the gardeners to hurry, when the first stirrings of dread seeped into her consciousness. Her stepmother had invited several bachelors to dine with the family that evening, and nobody refused an invitation from the Duke and Duchess of Inverary.

Snoring from the bed intruded on her thoughts, drawing her attention. Puddles was lying in the middle of her bed, all four limbs outstretched. The brindled mastiff looked like he was sleeping off a seven-day drunk.

Blaze wandered across the room to the cheval mirror. Studying her reflection, she wondered how she appeared to gentlemen.

Gawd, she hated her freckles, and her red hair accentuated the sprinkling of dots across the bridge of her nose. Blushing diminished the tiny flaws, but she could not blush every minute of every day for the remainder of her life.

If only she had inherited the Flambeau black hair and flawless complexion. A Scots ancestor—Aunt Bedelia Campbell, her father said—had sent the riotous red hair and freckles through time and space to land on her, making her the cuckoo in the nest. The classic Flambeau beauty had even touched her own twin, who looked nothing like her.

What sane gentleman would offer for a redhaired, freck-led-faced monkey? Blaze asked herself.

A blind man, came her honest answer, *or a man*

desiring a close connection with the influential Duke of Inverary.

She supposed her freckles did not matter, though. Attracting a husband did not appear on her list of priorities. Winning the thoroughbred races that season would give her the money to reach her goal. Or, at least, set her plan into motion.

And yet . . . A smile touched her lips when she recalled the handsome gentleman who had requested a dance at her sister's wedding the previous year. Waltzing with the Marquis of Somewhere-Or-Other had made her feel almost pretty. At least for the dance's duration.

The fond memory disappeared as quickly as it had come. The marquis had proceeded to dance with every female guest, no matter her age or appearance. Blaze could not fault the marquis for failing to request a second dance. She *had* stepped on his feet several times.

Gazing out the window again, Blaze noted the gardeners had finished their chores and gone. She grabbed the bulging sack stowed beside her bed.

"Outside, Puddles," she called, heading for the door.

Awakened by the word *out,* the black-masked mastiff bolted off the bed. He trotted beside her down the corridor.

Blaze stopped at the next door and peered into her twin's bedchamber. Working on ledgers, her sister sat at a table near the window.

"Bliss?"

"I'm too busy at the moment," her sister said without looking up. "Ask someone else."

Blaze closed the door. Her twin was always busy when she needed her assistance.

Continuing down the hall, Blaze paused at her sister Serena's bedchamber and pressed her ear to the door. The sound of muted voices in conversation reached her. She opened the door. Apparently, Serena was posing for Sophia, her artistic identical twin.

Blaze cleared her throat. "Sisters?"

Both twins looked at her, their gazes dropping to the sack in her hands. "No," they said simultaneously, and then giggled.

Blaze closed the door and walked the length of the corridor to her youngest sibling's door. She raised her fist to knock but heard her sister's voice.

"Come inside, Blaze."

That made her smile. Raven always knew things in advance. She wondered if her sister could tell her how successful the thoroughbred racing season would prove.

Blaze stepped into her sister's chamber. "Will you—?"

"I've been waiting for you," Raven interrupted, crossing the chamber, "but I am not digging."

"I will bury the deceased."

Raven smiled at that. "What if Her Grace catches you?"

"I'll say I was simply playing an April Fool's joke on her," she answered.

"You are sneaky."

Blaze gave her a sunshine smile. "Thank you for the compliment, sister."

"Do you have a shovel?" Raven asked, following her into the hallway.

"I hid one behind the gazebo." Blaze started to walk down the corridor to the main staircase.

Raven touched her arm. "Using the servants' stairs will be more discreet."

Blaze retraced her steps in the opposite direction. "You are almost as sneaky as I am."

Raven threw her arm across her shoulders in camaraderie. "Sneakiness must run in our family."

"Did we inherit our sneakiness from the Flambeaus or the Campbells?"

"Both, probably."

Hurrying down the back stairs to the garden door, Blaze and Raven stepped into an unseasonably warm April afternoon. They walked through the formal gardens and passed the maze's clipped hedges. Ahead of them stretched an expanse of manicured lawns and then the woodland, the white gazebo standing guard between the two.

Birdsong wafted through the air, catching Blaze's attention. She looked up at the sky. High, thin clouds diluted its blue brilliance, and a hawk was gliding on a breeze while searching for its next meal.

Walking around the gazebo, Blaze grabbed the shovel and returned to where Raven sat on the structure's top step. Puddles dashed around, enjoying his freedom like a felon released from Newgate.

With her right foot on the shovel, Blaze used her weight to lift the top layer of grass and gently set it aside. She repeated this again and again until she had the width and the length of the hole she wanted to dig.

"Life seems different with Fancy and Belle married," Blaze said as she worked. "You will be gone, too, in a couple of months."

"I may need to postpone the wedding," Raven told her.

Blaze stopped digging. "Why is that?"

"I feel one of my sisters may need to use the wedding plans for herself."

"Which sister?" Blaze asked, her blue gaze narrowing.

"I don't know everything," Raven said. "Why are you setting the grass aside?"

"Once the hole is filled," she answered, "I will replace the grass, and no one will notice the grave."

"That *is* sneaky," Raven said. "Alex will be arriving in Newmarket this afternoon."

"Are he and the constable investigating the jockey's murder?" Blaze asked, glancing at her.

"I suppose so, but they will be staying at his grandfather's estate," her sister answered. "Alex may be following the thoroughbreds when they leave Newmarket if the crime remains unsolved."

Blaze fixed her thoughts on her own thoroughbred, a gift from her father, and the filly's success during the racing season. She wanted to ask her sister if Pegasus would win but feared the answer.

"You will experience joy, sadness, and surprise," Raven said, her smile ambiguous.

"Do you mean Pegasus will win?" Her digging forgotten for the moment, Blaze sat beside her sister.

"Your filly will beat the others," Raven answered, "but she must overcome a slight problem first."

Her comment surprised Blaze. "What is the problem?"

"I don't know, but you will find the solution to it."

Blaze smiled at the encouraging words. "Pegasus loves running."

"Doesn't winning require strategy, too?"

Blaze considered the question. She hadn't thought about strategy in terms of horse racing. "I will speak to Rooney," she said, referring to her jockey.

"Wait until he's sober," Raven advised her.

"Rooney promised me no drinking during the season." Blaze rose from her perch and resumed digging. "Her Grace invited several bachelors to dinner this evening."

"Stepmama has invited three bachelors," Raven told her.

"That takes care of Bliss, Serena, and Sophia," Blaze said, her mood brightening. For the first time in her life, she enjoyed being overlooked. "Perhaps the duchess has accepted my preference for remaining unmarried."

"If I were you," Raven said, "I wouldn't wager on that. Why don't you want to marry?"

Blaze tossed a shovelful of dirt aside and then looked her sister in the eye. "Testicles cause trouble."

Raven laughed at that. "Sister, all three bachelors have been invited to meet you."

"Me?" Blaze stopped digging to brush a wisp of fiery hair away from her face. "That woman will not rest until she marries me off. I don't think she likes me."

"Stepmama is giving you a choice," Raven told her. "That means she likes you best."

"What if I don't want anyone?"

"That is *not* one of your choices." Raven smiled, adding, "Her Grace possesses a wealth of knowledge for living with troublesome testicles."

"Have you been following her advice?"

Her sister nodded. "I am becoming adept at confounding Alex."

"I should speak to Her Grace before the Jockey Club Ball," Blaze said, and then a troubling thought stepped from the shadows of her mind. "What if none of those bachelors interests me? What if I don't interest them? What if one interests me, but I do not interest him?"

"You think too much," Raven said. "Relax and enjoy the competition for your affections."

"Humph, Bliss says I do not think at all." Blaze tossed another shovelful of dirt aside. "The man I marry should love me even if I were not the Duke of Inverary's daughter, but how will I know which gentleman is sincere?"

"You will know in your heart."

"Gawd, you sound like Papa."

"Miss Raven."

Both sisters turned at the call and spied Tinker, the duke's majordomo, hurrying toward them.

"The Marquis of Basildon has arrived," Tinker announced, reaching them.

"Thank you, Tinker." Raven rose from her perch on the stair. "Tell the marquis I will be along shortly."

"Yes, Miss Raven." Tinker turned to walk away but paused, his gaze shifting from Blaze to the shovel in her hand and the hole.

"You did not see me digging this hole," she said.

The man's lips twitched. "I have not seen you all afternoon, Miss Blaze."

"Thank you, Tinker."

"You are very welcome." The majordomo started across the lawn toward the mansion.

Blaze looked at her sister. "How will you confound Alex today?"

"I will take the long way round," Raven answered. "Walking slowly, of course. I believe that will set the tone for his visit. I would never want him to think I had been waiting for him."

"Were you waiting for him?"

"Yes." With that, Raven walked away.

Blaze patted her dog's massive head. "Good boy, Puddles." Then she resumed her digging, pressing the shovel into the dirt with her foot before scooping it up and tossing it aside.

A sudden chill danced down her spine, and an uncanny feeling of being watched seeped into her senses. She could almost feel someone's gaze on her.

Blaze stilled, her gaze drifting to the mastiff lying relaxed in the sunshine. Which meant there was no imminent danger.

Nevertheless, Blaze could not shake the feeling. She scanned the woodland behind the gazebo but saw nothing. Then she whirled around to scan the lawns and formal garden. No one was lurking about.

Blaze lifted her gaze to the mansion's windows and caught movement in one of the second-floor rooms. That would be her father's office.

Damn, damn, damn. Trouble had found her again.

Blaze knew she would be getting another lecture from her father and stepmother on proper deportment. Digging in the dirt would never be considered a ladylike pursuit.

And then she smiled. Thank God for those bachelors. If they arrived early, the bachelors could save her from a dressing down.

What the hell is she doing?

Ross MacArthur, the Marquis of Awe, stood at the duke's office window and watched the petite redhead digging his kinsman's manicured lawns. He'd never seen a gardening girl, never mind one bent on ruining a fine lawn.

The marquis admired the girl's fiery hair glinting in the afternoon's sun. A smile touched his lips when she bent over to scoop another shovelful of dirt, offering him the sight of her backside's delightful shape in the light gown she wore.

When the girl looked over her shoulder, Ross scanned the area. He wanted to see what had distracted her, but the gardens appeared deserted.

Resuming her task, the gardening girl tossed another shovelful of dirt. A moment later, she paused again, this time facing the mansion.

Ross guessed the girl felt watched. She stood motionless, staring at the mansion, and he knew her gaze was traveling from window to window.

"Come here, Ross," the Duke of Inverary beckoned him. "I want to test your whisky knowledge."

"Ye pour the whisky into a glass and drink it," Ross said, turning away from the window, his dark gaze on his kinsman. "What more do I need to know?"

Ross smiled at the duke's irritated expression.

Heavily invested in the business, the duke and his own father believed whisky akin to chalice wine.

"Never joke about whisky or horses," the Duke of Inverary warned him.

Sauntering across the office, Ross dropped into a chair in front of the desk. Five chunky glasses, each containing a measure of whisky, stood in a line on the desk.

Ross wondered the reason he'd been summoned. Inverary was as wily as his own father, and Ross knew damn well that he hadn't been invited here for the purpose of tasting whisky.

"Isna investin' in Campbell whisky enough?" Ross managed to appear relaxed in the leather chair. "What scheme are ye and my father hatchin'?"

"I need to decide if you're worthy," the duke told him.

His dark gaze narrowed on the older man. "Worthy of what?"

The Duke of Inverary smiled. "I will tell you that by and by."

The duke's inscrutable smile meant trouble. His own father wore that same expression when he wanted something.

Ross slid his gaze to the Jockey Club's Triple Crown trophies, which the Inverary stables had won the previous year, reminding him of his perpetual second place finishes. He planned to win the coveted trophies this year, or at the very least prevent his kinsman from taking home the honor again. The same horse needed to win the three main classic races.

"Very well, Yer Grace." Ross lifted the first glass

and sipped the whisky, holding it in his mouth, letting the warmth of his tongue release its flavors. "Full-bodied, muscular, and bold." He set the glass on the desk. "Highland whisky, of course."

The duke smiled at the correct answer. "How is your father?"

"Da, Stepmama, and the Feathered Flock will be arrivin' in Newmarket before the Jockey Club Ball," Ross answered.

"What is the Feathered Flock?"

"My sister and stepsister will be bringin' Drucilla Gordon, Catriona Calder, and Felicia Burns," Ross told him. "I called them the Feathered Flock because they're constantly preenin' and twitterin' like canaries."

"All women preen and twitter, especially wives and daughters of aristocrats," Inverary said. "I recall your father was hoping for a match between you and the Gordon girl."

"My stepmother was pushin' for a match between me and my stepsister," Ross said, reaching for the second glass of whisky, "but I've no inclination to wed her or one of my sister's friends." He kept the liquid in his mouth a moment before swallowing. "Elegant and floral. Lowland whisky, no doubt."

The Duke of Inverary nodded at his answer. "I never hear your name attached to any ladies."

"I dinna trifle with maidens or marrieds."

"Do you keep a mistress?"

The question gave Ross an unexpected jolt, putting him on guard. "Why do ye ask?"

Inverary shrugged, his inscrutable smile appearing

again. "Simple curiosity while passing time with my favorite cousin's son."

Curiosity, my arse. Ross smelled a trap. Inverary had never been prone to idle curiosity. His duchess was another matter, though.

"Where has Douglas Gordon been hiding himself lately?" Inverary asked, changing the subject.

Ross relaxed again. "Dougie's been delayed in London, confounded by this Seven Doves Company undercuttin' his prices, but he'll arrive in Newmarket before the Jockey Ball."

"I suppose you'll be stayin' with Gordon once this Feathered Flock perches at your home," the duke said.

Ross shook his head. "I keep rooms at the Rowley Lodge to escape the twitterers."

"Did you hear what happened to Charlie?"

"I heard he'd been stabbed in a tavern brawl, God rest his soul," Ross said, reaching for the third glass of whisky.

"Thoroughbred racing's best jockey would never have been involved in a brawl two weeks before the first race," the duke said. "I've given Harry the nod to ride Thor."

"Perhaps Charlie was reluctantly drawn into the brawl."

"Someone murdered Charlie to prevent his winning me the Crown again this year," Inverary said. "Alexander Blake is arriving today for the races and helping Constable Black investigate the murder. Hiring London's most famous constable is costing me a fortune."

"Ye can afford it." Ross sipped the whisky. "This spicy taste screams Campbeltown whisky."

The Duke of Inverary smiled. "You are three for three, lad."

"What's this I heard aboot a monkey livin' with ye?" Ross asked, resting his tongue before continuing the whisky tasting.

"My daughter acquired a Capuchin monkey," Inverary said, rolling his eyes. "Blaze inherited my aunt Bedelia's affinity with animals. Did your father ever tell you stories about Aunt Bedelia?"

"Ye mean the witch?" Ross asked, reaching for the fourth glass of whisky.

"Bedelia was no witch," the duke said, "but she did possess several unusual gifts, one of which was communing with animals."

Ross sipped the whisky, savoring its flavor. "Speyside whisky, soft and lovely but no Lowland lady."

"Correct again, lad." Inverary continued his story, "Anyway, Blaze acquired Miss Giggles, but Roxie insisted the monkey needed to go."

Ross's lips quirked in a barely suppressed smile at the duke's predicament. "Monkeys are such wee, cute creatures."

"Do you know how a monkey expresses displeasure?"

Ross shook his head.

"The monkey tosses its feces," the duke told him, "and Miss Giggles took an instant dislike to my wife's good friend, Lady Althorpe."

Ross chuckled. "I wish I could've seen that."

"I needed to lose the monkey," Inverary said, gesturing to the last glass of whisky, "or I would lose my wife. On the other hand, I'd lose my daughter if I used my pistol on it."

"How did ye solve the problem?" Ross sipped the whisky, the warmth of his tongue releasing its distinctive taste. "Peaty and smoky, this Islay has been aged better than fifteen years, I'd say."

The Duke of Inverary nodded his approval and then finished his story. "I sat Blaze down and explained that Giggles, being an adult female, needed a husband. Though it broke her heart, my daughter saw the sense in that and agreed to give Miss Giggles to the Tower Menagerie. I bought the monkey a husband, and the two recently became parents. Problem solved."

"Good thinkin' on yer part," Ross said. "Now, tell me what I'm worthy of."

"You are worthy to marry one of my daughters," Inverary answered.

Ross coughed and reached for a glass of whisky. He gulped a healthy swig and shuddered as the potent liquid burned a path to his stomach.

"Russian princes are all very well," the duke was saying, "but I aim for some of my girls to wed sturdy Scotsmen."

"I'm honored," Ross hedged, "but our families dinna need another connection, ye and my father bein' cousins and all."

"My wife has decided," Inverary said, his gaze narrowing on the younger man. "Accept your fate, Ross. After all, you need to marry someone and get an heir."

"Which daughter does the duchess have in mind?"

"Blaze."

"The animal communicator?"

"You breed and race thoroughbreds," the duke said, "and my Blaze added to the Inverary coffers by picking last year's winners."

Ross slid his gaze to the Triple Crown trophies. "Did she ever pick a loser?"

"I don't believe so."

Ross knew he'd been hooked neater than any fish. "How does she do it?"

"You will need to ask her."

"I will certainly enjoy meetin' Blaze," Ross said, trying to sound casual.

"There is a minor problem," Inverary warned him. "Blaze refuses to marry and intends to win enough money this racing season—I gave her a filly—to open a refuge for unwanted horses, dogs, and cats. Naturally, Roxie worries the girl will end a spinster."

"Yer daughter has ambition," Ross said. "Which filly did ye give her?"

"I gave her Pegasus," the duke answered, "and Rooney will jockey her."

"Pegasus balks at goin' through holes," Ross said, "and Rooney is a drunkard. Ye've set yer daughter up for failure."

"Blaze needs to learn that horse racing can be a difficult and heartbreaking business," the duke replied.

"I dinna ken the reason ye keep Rooney on yer payroll," Ross added.

"My grandfather was his great-grandfather," Inverary answered, "though Rooney hails from the illegitimate branch of the family." The duke smiled, adding, "Rooney got Aunt Bedelia's red hair, too, and could pass as my daughter's brother. I thought you and Blaze could become acquainted under the guise of helping her."

"Mind ye, I amna agreein' to marriage at this moment," Ross said, "but I'm curious to know if yer plannin' to force the lass down the aisle."

"Roxie insists on giving this daughter a choice," the duke told him, "but she does favor you."

Ross loved nothing more than a challenge. "Who's my competition?"

"Prince Lykos Kazanov and Dirk Stanley have been invited to dine with us tonight."

"My stepbrother is a compulsive gambler."

"Roxie decided to give Blaze the choice of a prince, a marquis, and an earl," the duke said, "but we don't expect her to choose Dirk."

"I'll be lookin' forward to meetin' the lass and my royal competition," Ross said, stretching his long legs out. The racing season could prove interesting as well as lucrative.

"You'll like her," Inverary said. "My Blaze has a big heart along with a hot temper to match her fiery hair, which she also inherited from Bedelia Campbell."

Ross crossed the office to the window and gestured outside. "Is that Blaze?"

The Duke of Inverary joined him there. "What is she doing to my lawn?"

Blaze dropped the shovel and, opening a sack, pulled out a fur. Shaking her head, she folded the fur and placed it in the hole. Then she reached into the sack again, producing another fur.

"Good God, she's burying my wife's fur coats."

Ross shouted with laughter, and the Duke of Inverary chuckled. Neither heard the door opening.

"My lord, you were able to join us," a woman said, by way of a greeting.

Both men whirled around at the sound of the duchess's voice. They stood with their backs against the window to block her view.

"You gentlemen look guilty," Roxie teased them, crossing the chamber. "What are you hiding?" The duchess peered out the window through the space between their bodies, the girl's red hair catching her attention. "What is Blaze doing?"

"I believe she's buryin' yer furs."

"Oh, dear God." The duchess swooned at his words.

Ross caught her before she dropped to the floor and, with the duke's help, carried her to the sofa in front of the hearth. Inverary dropped on his knees beside his wife.

"Send a maid to fetch hartshorn," the duke instructed him, "and then go outside and save my wife's furs."

Ross started for the door but paused halfway across the chamber. "Yer Grace, I'll take the lass," he said, smiling, and turned to leave. "If she's agreeable to the match, that is."

"MacArthur wants to marry Blaze?" he heard the duchess exclaim in a surprisingly strong voice. "Even though the little witch is burying my furs?"

"I daresay the lad wants to marry her *because* she's burying your furs."

The door clicked shut behind Ross, but he'd heard the laughter in his kinsman's voice. His conniving father must have told the duke how to pique his interest.

Ross decided he would play along. After all, he was competing against a prince and an earl, a foreigner and a gambler. He enjoyed winning, and his stepbrother was inferior competition. The prince might give him a bit of trouble, but that would make winning so much sweeter.

The lass would not prove a problem, but her dog was a monster. Wheedling a few treats from the cook would suit his purpose in keeping the dog sweet.

Once armed with the dog's favorite cinnamon cookies, Ross strolled across the duke's lawns in the direction of the gazebo, his gaze fixed on the petite redhead's backside as she bent over. His future bride had herself a fetching arse. True, she was no bigger than a mite, the perfect size for a jockey had she been born male.

Lucky for him, the lass had been born female. That glorious red hair positively screamed stubborn determination. Life with her would never bore him.

Ross recalled the dance they had shared at her sister's wedding. Her small, perfectly proportioned breasts had enticed him. The fine sprinkling of freckles across the bridge of her delicate nose had intrigued him, and he'd wondered if she sported freckles anywhere else on her body.

He'd been tempted to seduce her that night, but no sane man trifled with Inverary's daughters. Besides, seducing maidens and marrieds was dangerous in the extreme.

Apparently, both Inverary and his own father

wanted him to marry her. He would demolish the other two contenders and win the lass's hand in marriage. By fair means or foul.

Ross glanced at the mastiff, wagging its tail at his approach. No protection for her there.

Standing with his hands on his hips, Ross willed her to turn around. She was muttering to the dog about the slaughter of animals and remained oblivious to his presence.

"Drop the fur, lass."

Blaze gasped and whirled around. Surprise made her stumble back, but she managed to remain standing. Beside her, Puddles was wagging his tail like a conductor's baton, which meant the mastiff sensed no danger.

She recognized the intruder. They had waltzed together in dozens of her daydreams during the previous year. Now he stood in front of her.

More than six feet tall, the Marquis of Somewhere was not a man easily forgotten. He reminded her of a warrior, his broad shoulders and tapered waist shown to best advantage in expensive clothing.

His face was arrestingly handsome, his lips generously chiseled. The hint of a dimple on his chin softened the aura of ruggedness. His hair was blacker than a moonless midnight, his eyes gleaming black diamonds.

Gawd, the Marquis of Somewhere reeked of masculinity.

His expression irritated her, though. He was staring as if he'd never seen her before, never shared a dance at her sister's wedding.

That hurt.

Blaze knew no one would consider her an acclaimed beauty, but no one would lose lunch by looking at her face. The insult rankled, demanding she repay him in kind.

"Who are you?"

"Ye wound me, lass." He placed a hand over his heart. "Dinna ye recall us sharin' a dance at yer sister's weddin'?"

Blaze tilted her head, studying his face, and then shrugged. "I cannot remember every gentleman who requests a dance." A tightening of his lips told her she'd hit her mark.

"Allow me to refresh yer memory," he said. "I am Ross MacArthur, the Marquis of Awe."

"A pleasure to make your acquaintance. Again, I mean." Blaze waved her hand in a shooing gesture. "Run along, my lord. I am in the middle of a funeral."

The marquis chuckled. His response did not sit well with her.

"Yer father sent me to stop the burial." Ross lifted the fur out of her hand. "Her Grace caught yer act and swooned."

Blaze looked at Puddles. *Scare man.*

The mastiff stood, hackles raised, baring its fangs and growling. Drool dripped from its muzzle.

Keeping his gaze on the dog, Ross reached into his pocket and produced a cinnamon cookie. He held it in the palm of his hand, offering it to the dog.

Puddles whined and wagged his tail, inching closer and closer to the treat. Gently, the mastiff took the cookie. *Man good.*

That surprised Blaze. She would have called the mastiff a traitor, but he did not know the word.

"What's yer dog's name?" Ross asked, folding the fur and placing it into the sack.

"I named him Puddles, for the usual reason."

Ross smiled at that and retrieved the other furs from their grave. After shaking them out, he returned them to the sack.

"You take the duchess her dead animal skins," Blaze said, grabbing the shovel. "I will fill the hole."

"I dinna take orders from ye or anyone else." Ross lifted the shovel out of her hand and tossed it aside. "The gardener will do it." He gestured to the gazebo, saying, "Sit there. I want to speak with ye aboot the racin' season."

Blaze would have mentioned that she did not take orders either, but curiosity stifled the urge to walk away. Without argument, she climbed the gazebo stairs and sat on a bench.

After tossing the mastiff a couple of cookies, the marquis followed and dropped beside her on the bench. Her gaze downcast, Blaze noted his thigh flirting with her skirt and inched away, which gave him the space for a relaxed sprawl. She shied away when his thigh touched her skirt again.

"Ye'll fall off the edge if ye keep movin'."

Blaze heard the smile in his voice and looked up. His black gaze disturbed her as did his amusement at her expense.

"I race thoroughbreds so I know somethin' aboot the business," the marquis said. "Yer father tells me he gave ye a horse."

Pegasus. Blaze smiled, thinking of her Arabian.

"Yer filly finished last in her only two races," Ross told her.

"Pegasus runs faster than any of my father's horses," Blaze said, dismissing his statement. "We will qualify and take the Classic Three to win the Triple Crown."

"I admire yer confidence," he said, "but speed doesna matter if yer horse balks at goin' through holes."

Holes? Blaze had no idea to what he was referring and too proud to ask. Pegasus loved running and had even beaten her father's Thor in trial matches as well as the previous year's champion, Zeus.

"I'll help ye," the marquis said, "but I canna promise success in overcomin' the flaw."

"Why do you want to help me beat you?" Blaze could not mask the suspicion in her tone.

Ross gave her an easy smile. "I like red hair and freckles?"

Stiffening at the mention of her flaw, Blaze struggled against the urge to hide her freckles behind a hand. "I appreciate your offer"—she managed an insincere smile—"but I prefer to solve my own problems."

"I'm insistin', not offerin'." Ross lifted a hand, but she shrank back. "Ye've a smudge of dirt, lass." Holding her chin in one hand, he brushed a thumb across her cheek.

Blaze froze, torn between enjoying the warmth of his touch and fleeing. Her blue eyes widened as his face inched closer, closer, closer.

"Don't kiss me." Blaze bolted off the bench, needing to distance herself from the possibility of her first kiss and his mere presence.

Ross grinned. "Ye canna condemn a man for tryin' to steal a kiss from a pretty girl."

He thought her pretty?

Blaze knew she was behaving badly, but she had no experience with gentlemen. There must be a way to discourage a gentleman without causing a scene. She needed to speak with her stepmother as her sister had suggested.

"I will not condemn you," Blaze said, gathering her dignity, "nor will I allow you a kiss." She turned away, calling, "Come, Puddles."

"Will ye sit with me at dinner?"

Damn, the Scotsman was one of the bachelors.

Blaze opened her mouth to refuse but lost her courage, his gaze stealing her words. If she couldn't find her voice with him looking at her, how could she manage eating dinner?

Opting for an easy escape, Blaze cleared her throat. "My stepmother decides who sits where." Then she left the gazebo, her dog trotting beside her.

Blaze walked in the direction of the stables instead of crossing the lawns to the mansion. Was the marquis watching her? She imagined his black gaze on her back.

Unable to control herself, Blaze peeked over her shoulder and then felt a heated blush rising on her cheeks. MacArthur stood near the gazebo, a smile on his face, his gaze fixed on her. And then he wiggled his fingers at her.

Blaze quickened her pace, which elicited his laughter. The sound of his amusement echoed in her ears and chased her down the path to the stables.

Chapter Two

The Scotsman possessed an inflated opinion of his own charms. She did not like him, nor did she trust him an inch. He must have wheedled a dinner invitation from her stepmother and offered her his assistance in order to spy on Pegasus or her father's Thor.

Could this hole be the problem Raven had sensed? If so, she would solve the problem without the marquis's help.

Blaze walked into the stable, her dog beside her. She paused inside the door, letting her eyes become accustomed to the shadows.

The musky odor of horses mingled with the scents of hay and oiled leather. The familiar sounds of snorting horses and their hollow clumping movements calmed her.

"Rooney?"

No answer.

Blaze strolled down the stable's straw-covered floorboards to one particular stall. Pegasus snorted a greeting, and she stroked the Arabian's dish face.

"Hello, my beauty," Blaze whispered, her tone a loving caress. And then faint mumbling drew her attention. "Rooney, are you here?"

The mumbling grew into grumbling.

Leaving her horse, Blaze peered into the last stall. With a bottle in his hand, her jockey was rising from the straw.

"I heard you," Rooney said, swaying on his feet. "You don't need to shout."

The jockey was short and slight, his shocking red hair surpassing hers in brilliance. Her own freckles seemed minuscule when compared with his.

Without a word, Blaze lifted the bottle out of his hand and sniffed its contents. Spirits.

Her anger rising, Blaze suffered the urge to smash the bottle of swill into pieces. Her mother's image rose in her mind's eye, taking her to another place and time. She could not repeat the worst day of her life.

Holding his glazed eyes captive, Blaze poured the bottle's contents onto the floorboards. "You promised me no drinking during racing season."

"Racing begins a week from today," Rooney defended himself.

Blaze arched a copper brow at him. "Do you want to win the Triple Crown?"

"Every jockey in England wishes for that."

"I'll take your statement as a *yes*," Blaze said. "Do you want to win enough to quit drinking? If not, tell me now, and I'll find another rider."

"Pegasus is a filly," Rooney said, "and she will never beat your father's Thor or MacArthur's Hercules or even Dirk Stanley's Emperor."

"She *will* win." Blaze turned to leave. "You're fired. I'll find another rider."

"Wait," Rooney stopped her. "How do you know Peg can beat those colts?"

"She told me."

Rooney shouted with laughter. Her hands itched to slap him, a most unladylike urge.

"Pegasus deserves better than a faithless drunk," Blaze said, her voice dripping contempt. "I'll send a footman with another bottle of poison, and you can guzzle yourself into an early grave."

"I'll ride her," Rooney said, his hand on her arm. "I won't take another drink, not a sip."

Blaze studied his face, trying to gauge his sincerity and, more importantly, his inner strength. Living with her mother had taught her that drink could waylay the best intentions.

"I promise," Rooney added, "but His Grace gave you a flawed horse."

The hole.

"The Marquis of Awe mentioned that Pegasus balks at going through holes," Blaze said. "Explain the hole."

"The empty space between two horses is called a hole," Rooney told her. "Though Peg is the fastest horse I've ever seen, she refuses to pass through holes to get ahead."

"What about going around the horses?"

"That wastes time," Rooney answered, "which is the reason Peg finished last in her only two races. Once the other jockeys discovered the flaw, they teamed up to use it against her."

"Why do you think she refuses to go through holes?"

Rooney shrugged. "Ask her."

That brought a smile to her lips. "Curing Pegasus will surprise those jockeys."

"How do we cure her?"

"Bring Pegasus and two other riders to the track at first light tomorrow," Blaze instructed him. "I will pay for their services and silence."

Hope and uncertainty warred on the jockey's face. "Do you really believe we can cure Peg's problem and win the Triple Crown?"

Blaze gave him a smile meant to encourage. "I know we can."

Dinner with the bachelors loomed before her.

Blaze wished her stepmother had started this nonsense after the racing season. She did not need any distractions stealing her focus from Pegasus and the races.

Delaying the inevitable, Blaze lingered in her bedchamber to study her reflection in the cheval mirror. She wore a pale yellow silk gown with a scalloped, lace-flounced hem and short, puffed sleeves. Thankfully, her stepmother had impeccable taste, and the pale shade complemented her red hair.

Life would have been easier if she had lived during an earlier time when ladies powdered their hair. On the other hand, she might have suffered the same fate as the other Flambeaus and lost her head to the guillotine.

Blaze recalled the stories her mother had told her

and her sisters about fashionable French society. And then the Terror erupted to claim the entire Flambeau family, leaving her mother an orphaned and penniless child countess who had matured into an insecure woman.

Inspecting her complexion in the cheval mirror, Blaze decided her freckles were less noticeable if she squinted but doubted her stepmother had invited squinting bachelors. The marquis hadn't squinted once during their conversation.

The bright side of the situation was she did not want to marry. Her unfashionable red hair and smattering of freckles would discourage suitors. She did not relish rejection, though.

The door swung open, drawing her attention. "You look lovely," Raven said, crossing the chamber.

Blaze eyed her sister's pink gown. "I wish I could wear that color."

"You radiate vibrancy without bright colors," Raven told her. "I would look sallow if I wore your gown."

Blaze appreciated her sister's kindness, but Raven had never looked sallow in her life. Ebony hair and ivory complexions could carry any shade.

"Where are Bliss, Serena, and Sophia?" Blaze asked her.

"Our sisters are hiding in their chambers."

"Cowards."

Raven smiled. "I bring you a message from the duchess."

Blaze grimaced and rolled her eyes. Her Grace was definitely raging about the furs, but the bachelors were delaying the inevitable dressing down.

The only two things her stepmother loved more than furs were expensive jewels and the duke.

"Stepmama's message is to bury all the furs you want," Raven said, surprising her, "because Papa promised to buy her replacements."

Blaze frowned at the thought of more dead animals. She had not considered that alarming possibility. Her stepmother was more cunning than a fox.

"Do not fiddle with your food," Raven added. "Whoever you marry can discover your eating habits after the vows are spoken."

"I am no cannibal," Blaze said, shuddering delicately to emphasize her revulsion. "Would dearest Stepmama prefer I force myself to eat meat and then regurgitate it?"

"Darling, society frowns upon public puking," Raven drawled, imitating the duchess. "Eating meat, fish, and poultry does not constitute cannibalism."

"You wouldn't say that if you could communicate with animals," Blaze said.

"I understand," Raven said, "but most people do not converse with animals."

"Animals do not converse," Blaze told her. "I communicate with them, not engage in conversation."

"You possess a rare gift."

"One woman's gift is another's curse," Blaze said. "Cutting the meat into pieces and swishing them around in my plate will make it appear as if I'd eaten my fill. Don't you think?"

"What a sterling idea." Raven turned toward the door.

Blaze touched her sister's arm. "Are my freckles very noticeable?"

"You see freckles," her sister answered, "but I see pixie dust enhancing your beauty."

Blaze opened the door for her. "I never noticed your poetical nature before."

"Darling, your freckles are setting a trend," Raven drawled, stepping into the hallway. "I predict the other ladies will be painting freckles on their noses before racing season ends."

Blaze smiled at that and fell into step beside her sister. "Tell me what you have learned about gaining the upper hand with gentlemen."

"A positive attitude means everything," Raven said. "Strategy is important because no man can resist a challenge, the most difficult to obtain being the most desired. A serene smile softens tart words and confounds the opposite sex."

"How can I remember all that?"

"Be yourself," Raven advised her, "and the gentlemen will be vying for your attention."

If she behaved as usual, Blaze thought, no gentleman would pursue her. Which would leave her free to concentrate on the racing season.

Blaze doubted any of the gentlemen invited to dinner would court her for a connection with her father. Her stepmother would begin her matchmaking with society's wealthiest, most sought-after eligibles.

"The gents will adore me," Blaze said, exercising her positive attitude, "but what if I cannot like them?"

"What an excellent attitude," Raven complimented

her. "Stepmama will parade bachelors in front of you until one catches your fancy."

The old witch must really want to get rid of me, Blaze thought.

They descended the stairs and headed in the direction of the drawing room. "When Stepmama praises your behavior," Raven whispered, "tell her you have been following her example."

"Do you mean lie?" Blaze asked.

"White lies never hurt anyone," Raven answered.

"Your feeling about Pegasus was correct," Blaze told her, pausing outside the drawing room. "Peg balks at going through holes to get ahead. The Marquis of Awe offered to help me solve the problem. What do you think?"

"Ross MacArthur is wealthy, titled, and handsome," Raven said, "and he loves animals."

"How do you know that?"

"I know because I know," Raven said, irritation tingeing her voice. "Do yourself a favor, and accept the marquis's offer. Otherwise, Pegasus will win no races."

"You know this?"

"I do."

Raven stepped inside the drawing room. Blaze had no choice but walk with her.

The drawing room was invitingly comfortable, more to Blaze's taste than the opulent formality of the duke's London mansion. The cream-colored walls created the perfect background for portraits and matched the gold, cream, and blue Aubusson carpet. Upholstered chairs, sofas, and settees in jewel colors formed intimate groupings around the chamber.

The present duchess's portrait hung above the white marble hearth. On a side wall in a secluded corner was the portrait of her own mother, Gabrielle Flambeau, looking achingly young and carefree as Blaze had never seen her.

Sometimes Blaze sat alone in front of her mother's portrait and talked to her. All her one-sided conversations began with the words *I'm sorry, Mama.*

Her father and stepmother stood near the hearth and conversed with four gentlemen. Blaze recognized Alexander Blake, the Marquis of Basildon, her sister's betrothed. The Marquis of Awe stood with his back to the door as did two other gentlemen, one dark-haired and the other blond.

"Ah, here are two of my lovely stepdaughters," the duchess announced.

All masculine gazes shifted to watch them. Blaze wished her stepmother hadn't done that. Accustomed to being lost in the crowd of six sisters, she disliked being the center of attention.

"Attitude," Raven whispered.

Blaze pasted an ambiguous smile onto her face and glided across the carpet toward them. Eyeing the pianoforte, she prayed no gentleman would request a performance. Her skill offended audiences, and she preferred to do the rejecting.

"You look beautiful, Brat," Alexander Blake was saying to her sister, before sliding his gaze to her. "How are you doing, Freckles?"

Hearing MacArthur's deep chuckle, Blaze managed not to blush through sheer force of will. Her sister's fiancé was expecting a tart response, but she refused to accommodate his teasing.

"Alex, what a kidder you are," Blaze said, her smile serene, enjoying his expression of surprise at the gentleness of her rebuke. "I believe you envy my unique beauty."

"I agree with your self-assessment, my lady," another voice spoke. "Yours is a rare beauty."

"Your Highness," Blaze said, turning to Prince Lykos Kazanov, "I did not realize you were joining us tonight."

"I have told you several times to use my given name," Lykos said, bowing over her hand. "I command you to do so."

"Lykos," Blaze murmured, willing herself to blush.

The prince's presence surprised her. She should have known her stepmother would seek a match with royalty, even if it was foreign.

With black hair and blue eyes and strong, angular features, Prince Lykos Kazanov would be a jewel of a catch. His title and vast wealth made him her stepmother's choice. A third prince marrying into the family would be an astounding feat, much envied for decades.

Blaze suspected that MacArthur, a Scotsman, was her father's preference. She had learned during the previous year that her father viewed the Highlands in a romantic light while her stepmother was always pragmatic. The blond gentleman, of course, was a weak offering designed to fool her.

"Too many months have passed since I have seen you," the prince was saying, still holding her hand. "Do you recall our dance at your sister's wedding?"

"I could never forget our waltz, Lykos." Blaze flicked a glance at the marquis's tight-lipped expression. "Your feet must carry the scars from my missteps."

Everyone, including the marquis, smiled at that.

"You danced like a dream," the prince said.

"What an interesting ring," Blaze said, her gaze dropping to the prince's hand.

Lykos held his hand up, freeing her hand. On the third finger of his right hand was a gold ring shaped like a wolf's head, two rubies its glittering eyes. "My parents gave me this when I graduated university."

"You must have done well to earn such a reward," Blaze said.

"On the contrary," Lykos said with a smile, "I could see no good reason a wealthy prince needed to study but did manage to graduate. Their gift reflects my parents' relief, not pride."

"Ahem." The Duke of Inverary cleared his throat, indicating their conversation should end. "I believe both my daughters have met the Marquis of Awe."

"A pleasure to see you again," Raven said.

Blaze gave the marquis an ambiguous smile. "His Lordship and I enjoyed a"—she glanced at her father—"a most *informative* conversation this afternoon."

"Call me Ross." The marquis bowed over her hand.

His dark gaze and easy smile had an odd effect on Blaze. Her knees felt suddenly weak, and butterflies winged in the bottom of her belly. Masking this dizzying response behind a frozen smile, Blaze dropped her gaze. Unlike the prince, MacArthur wore no rings, and his hands appeared roughened from working with horses.

"Where is that dog of yers?" Ross asked her.

"Puddles is sleeping off those cookies you fed him."

Her father injected himself into the conversation. "Blaze and Raven, you have never met Dirk Stanley, the Earl of Boston."

Blaze turned to the earl, easily the handsomest of the three. His blond hair, green eyes, and perfectly formed features lent him an angelic expression, but the gleam in his fabulous green eyes was pure mischief.

Dirk Stanley bowed over her hand. "A pleasure to make your acquaintance, my lady."

"I am merely a miss." Blaze noted the diamond ring the earl wore on his pinky finger. His unblemished hands had never met any work.

"Ross and Dirk are brothers," her father said.

That surprised Blaze. She looked from one to the other but could see no resemblance.

"We are *step*brothers," Ross corrected her father.

"After mourning the loss of their respective spouses," Dirk said, "his father and my mother married to assuage their loneliness."

"Their spouses died together?" Blaze blurted in surprise and then caught her stepmother's grimace.

"You misunderstand me," Dirk said. "My own father had already died, and when my brother's—"

"*Step*brother," Ross corrected him again.

Blaze could almost feel the tension emanating from the marquis. She had truly stepped into a *faux pas.*

"When my stepbrother's mother suffered an untimely passing," Dirk explained, "his father married my mother."

"I apologize for prying," Blaze said, and peeked at the marquis. MacArthur was staring at his step-brother with an expression of contempt.

"Yer Highness, I didna realize ye had an interest in thoroughbreds," Ross said, turning to Kazanov.

"Call me Lykos," the prince said. "Thoroughbred racing is a pleasurable and sometimes profitable pursuit. Dealing in diamonds and other precious gems is my business."

"I thought Russians peddled vodka," Dirk injected himself into the conversation.

"Russian princes do not peddle," Lykos told the earl.

"Forgive my poor choice of words, Your Highness," Dirk apologized, his smile ingratiating.

"I forgive you, Dick."

"Dirk."

Blaze swallowed a bubble of laughter. She would bet her last penny the prince had purposely mispronounced the earl's name, and she noted no permission granted to use his given name.

Three rivals vying for her attention could be amusing. She did not need to marry any of them, merely enjoy the bloodletting.

"Lykos is an interestin' name," Ross was saying. "Does it carry a special meanin'?"

"Lykos means wolf," the prince answered.

"Ah, I understand the significance of your ring," Blaze said.

"Shall we go down to dinner," the duchess suggested.

Prince Lykos offered Blaze his arm. "I will escort you, my lady."

"How kind." Blaze accepted his arm but caught the marquis's unhappy expression.

Her father did not appear pleased, either. In fact, he was giving his wife a hard look, and she responded with a vacuous smile.

Her stepmother was the least vacuous woman in the realm. The shrewdest of women, the duchess had more matchmaking tricks than the combined battle strategies of Wellington and Napoleon.

A rectangular mahogany table stood beneath a crystal chandelier in the center of the dining room. The footmen had laid eight place settings of the finest porcelain plates, crystal goblets, and shining silverware.

Tinker, the duke's majordomo, awaited the signal to serve. With him stood two footmen.

"Ross, you are seated on my left," the duchess instructed from her position at one end of the table, "and Lykos will sit on my right. Blaze take the chair on the marquis's left between him and Alexander. Raven, sit between the prince and the earl."

"Where do I sit?" the duke teased his wife.

"Dearest, you sit at the head of the table as usual." The duchess signaled the majordomo.

Prince Lykos assisted Blaze into her chair. She glanced at the marquis, smiling at the prince.

"I will take good care of the lady," Ross needled the other man.

Sitting beside the marquis was not Blaze's preference. His close proximity disturbed her. She could almost feel the warmth of his body. Or was that her imagination? The good news was she need not stare into his fathomless dark eyes that seemed to see into her soul.

Blaze distracted herself by considering the seating arrangements. Flanking the duchess, Prince Lykos and Ross MacArthur were the honored guests, and placing her beside MacArthur meant the duchess favored the Scotsman. That puzzled her. She would have wagered the duchess was aiming for royalty.

Tinker and the footmen began serving dinner. When the majordomo set a bowl of springtime soup in front of her, Blaze felt a surge of relief. She could eat this first course of vegetables and broth. No creature's flesh tainted the dish. Even the stock was made from vegetables.

Blaze dipped her spoon into the soup and lifted it to her lips. The broth tasted delicious, and the knowledge that no animals had died comforted her.

When she peeked at the marquis, her relaxation vanished. The man was watching her, the hint of a smile on his lips.

"Is something wrong?" she asked him.

MacArthur shook his head, his dark gaze drifting to her lips. "All is perfection, my lady."

Was the marquis flirting with her? That was as surprising as his being favored by her stepmother. She wondered what the old vixen was planning.

Attitude, Blaze reminded herself, giving the marquis an ambiguous smile. "Close, my lord, but no one is perfect."

Amusement shone from his dark eyes. "Almost perfection, then."

Tinker poured wine into their goblets, leaving only Blaze's empty. A footman appeared with a pitcher of lemon barley water.

"Ye dinna care for wine?" Ross asked, reaching for his goblet.

"I dislike spirits," she answered.

Ross set his goblet on the table. "Tinker, I prefer lemon barley water."

"Lemon barley water?" Prince Lykos echoed. "I will try that, too."

"I love lemon barley water." Dirk Stanley gestured to the majordomo. "We English consume too much alcohol, especially gin."

Blaze looked from the marquis to the prince and then glanced at the earl. Were they so eager to please her? This contest to win her affection was becoming more amusing by the minute.

"Has there been an arrest for your jockey's murder?" the earl asked the duke.

"Sadly, no." Her father shook his head. "Blake will be investigating the incident."

"I expect Constable Black in Newmarket tomorrow," Alexander told them.

"Amadeus Black?" the earl echoed, paling by several shades.

Watching him, Blaze knew one thing for certain. Even innocent men trembled at the mention of London's most illustrious constable.

Her ears prickled with the need to hear every word when the earl began discussing the racing season with her father. All her attention focused on their conversation, but she pretended to concentrate on her lemon barley water and soup.

"I will be placing better than last season's third," the earl was telling her father. "Emperor is running in the less prestigious races to practice for the Classic Three."

"Emperor will never beat my colt," her father replied. "Thor runs faster than Zeus did last year."

"Pegasus beat Thor in the trial heats," Blaze said, her pride evident. She caught her father's gaze, adding, "I will cure her of that slight flaw."

The flaw you failed to mention was left unspoken.

Her father cleared his throat. "I am glad to hear it, daughter."

"Tell me about your thoroughbred," Prince Lykos said.

"Pegasus is a white Arabian," Blaze began, her pride evident in her voice.

"Ye mean gray," Ross MacArthur corrected her.

"Pegasus is white," Blaze repeated, noting the marquis's smile.

"White horses are considered gray," Ross told her.

"Pegasus is white," Blaze insisted. "What color you consider her is unimportant."

The marquis opened his mouth as if to speak, but the footmen removing the soup dishes interrupted whatever he would have said. Calf's liver salad, the dinner's second course, consisted of various kinds of greens and well-trimmed calf's liver.

Blaze looked at her plate and then glanced across the table at Raven, who gave her an encouraging nod. Then she shifted her gaze to her stepmother. The duchess's expression dared her to complain.

"Mmm, this looks delicious," Blaze said to no one in particular.

"Cook does excel at calf's liver," the duchess remarked.

Blaze cut a sliver of liver into two minuscule pieces. Instead of eating the meat, she moved the pieces to the side and speared a lettuce leaf. She chewed the lettuce slowly and longer than necessary, trying to waste time until the third course arrived. Then she reached for her lemon barley water.

Peeking at their guests, Blaze noted that no one noticed her liver avoidance. She repeated this procedure again and again and again while conversations swirled around her.

"Jeez, lass, are ye eatin' the liver or playin' with it?"

All conversation ceased. All eyes shifted to Ross and Blaze, her complexion reddening.

"I am eating what I prefer," Blaze answered, her irritation apparent in spite of her smile. "I suffer urticaria from certain foods."

The Marquis of Awe raised his eyebrows at that, and Blaze could have sworn the corners of his lips twitched. She peeked at her stepmother and then her father. Both were staring at her in unmistakable surprise.

"Is that serious?" Dirk Stanley asked. "Or contagious?"

"The lady gets the hives," Ross informed his stepbrother.

"Which foods cause that?"

"Meat, fish, and poultry," she answered.

Dirk Stanley wore an expression of sympathy. "What a pity."

"All those foods give ye the hives?" Ross asked,

his expression incredulous. "No wonder yer no bigger than a mite."

Blaze blushed, but Tinker rescued her from more embarrassing comments by instructing the footmen to serve the third course. Roasted duck with espagnole sauce, fricassee of turnips, and vegetable pie arrived next.

"Ye'd better set the turnip platter in front of the lady," Ross told Tinker, making everyone smile.

Except the lady.

Blaze leveled a deadly look on the marquis, but he surprised her with an infectious grin. Though the joke was on her, she returned his irresistible smile.

"So, you own a *white* filly," Prince Lykos said, catching her eye.

"My father gave me Pegasus," Blaze told him, "and I intend to race her."

"Colts possess more stamina," Dirk said.

Blaze looked down the table at him and then wished she hadn't. The earl was sucking on a duck bone, his perfect white teeth scraping its roasted flesh.

Nausea churned her belly. Fighting her revulsion, Blaze set her fork down and reached for the goblet of lemon barley water.

After taking a sip, she replied to the earl's comment without looking at him. "Take my advice, my lord, and wager on my filly."

"Blaze picked last season's winners," the duke boasted. "Her advice fattened my purse."

"How did you divine the winners?" the earl asked her.

"Horses never lie," she answered. "I asked them."

Everyone laughed. Blaze peeked at her stepmother,

whose expression resembled a woman with a pin stuck in her unmentionables.

"The lady doesna care to share her secrets," Ross said, covering for her.

"Ladies are entitled to keep their secrets, Dick," Prince Lykos agreed.

"Dirk, Your Highness." The earl looked at her, gesturing with the duck bone in hand. "You should enter your filly in the filly-only races."

Blaze blanched at the sight and dropped her gaze to her vegetable pie. "A filly can beat a colt, my lord."

"Darling, a lady acknowledges a gentleman by looking at him when he speaks," the duchess said, clearly irritated.

And a lady never corrects another's behavior in public, Blaze thought, her expression mutinous. Raven was correct; she needed to be herself, no matter how outrageous others considered her.

"I apologize for my lapse in manners," Blaze said, meeting the earl's gaze, "but I dislike watching people suck on dead animal bones."

The Duchess of Inverary gasped, and the Duke of Inverary covered his mouth though his shoulders shook with mirth. The others at the table could not suppress their laughter.

"That's my girl," the marquis whispered, leaning close. "Speak yer mind freely."

Blaze froze at his nearness, his warm whisper against her ear creating a riot inside her belly. The marquis's scent of mountain heather sent her senses reeling. She was torn between bolting off the chair and flattening herself against his hard, muscular body. Neither of which her stepmother would approve.

"Bone marrow is good for your health," Dirk Stanley was saying, his easy smile making her feel guilty. "I will, however, refrain from sucking animal bones if you ride with me to the village tomorrow afternoon."

"I would love to accompany you," Blaze lied, "but I have already accepted Lord MacArthur's invitation to tour his estate and stables." She flicked a sidelong glance at the marquis and hoped he would not dispute her words.

Dirk Stanley cocked a blond brow at his stepbrother. "Alone?"

"Alexander and I will be joining them," Raven spoke up. "Isn't that so?"

"I can hardly wait to tour the marquis's estate," Alexander agreed.

"The estate belongs to his father," the earl said.

"I own the thoroughbreds," Ross said, "and ye arena invited to tag along."

Blaze felt sorry for the man. "Come to tea another day."

The earl's expression brightened. "I would enjoy that."

"What about me?" the prince asked.

Blaze sent him a flirtatious smile. "Your Highness—I mean, Lykos—you are welcome to tea every afternoon."

When dinner ended, the ladies rose from their chairs to leave the gentlemen with their port. Ross MacArthur stood when they did.

"Excuse me for a moment," he told the others,

and followed the ladies into the corridor. "Yer Grace, I beg a private word with Blaze."

The Duchess of Inverary nodded, her dimpled smile decidedly feline. "Take as long as you like."

Blaze faced the marquis but dared not meet his black gaze. "Thank you for not contradicting me," she told his chest.

"Look at my face." When she did, the marquis warned her, "Ye'll need to follow through on our outin' lest Dirk discover the lie."

"I will tour your estate if it isn't too much trouble."

"No trouble at all, lass."

"I've decided to accept your help with Pegasus," Blaze told him.

He smiled with apparent satisfaction. "Ye've made a wise decision, lass."

"That remains to be seen," she said, wiping the smile off his face. "I'm meeting Rooney at the track in the morning."

Ross nodded. "I've arranged everythin'."

Blaze narrowed her gaze on him. "What do you mean?"

"Bobby Bender and I will be the other riders," he answered.

"Bender is my father's trainer," she said. "He'll squeal to my father."

"Bobby willna say a word," Ross assured her. "The other two would've spilled their guts to curry yer father's favor."

Blaze disliked the marquis controlling the situation. Pegasus was her filly and her responsibility. She was the boss, not he.

"Ye know, I thought ye didna like me."

She arched a copper brow, assuming a haughty expression. "I don't like you."

Ross raised his brows. "Ye dinna mean that."

"Yes, I do."

"What's wrong with me?"

"How much time do you have to listen?"

"Very funny, lass."

Blaze gave him her sweetest smile. "Shall I begin with bossy and arrogant?"

His lips twitched. "Oh, that."

"You disturb me," she added.

"Thank ye for the praise." Ross turned toward the dining room door. "I'm in dire need of whisky to wash the foul lemon taste from my mouth."

"I thought you liked lemon barley water."

"I lied." He winked at her and then disappeared into the dining room.

Chapter Three

The bachelors were stealing her focus.

With her lips in a grim line, Blaze trudged across the lawn early the next morning on her way to the path leading to her father's private track. Troubled thoughts had disturbed her sleep, her mind consumed with a newly discovered flaw.

Cowardice. She was a coward, no doubt about it.

Pleading a headache, Blaze had escaped the bachelors by retreating to her chamber and bolting the door against intruders. Locking the door had been a wise move. Later, her stepmother had knocked and called her name, but Blaze had jerked the coverlet over her head and pretended deafness.

She could return to the old Flambeau family home in Soho Square. Unfortunately, that would mean forgetting her dreams for the racing season and a refuge for unwanted animals.

In spite of a lack of sleep, Blaze felt her fighting spirit reviving. Would she allow three bachelors to send her scurrying back to London? Certainly not. She would string them along to keep her stepmother quiet. At least, until the racing season ended.

All three bachelors were wealthy, titled, and reasonably good-looking. Her stepmama would have barred the door against them if they hadn't possessed those first two qualities.

Choosing a husband on the basis of prestige meant marrying Prince Lykos Kazanov, but his wanting to court her stretched the limits of credulity. For some unknown reason, Lykos wanted to irritate MacArthur and had chosen her as his instrument.

Dirk Stanley's blond hair, green eyes, and angelic expression would win him the beauty contest. Blaze knew she could never marry a man prettier than she, nor could she erase the sickening sight of the earl sucking on the duck bone.

That left the Marquis of Awe. Marrying MacArthur would be almost as prestigious as marrying the prince. Though he lacked an angelic expression, the Scotsman possessed a ruggedly handsome masculinity. She could not envision herself marrying a bossy, arrogant man.

Blaze smiled at the idea of marrying the marquis. The peace would last less than two minutes. She could almost hear the sound of the crockery crashing.

The three bachelors were simply unacceptable. The next three paraded in front of her would not be any better. Nor would the following three.

Her plan to keep the bachelors dangling was stepmother-proof. Once the racing season ended, she would inform all three that she could not develop a fondness for them. Then she would steel herself for the meddling woman's next parade of bachelors.

Chirping birds, aroused from their night's sleep, awakened Blaze to her surroundings. The April morn was crisp, promising warmth once the sun rode high in the sky.

Blaze reached the end of the path. Morning fog clung like a lover to the open track.

Ross MacArthur, Bobby Bender, and Rooney huddled together and spoke in hushed conversation. Two chestnut horses and Pegasus stood nearby, the Arabian's white coat creating the illusion of a mythical horse goddess.

The three men watched her approach. Greeting them with a nod, Blaze headed straight for Pegasus.

She stroked the filly's face. *Love Peg.*

Me love, the thought popped into her mind, making her smile.

Walking back to the men, Blaze knew the marquis would not be easily controlled. She needed to assert her authority.

"Good morning." Blaze looked at Bobby Bender. "You won't mention this to my father?"

The trainer shook his head. "My lips are locked."

"Good mornin'." Ross slid his gaze from her freshly scrubbed face to her body. "What are ye wearin'?"

Blaze glanced at her stableboy garb. She wore black breeches and a shirt topped by a leather jerkin for warmth. She'd woven her hair into one thick braid and tucked it beneath a cap.

"I am wearing appropriate clothing," she answered.

"Well, ye make a bonny jockey."

"Thank you for the praise," she said, echoing his words from the previous evening.

Then Blaze became all business. She knew the trainer and the jockey would follow her orders. The marquis was an entirely different matter.

"Mount your horses," she said, "and show me this balking."

Ross MacArthur cocked a dark brow at her. "Are ye orderin' me?" His tone challenged, not questioned.

"I must see the balking in order to solve the problem," Blaze said, evading a direct answer.

The marquis did not budge. "I told ye I would solve the problem."

"Demonstrate the balking." Blaze gave him an ambiguous smile. "Please."

"That's better." The marquis turned to the others. "Let's show her."

MacArthur gave Rooney a leg up on Pegasus. Then he and the trainer mounted their own horses.

"Give Bender and me a four or five length lead down track," Ross instructed the jockey. "We'll keep a hole between us."

Rooney nodded.

"Wait." Blaze approached the jockey and held her hand out. "Nobody uses a whip on my horse."

Rooney rolled his eyes at the other two men but passed her the whip.

Ross called to Bender, "One, two, three, *go*."

The marquis and the trainer spurred their horses into action. Swishing and thudding, their horses galloped down track. When they were fifty feet from the line, Rooney and Pegasus started after them. Within mere seconds, the Arabian caught them but slowed near the hole. The filly refused to pass between the galloping horses.

Slowing their mounts, the three men halted farther down track. They turned their horses in unison and returned to the start line.

"I can see the problem," Blaze began. "Perhaps if we—"

Rooney ignored her, turning to the marquis. "Do you think blinders would work?"

"I suppose blinders could help," Ross said, and then looked at the trainer. "What do you say, Bobby?"

Bender shook his head. "We tried blinders in her second race last year. She balked all the same."

Blaze did not like the way this was unfolding. She owned the filly, but the men were ignoring her.

Sounding more confident than she felt, Blaze lifted the reins out of the jockey's hands, telling them, "I can solve this problem once I know the source."

Blaze led the filly away, feeling the men's gazes on her back. They were smiling behind their hands at her foolishness, but she would make them believers before the season ended.

Love Peg, Blaze thought, stroking the filly's face.

Me love.

Peg run between horses?

Lonely. Scared.

Seeking to comfort, Blaze put her arm around the filly's neck and pressed her face against her cheek. Then she led the filly back to the watching men.

"Dinna kiss me until ye wash yer face," Ross teased her.

"I would rather kiss a frog," Blaze said, remembering to give him a serene smile. "Perhaps the frog would turn into a Russian prince?"

That wiped the smile off the Scotsman's face.

Blaze shifted her gaze to the trainer and the jockey. "Peg feels lonely, which makes her afraid to go through the hole. She needs to feel the jockey is with her."

Bobby Bender and Rooney stared at her in open-mouthed surprise. The marquis was not so polite.

Ross shouted with laughter. "Horses canna feel lonely."

"What does it mean when a dog growls or bites?" Blaze asked, rounding on him, her hands on her hips.

Ross rolled his eyes at the other men, making them smile. "Most likely, the dog is angry."

"And if the dog wags its tail?"

"The mutt likes ye."

"How about a purring cat?"

The marquis's expression said he knew where her questions were leading. "The cat feels contented."

"If dogs and cats can feel anger, friendliness, and contentment," Blaze said, "then a horse can feel lonely."

"Have it yer way, then." He threw his hands up in feigned surrender. "Ye women always do."

"Try again," Blaze ordered Rooney. "While you ride, reassure Peg that she's not alone."

The three men mounted their horses while Blaze

watched from the sideline. Again, the filly balked at passing through the hole.

"Rooney isn't connecting with her," she told them. "Do it again, and I will try connecting with her from here."

Blaze leaned against the track's fence. The three men lined their horses side by side, and then the marquis and the trainer spurred their mounts forward into a gallop. Rooney and Peg gave chase.

Love Peg. Love Peg. Love Peg.

Blaze chanted inside her mind, her lips moving with the repetitive thought.

Peg through hole. Peg through hole. Peg through hole.

Rooney reached the marquis and the trainer. Pegasus started through the hole but slowed at the last minute, allowing the other horses to pull ahead.

Blaze closed her eyes in disappointment. Communicating from a distance was proving more difficult than she could have imagined. She did not doubt her eventual success, but weeks of practice would be needed.

"Give it up," Rooney said, dismounting. "Winning requires heart, not speed."

"Peg can do this," Blaze insisted. "I'll take her through the hole."

"Women do not jockey racehorses," Rooney told her.

"If you get on that horse," Bender said, "your father will slit my throat."

In desperation, Blaze turned to the marquis. His expression was unreadable, but he wasn't laughing anymore.

"Raven insisted we will solve Peg's problem." A pleading note crept into her voice. "She said you would help us."

"How does your sister know we can solve the problem?" Rooney asked, drawing her attention.

"Raven knows because . . . because she knows."

Ross struggled against the urge to laugh in her face. He could never have imagined how entertaining his future bride would be. Her pleading expression became glacial when he said nothing.

By fair means or foul, Ross reminded himself. He aimed to persuade her into marriage even if it required dragging the damn filly through the hole.

"I'll give ye a leg up," Ross said, gratified when her expression thawed into pleased surprise. He turned to the trainer. "I'll shoulder the blame if she gets hurt. Rooney, ride my horse while I watch."

Ross cupped his hands together and hoisted Blaze up, admiring her derriere as she swung her leg over the horse and settled into the saddle.

"Crouch low over Peg," he instructed her. "Ye must connect with yer horse physically as well as mentally. A winnin' jockey and horse become one. Ye ken?"

Blaze gave him a smile that made rising early worth every minute of lost sleep. She nudged her horse forward to the start line.

"Wait until they're eight lengths ahead of ye," Ross called.

He kept his gaze fixed on Blaze. Her lips were moving in silent communion with the filly, who seemed to stand more confidently. Or was his imagination running wild? Horses did not feel confident or anything else.

"One, two, three, *go*."

Bender and Rooney spurred their horses into action, galloping down track.

"Go now, lass."

Blaze and Pegasus bolted away. The filly chased the two horses down track at an amazing speed. Blaze's lips never stopped moving as the filly ate the distance like a starving man at a feast.

And then it happened. Pegasus flew through the hole between the two horses.

"God's balls, she did it," Ross shouted.

Blaze slowed the filly and turned toward the start line. He could see her smile even from this distance.

Ross helped her off the horse. Before speaking, she paused to stroke the filly's face. "Love Peg," he heard her whisper.

"Pegasus, I do believe ye'll win a few races," Ross said, patting the filly.

"What good is Blaze taking her through the hole if Rooney will be riding?" Bobby Bender argued.

Raising his brows, Ross looked at Blaze. His dark gaze demanded she answer the trainer.

"We'll practice every day," Blaze said, "and Peg will learn to go through the hole while I guide her from the sidelines. Communicating from a distance takes practice."

"Time is short," Rooney entered the argument. "Peg cannot learn by Monday."

Ross recognized the worry in Blaze's eyes. To her credit, she managed a confident smile for the trainer and the jockey.

Did the lass believe in miracles? Why would God grant her a miracle when so many others needed a miracle more than she?

By fair means or foul.

"Blaze will ride Pegasus in The Craven next Monday," Ross announced, startling everyone.

"I will?" Blaze looked flabbergasted.

"I refuse to become an accomplice to this," Bender said.

"Bobby, ye need to go along to get along," Ross said, giving the man an easy smile. "I'll make it worth yer while and shoulder the blame."

"The Jockey Club will revoke your membership," Bender warned him.

"I've read the book," Ross countered, "and I canna recall any specific rule banning female jockeys."

"Inverary will never permit his daughter to race."

"Bobby, ye worry too much aboot life's little thin's," Ross told him. "Ye should be worryin' aboot findin' employment if ye dinna go along with me."

"I knew I should have stayed in bed this morning," the trainer muttered.

"They'll disqualify her for being female," Rooney argued, and the trainer bobbed his head in agreement. "She won't even make the starting line."

"Both of ye sport red hair and freckles," Ross said. "Once dressed for racin', no one will suspect she isna ye."

"What about her"—Rooney dropped his gaze to her chest—"her you-know-what?"

Ross laughed at Blaze's blush. "She'll bind them." He looked straight into her blue eyes. "Give me an honest answer, lass. Do ye want to win enough to ride Peg if need be?"

Blaze bobbed her head. "I'm game."

"Mind ye, this can only work at Newmarket," Ross warned her. "When the horses move to Epsom, the other track willna allow deception. Ye'll need to use the next two months trainin' Peg to go through holes with Rooney."

"I understand."

"I've a plan that can work." Ross looked at the trainer. "Bobby, I'd be grateful if ye showed each mornin' for practice and escorted the lass onto the track on race day. Ye dinna need to know more than that. If we're caught, ye can claim ignorance."

"I'll do it," Bender agreed, and then walked away grumbling to himself.

"Crush a large stash of Stinkin' Billy," Ross said, turning to the jockey. "Ye must carry some in yer pockets day and night. Smudge a bit of dirt on yer face each mornin', and carry an empty flask of gin at all times."

"I know what you're planning." Rooney laughed, grasped Peg's reins, and led the filly toward the stables.

"What is this Billy?" Blaze asked him.

"Stinkin' Billy is the most foul smellin' weed on earth," Ross answered. "The stink keeps people away better than dung. Ye'll need to carry it on race day."

"Why is it called Stinking Billy?"

"We Highlanders named the weed after the Duke of Cumberland."

"Who is he?" Blaze looked confused. "Does my father know him?"

"I keep forgettin' how young and English ye are," Ross said, touching her cheek. "I'll tell ye the tale of Cumberland one day, but trust me on this. Dinna ask yer father aboot Cumberland lest ye arouse his suspicions."

"Why does Rooney need to carry a flask and smudge his face with dirt?" she asked him.

"We want the whole of Newmarket to believe Rooney is drinkin' again," Ross answered. "Drinkin' and stinkin'."

"You *are* sneaky."

"Thank ye for the high praise, darlin'." Ross grabbed his horse's reins. "Come on, and I'll walk ye home."

"No, thank you." Blaze gestured to her garb. "I need to sneak inside via the back door."

"Ye've a ways to go before ye reach my level of sneakiness," Ross said. "I'll see ye at two o'clock for our tour."

"I will count the minutes."

He winked at her. "See that ye do."

Why is the marquis courting me? Blaze wondered, inspecting herself in the cheval mirror.

She doubted he was spying on Thor or Pegasus. Hercules, his own colt, was a formidable competitor. That left her father's influence and fortune, neither of which he needed.

With a critical eye, Blaze stared at her reflection. She wore a pale peach gown topped with a white cashmere shawl, its bottom edge embroidered with dainty peach blossoms.

Turning around, Blaze glanced over her shoulder to see her backside. All seemed in order. Then she turned sideways and, not for the first time in her life, wished her bosom were more developed.

Would the marquis try to kiss her? That disturbing possibility leaped into her mind. She needed to speak with her stepmother before leaving.

Crossing the bedchamber, Blaze lifted the white hat with peach ribbons off the bed. She would carry her bonnet while seeking her stepmother's advice and then ditch the hat in the foyer on the way out.

Blaze met the majordomo on the second-floor landing. "Do you know Her Grace's whereabouts?"

"Their Graces are consulting in his office," Tinker answered. "May I add how lovely you look, Miss Blaze."

"Thank you, Tinker."

Reaching her father's office, Blaze lifted her hand to tap on the door. She hesitated, hearing her stepmother's voice.

"Magnus, please trust my strategy." The duchess sounded exasperated. "I promise all will end as you desire."

Her father muttered a reply, his words inaudible. His tone did not sound especially happy.

Blaze tapped on the door and then peered into the office. In an instant, her father and stepmother pasted smiles onto their faces. Had they been discussing her?

"Come inside, darling." Her stepmother beckoned her. "How beautiful you look for your outing."

"Thank you for noticing." Blaze dropped into the chair beside her stepmother's.

Her father's office was a bastion of masculinity. Sturdy oak furnishings and muted colors lent the room a somber atmosphere. No feminine frills distracted the eye or the mind from business dealings.

Blaze fixed her gaze on her stepmother. "Are you trying to get rid of me?"

"I am trying to do right by you." The duchess's dimpled smile appeared. "Darling, marrying a wealthy gentleman means you can save more animals."

Blaze said nothing. Wealth did afford its owner freedom, a valuable commodity to a woman. Money meant doing as one pleased. Within reason, of course.

"If you do not like the three gentlemen you met last night," the duchess said, "I can introduce you to others."

Uh-oh. Her strategy for the racing season required pitting the marquis, the prince, and the earl against each other.

"I am content for the moment." Blaze practiced her serene smile on her stepmother. "Choosing a husband must be done carefully."

The duchess gave her husband a triumphant smile. Her father looked suspicious, though.

Blaze realized the trainer had been correct. Her father was not easily fooled, but she would give him something to worry about other than her sincerity.

"What should I do if a gentleman tries to kiss me?" Blaze asked her stepmother.

"Slap his face," her father answered.

The duchess gave her husband a pointed look. "Magnus, let me handle this."

"She's *my* daughter."

"Kissing gentlemen is *my* expertise."

"What?"

"You know what I mean," the duchess said, and then turned to Blaze. "If you do not welcome his kiss, show him your cheek and step back a pace or two. If you do welcome it, simply allow him the kiss."

"No tongues," the duke added.

"Tongues?" Blaze echoed in confusion. "People kiss with their lips, don't they?"

"Yes, dearest, people use their lips for kissing," the duchess said. "I hope that settles the matter for you."

"What should I do with my hands?" Blaze asked her.

"No touching," the duke ordered.

"Ignore your father," the duchess told her. "When you desire a gentleman's kiss, your hands will do what comes naturally."

"Good God, I've got a headache," the Duke of Inverary muttered, both hands holding his head.

"Leave your father and his headache to me," the duchess said, gesturing her out. "Enjoy your afternoon with the marquis."

Wondering about her father's hands and tongues comments, Blaze crossed the chamber and opened the door. She heard her father asking in a loud voice, "Are Alex and Raven accompanying them?"

"Don't be ridiculous," the duchess said, and the door clicked shut.

Blaze struggled against laughing at the anxiety she'd heard in her father's voice. He didn't know he had nothing to fear. She planned never to marry, nor would pregnancy trap her into marriage.

When she reached the foyer, Tinker was opening the door for Ross MacArthur. Tall and broad-shouldered, the marquis cut an imposing figure in his perfectly tailored clothing.

Her knees weakened at the sight of him. The damn butterflies had returned, winging inside her belly.

"Ye look peachy and good enough to eat," Ross said, his smile charming. "I bet ye taste sweet, too."

Attitude, Blaze reminded herself.

"I'm as sweet as lemons," she said, making the majordomo chuckle.

Blaze passed him her bonnet. "Tinker, hide this until I return."

"I understand, Miss Blaze." Tinker opened the door. "Enjoy your afternoon."

Ross escorted her to his phaeton, its hood folded down. He helped her onto the seat and climbed up beside her. "Shall I put the hood up?"

Blaze shook her head. "I love feeling breezes and the sun's warmth."

"In that case"—Ross plucked the pins from her hair, letting the fiery mane cascade around her—"enjoy the ride."

Blaze felt uncomfortable sitting so close to him and wished the marquis had arrived with a coach and a driver instead of the two-seater phaeton. His thigh flirted with her skirt, and she caught his mountain heather scent.

Intelligent conversation eluded her. She had never been completely alone with any gentleman except Alexander Blake, and he was more brother than gentleman. Though born on the wrong side of the blanket, she and her sisters had been sheltered as befitted a duke's daughters.

At the end of the private lane, Ross steered the phaeton onto Bury Road. He turned onto Fordham Road before reaching Newmarket proper.

Blaze peeked at the marquis and caught him smiling at her. She averted her gaze and concentrated on the passing scenery. Various wildflowers were blooming along the roadside, and lilacs scented the air. An occasional robin darted past, carrying grass for its nest.

"Pleasant small talk makes a coach ride more enjoyable," Ross said, "like when yer waltzin'."

Blaze looked at him. "I never engage in pleasant small talk."

"Ye had plenty to say this mornin'," he teased her.

"How far is the MacArthur estate from my father's?" she asked. "Is that talk small enough for you?"

Ross laughed out loud, making her smile. "I do believe the only thin' smaller would be aboot the weather. To answer yer question, MacArthur House lies two miles or so from yers, shorter as the crow flies."

"Your house is beyond the woods on the far side of my father's track?" Blaze asked.

"Ye've a keen sense of direction," Ross said, steering the phaeton onto a private lane. "We'll visit the stables and then stop at the house for refreshment."

Blaze noted several enclosures. Foals frolicked beneath their mother's supervision in the pens closest to the stables. In the distance, a lone horse grazed in its own enclosure.

"Why is that horse alone?" She pointed toward the enclosure.

"We keep the barrens separated from the others," he told her.

"What do you mean?"

"A mare that hasna delivered a foal in three years is considered barren," he answered. "We'll be sellin' her."

His cool detachment surprised Blaze. "Who will purchase a barren mare?"

Ross shrugged. "The knackers will give us the best offer, most likely."

"You mean to slaughter her?" Her surprise became horror. "That's cruel and unfair."

God's balls, Ross thought, *honesty is overrated.* He'd really stepped in dung this time and should have known better. A woman who held funerals for furs was bound to object to selling a horse to the knackers.

"Drive to that pasture," Blaze said.

Was she ordering him again? Ross managed a conciliatory smile. "We'll stop to visit her another day."

She arched a copper brow at him. "I won't forget."

"I know ye willna forget." The lass had a mind like a steel trap.

"I can never marry a man who sells a horse to the slaughterhouse."

"I dinna recall askin' to marry ye."

Blaze blushed, her gaze skittering away. She'd walked into that. Would she never learn to keep her thoughts to herself? On the other hand, why would he waste his time if he wasn't intending an offer of marriage? She resolved to keep her mouth shut until Pegasus won the Triple Crown. If the marquis sent the mare to the slaughterhouse, his offer of marriage would go the same way.

Ross halted the phaeton in the stableyard and stepped down. By the time he circled the phaeton to assist her, Blaze had already climbed down.

"Ladies always wait for a gentleman's assistance," Ross told her.

"A true gentleman does not send horses to the slaughter," Blaze countered.

Ross ignored her comment and gestured to the stables. "I want to show ye Hercules, my best hope for winnin' this year's Crown."

The MacArthur stables resembled her father's stables. The lighting was dim but sufficient, and the straw-covered floorboards muffled the sounds of their boots. The scents of hay and musky horses hung in the air along with a faint dung odor.

Hercules, a powerfully-built chestnut colt, stood proudly in his stall as if he'd already won the Triple Crown. He snorted a greeting at his owner and then turned doleful eyes on his owner's companion.

Blaze touched the colt's face and gazed for a

long moment into his eyes. "Juno is the barren mare and Hercules is her son."

Ross stared at her in surprise. "How do ye know?"

"Banishing Juno has upset Hercules," Blaze told him. "He worries about your selling his mother to the knackers."

Ross smiled at that. "How can Hercules know what I plan?"

"He hears talk around the stables."

"She's got the gift."

A stocky, middle-aged man stood a few feet away. His clothing and leather apron proclaimed him the farrier.

"You believe in such thin's?" Ross asked him.

The man nodded. "I do."

"Meet Duncan MacArthur," Ross introduced them. "Duncan, this is Miss Blaze Flambeau, Inverary's daughter."

"Hercules's left shoe is loose," Blaze told the farrier.

"I know aboot the shoe," Duncan said, "but the forge is already dark. I'm plannin' to fix it in the mornin'."

Ross could not credit what he was hearing. He watched Blaze press her hand against the colt's cheek. Then she closed her eyes.

"What's he tellin' ye?" Ross asked.

"Hercules thanks me in advance for saving his mother from the knackers." Blaze gave him a flirtatious smile. "Will you give me Juno?"

"I dinna give horses away," Ross refused her.

"Will you sell me Juno?"

"A useless mare wastes food and stable space," Ross said, gesturing to the door.

"I plan to mate Juno with my father's Zeus."

Ross laughed. "Yer father willna agree to that."

"Apparently, you understand nothing about fathers and daughters." Blaze lifted her nose into the air and walked out of the stable.

Tidy lawns and dark green manicured shrubs led to the MacArthur House. Its understated opulence and serene atmosphere came from decades of social and financial security.

"Good afternoon, my lord," the MacArthur majordomo greeted them, opening the door before they reached it.

Blaze wondered if the man lived in anticipation of guests coming and going. He reminded her of Tinker, who always knew when to open the door.

"We'll take tea in the dinin' room," Ross instructed his man.

"Yes, my lord." The majordomo gave her a speculative glance and then shifted his gaze to the marquis. "Ahem."

"Pardon my lapse in manners," Ross said, his tone dry. "Blaze, I present Dodger. Dodger, meet Miss Flambeau, Inverary's daughter."

"A pleasure to meet you, Dodger."

"The pleasure is mine, Miss Flambeau." The majordomo headed down the corridor to fetch their tea.

"The dinin' room is this way," Ross said, leading her in the direction the majordomo had gone.

"Do you usually introduce guests to Dodger?" Blaze asked.

"Dodger has never requested an introduction before," Ross answered. "The old sneak usually eavesdrops on conversations."

"Tinker knows more than anyone else what is happening at home," Blaze said. "I swear that man would be richer than my father if he resorted to blackmail."

The MacArthur dining room reminded her of her father's. The rectangular mahogany table with matching chairs stood in the middle of the dining room. Overhead hung a crystal chandelier. Even the blue and white porcelain Worcester service in the center of the table seemed eerily familiar.

Blaze thought the social elite were monkeys mimicking one another. No one dared to be different in words, deeds, or possessions.

"Hercules will win no races if you send Juno to the slaughterhouse," Blaze said, sitting beside the marquis.

A smile touched his lips. "He told ye so."

Dodger arrived with the tea and pastries, saving her from answering. "Will there be anything else, my lord?"

"Privacy."

"Yes, my lord." The majordomo started to leave.

"Close the doors, Dodger."

"Leave the doors open," Blaze countermanded the order.

"Yes, Miss Flambeau."

Ross winked at her and whispered, "Ye do realize Dodger will be eavesdroppin' on our conversation."

"No eavesdropping, Dodger," she called.

"Yes, Miss Flambeau."

"Tomorrow mornin' after practice, I'll take ye to the Rowley Mile," Ross said, his voice low. "Pegasus must pick up speed before the Devil's Ditch because the race ends uphill."

"Peg's problem is not speed."

"There's a copse of trees beyond the finish," Ross told her. "If ye win, ride straight into the path to switch places with Rooney."

"Why do we need to switch places?"

"Ye canna take yer place in the winner's circle if yer ridin' her," Ross answered. "I'll be waitin' with Rooney and hurry ye back to the winner's circle. Wearin' yer gown beneath breeches and racin' silks will even the weight between Rooney and ye."

Blaze could not suppress her doubts. "Do you think this will work?" She believed in her horse but not their ability to succeed in deception.

Ross shrugged, his black gaze holding hers captive. "Do ye believe Pegasus can win?"

"Yes." No hesitation there.

With their tea finished, Ross rose from his chair. "I'll take ye home now."

Blaze stood when he did, her thoughts on the lonely mare in the pasture. "Will you please sell me Juno?"

"I'll consider yer offer," Ross said, stepping closer, "if ye allow me a kiss."

Staring into his dark eyes, Blaze remained silent for a long moment. Surely, one kiss was a small price to pay to save the mare's life.

"What should I do?" she whispered.

The innocence of her question brought a lazy smile to his lips. "Close yer eyes, darlin'."

When she did, Blaze felt his fingers caress her cheek. She heard him murmur, "Soft and sweet."

And then their lips touched.

His lips were warm and firm, his scent reminding her of mountain heather. The muscular planes of his body pressed against her, his warmth heating her, and Blaze relaxed against his powerful frame.

"Are you bringing your doxy into my home?"

"Mind yer manners, Celeste."

Blaze leaped away from the marquis and whirled toward the intruders. The image of Ross as an older man stood there. Beside him was a middle-aged woman.

The Duke of Kilchurn possessed the same black hair and rugged good looks as his son. And he was smiling at her, warmly, as if he knew her.

The Duchess of Kilchurn was an attractive blonde, graying at the temples. And she was definitely *not* smiling at her. In fact, the duchess appeared hostile.

"Yer Graces, I present Miss Blaze Flambeau," Ross said, holding her hand. "Blaze, the Duke and Duchess of Kilchurn."

"A pleasure to make your acquaintances," Blaze said, managing an ambiguous smile.

"We're happy to meet ye," the duke said. "Celeste?"

"Ecstatic." The duchess's frigid gaze shrieked the word *bastard* at Blaze.

"Child, ye resemble yer father's aunt Bedelia," the duke told her. "We shared high times with Bedelia and her long-sufferin' husband, Colin."

"My father told me." Blaze smiled at the duke,

adding, "I wish his aunt Bedelia hadn't given me her freckles, though."

"Freckles do handicap to a young lady's appearance," the duchess agreed, and then looked at Ross. "You will dine with us this evening?"

"Unfortunately, no." Ross ushered Blaze toward the door. "I will be movin' my belongin's into the Rowley Lodge."

"The girls want to visit with you," the duchess said.

"I'll see them before leavin'. By the way, where is the Feathered Flock?"

"The flock is soarin' in the village," the duke answered, and then looked at Blaze. "Tell yer father I'll see him soon."

"I will, Your Grace." Blaze smiled with genuine pleasure at the Duke of Kilchurn. She flicked the duchess a frigid glance and then walked out of the dining room.

Standing in the foyer, Dodger opened the door for them. "Enjoy your ride home, Miss Flambeau."

"Thank you, Dodger."

Climbing into the phaeton beside her, Ross asked, "Well, did ye enjoy the tour?"

"I never appreciated my own wonderful stepmother until I met yours."

"In a bygone era, the villagers would have burned Celeste as a witch," he agreed.

Ross drove the phaeton down the private lane leading to Fordham Road. They retraced the route taken earlier.

"What is a Feathered Flock?" Blaze asked.

"The flock consists of my sister Mairi, my stepsister Amanda, and their friends," Ross answered, steering the phaeton onto Bury Road. "I dubbed them the flock cuz of all their preenin' and twitterin'."

"Preening and twittering like canaries?" Blaze giggled at the provoking picture. "Your stepmother doesn't like me."

"What makes ye say so?" Ross gave her a sidelong smile. "Did Hercules tell ye?"

"Very funny." Blaze was silent for a moment and then told him, "I saw hostility in her eyes."

"Celeste dislikes everyone," he said. "Besides, she was hopin' for a match between Amanda and me."

Ross halted the phaeton in the Inverary courtyard. "I'll see ye at the track in the mornin'."

"I need to ask you something." Blaze stared into his black eyes, hoping to discern the truth in his answer. "Did you ever kill an animal?"

"I canna lie to ye," Ross said, his expression serious. "I've stepped on my share of ants."

"I knew I heard screams coming from the direction of MacArthur House." Blaze smiled at him and walked away.

His laughter followed her into Inverary House.

Chapter Four

"Hello, Tinker." Blaze held her hand out.

The majordomo passed her the bonnet. "I trust you enjoyed your outing."

"I did enjoy myself," Blaze told him, "but the marquis's stepmother makes mine seem like Little Bo Peep."

"Her Grace prays only for your happiness," Tinker said, smiling.

"Do you know my father's whereabouts?" she asked.

"His Grace is meeting with business associates," the majordomo answered. "He has another meeting scheduled afterwards."

"Thank you, Tinker."

Blaze climbed the stairs to the second floor, her thoughts on her mission of mercy. This scenario was better than she could have hoped. Her father's business meeting was divine intervention. He could not refuse her request in front of others. Doing so would show him in a bad light. After all, no gentleman would conduct business with a man who refused to rescue a defenseless animal from certain death.

Pausing outside the office's closed door, Blaze took a deep breath. She needed to appeal to his kind heart and logical business mind, and she needed her wits.

Dealing with her father could sometimes prove difficult. He resisted rebellious challenges but appreciated mental agility and boldness. Like all men, her father caved when faced with feminine tears, but she would save that as her last resort. For once in her life, resembling his adored aunt Bedelia could prove useful.

Blaze tapped on the door, opened it without waiting for permission, and stepped inside. Princes Rudolf and Lykos Kazanov glanced over their shoulders. Her father raised his gaze to her.

"I apologize for interrupting," Blaze said, her smile sheepish, "but I must speak with you, Papa."

The Duke of Inverary gestured to the princes. "We are discussing business, and I have scheduled another meeting directly afterwards."

"My emergency cannot wait," she told him.

"In my vast experience, women scream during an emergency," Prince Rudolf teased her. "Why are you not screaming?"

Blaze narrowed her gaze on him, her expression warning him to silence. "You have never experienced me in an emergency."

Prince Rudolf grinned. "True enough."

"Can this emergency wait?" her father asked her.

"This concerns life or death," Blaze answered, "and I will take only a few minutes."

The duke rolled his eyes at the smiling princes. When Lykos started to rise from his chair, the duke gestured him to remain where he was and then beckoned her forward.

"Do you need privacy?"

"No, Papa."

Blaze sat in the vacant chair between the princes. She paused before speaking to acknowledge Prince Lykos with a smile.

The duke cleared his throat.

Blaze shifted her attention to him. Her gaze touched the glasses of whisky and vodka on his desk, reminding her of her mother.

"What is the emergency?" the duke prompted her.

"I need money," Blaze blurted out.

The Russian princes burst into laughter, which made her father smile. She hadn't meant to speak so abruptly and definitely needed her stepmother's instruction concerning feminine wiles.

"Running out of pin money with more than three weeks remaining in the month is an emergency of epic proportions," Prince Rudolf teased her.

Blaze ignored him.

"How much do you need?" her father asked her, his tone long-suffering.

"You should ask her the reason before opening your pockets," Prince Rudolf said. "My children receive a monthly allowance and no more."

"If I agree to her request," her father said, "then she will leave us to our business." He shifted his gaze to her, saying, "How much do you need and why do you need it?"

"I need enough money to buy a horse," Blaze told him.

"I gave you Pegasus," he reminded her. "Purchasing a horse does not qualify as a life-or-death emergency."

"You don't understand," Blaze said. "Ross Mac-Arthur plans to sell Juno to the knackers unless we buy her."

"MacArthur is sending a horse to the slaughter-house?" Prince Lykos echoed in surprise.

Blaze nodded. "Papa. I must save Juno. The marquis is selling her because he believes her barren."

"I commend your tender heart," her father said, his tone softening, "but horse racing is a business. A barren mare does not contribute to the owner's profit."

"Her Grace and you do not have children," Blaze argued. "Will you be sending Her Grace to the knackers?"

At that, the Kazanov princes shouted with laughter. Her father did not look pleased, but the corners of his lips twitched as if he wanted to laugh.

"Going to the knackers is no laughing matter," Blaze scolded the princes.

The Kazanovs laughed even harder. Even her father chuckled.

This negotiation was not succeeding. She needed another path to her goal. Tears. Though she disliked weeping in public, Blaze knew Juno was depending on her.

Bowing her head, Blaze raised a hand to her eyes and willed herself to weep. Her bottom lips trembled when she thought about the kitten she'd been unable to save all those long years ago. That poor broken kitten reminded her of her mother's death, which did send warm tears rolling down her cheeks.

The masculine merriment ceased. A good sign.

"I will send Ross a note."

Blaze looked at her father, an expression of misery etched across her face. "Thank you, Papa." Her voice was an emotion-choked whisper. "I knew you would understand."

When she moved to stand, her father gestured her to sit. "How will you repay my generosity?"

"I will refrain from baiting Her Grace," she promised.

Smothered chuckles erupted from the princes.

"Will you marry the man of my choice?" her father asked her.

Blaze paused for several moments, considering his words, and then stared straight into his eyes. "Let me answer this way," she said. "Were you planning to learn this year's winners from me?"

The princes' chuckles were no longer smothered. Their amusement was not helping her.

Father and daughter stared at each other, and then he grinned. "You remind me of Aunt Bedelia."

"I take that as a compliment." Blaze gave her father her sweetest smile. "You will pay MacArthur's asking price without haggling?"

"I will do what is necessary."

"Thank you, Papa, but I need one more tiny favor."

Blaze heard coughing on either side of her and knew the princes were laughing again. Her father's expression said she was pressing her luck.

"I want Juno mated with Zeus," Blaze told him, and then blushed at her own frankness.

"What?" the duke exclaimed, his tone incredulous. "In thoroughbred circles, we breed the best to the best. That means I cannot send my champion to the breeding barn for a barren mare."

Blaze leaned forward, ready to haggle for what she wanted. "I will pay for the stud service"—she blushed again—"with my winnings from The Craven next week."

Her father smiled, hopefully reminded of his beloved aunt Bedelia. "I agree to your terms, but if you lose, will you marry the man of my choice?"

"Trust me, Papa," she sidestepped his question. "Pegasus will win The Craven."

"I hope she does win," her father said, "but do you agree to my terms?"

"I agree." No hesitation there.

"You may now leave us to our business."

"I met the Duke of Kilchurn at MacArthur House," Blaze said, standing to leave. "I wonder the reason he speaks with an accent, but you do not."

"Aunt Bedelia decided I needed to sound English in order to move successfully through life." The Duke of Inverary smiled at the memory. "Jamie and I took elocution lessons but tormented the tutor. Bedelia banished Jamie, and without an accomplice, I lost my taste for bad behavior."

A knock on the door drew their attention. Tinker walked into the office, announcing, "The Marquis of Basildon and Constable Black have arrived."

"Ask them to wait ten minutes," the duke instructed his man. He looked at Blaze. "Run along and let me finish this meeting."

"You won't forget about Juno?"

"I doubt you will allow me to forget."

"Wager on my filly," Blaze advised the princes. "You will win a fortune."

"How can you be certain?" Prince Rudolf asked her.

"Pegasus told me."

Two miles west of Inverary House, shorter as the crow flies, Ross MacArthur lifted the satchel and left his bedchamber. He would return another day if he'd forgotten anything.

Descending the stairs to the foyer, Ross set the satchel down beside three others. "I want these delivered to Rowley Lodge," he instructed the majordomo, "and send someone to bring my horse around."

"Yes, my lord. Their Graces are expecting you in the drawing room."

Ross grimaced. He should have known his stepmother would delay his escape. "Thank ye, Dodger."

"You don't look thankful," Dodger drawled. "I can tell them I forgot to relay their message."

"I wouldna put ye in that position," Ross said.

"I have lied for you before," the majordomo reminded him.

"True, but we need to save lyin' for emergencies." Muttering to himself, Ross climbed the stairs and marched down the corridor to the drawing room.

The scene was worse than he could have imagined. Though his sister's twittering friends were missing, Dirk Stanley had arrived. He preferred the twitterers.

"Here comes your son," Celeste MacArthur told her husband. "Ross, sit on the settee beside Amanda.

Perhaps the girls will entertain us on the pianoforte and the harp."

"I dinna have time for a concert." Ross dropped onto the settee beside his stepsister and smiled a greeting.

Amanda Stanley returned his smile. "Good to see you, Ross." Blond and green-eyed like her mother, Amanda shared her brother's angel face and could have posed for one of the masters.

"How are ye, Poppet?" Ross teased his sister.

"How are ye, Aged Sibling?" Mairi countered, a sparkle of merriment in her dark eyes.

Dark-haired like him, Mairi MacArthur was petite and had inherited their mother's fire instead of his own easy nature. Her pure Highland blood emboldened her unlike the shy blonde by his side.

Dirk Stanley sat on the settee beside Mairi while he sat beside Amanda. Ross would bet his last shilling his stepmother was trying her hand at matchmaking. Celeste MacArthur had never accepted that he did not want to marry her daughter, a sweet twit who deferred to her mother in all matters.

Ross always took himself to the Rowley Lodge lest Celeste engineer a compromising situation that would force him to marry Amanda. Perhaps he should warn Mairi to bolt her chamber door at night.

"Dark and light make a pleasing picture," Celeste was murmuring. "Don't you think so, James?"

"I suppose so," the duke answered, sounding bored.

"Where are the missin' twitterers?" Ross asked his sister.

"We dropped them at their family estates," Mairi answered.

"Ross, help yourself to a cucumber sandwich," Celeste said. "Shall I pour you tea?"

"No tea." Ross reached for a sandwich from the platter. He disliked cucumber sandwiches.

Blaze Flambeau popped into his mind. The petite redhead would adore them. No meat, no poultry, no fish.

"Dirk tells us you dined with the Inverarys last night," Celeste remarked.

His stepmother was fishing for information.

Eating precluded conversation. Ross swallowed the last bit of cucumber sandwich and reached for another.

He lifted his gaze to the portrait of his own mother with her dark eyes, so much like his sister. God, he missed her. If she'd lived, Celeste would not be sitting here playing at being a duchess.

"Ross dear, you are hungry," his stepmother said. "Stay for dinner."

"I'm meetin' Douglas Gordon," Ross said in a polite refusal.

"The Inverarys are hosting the Jockey Club Ball this year," Celeste told the younger women. "We met the poor Flambeau girl this afternoon."

That got his attention.

Ross snapped his black gaze to his stepmother. "Why do you call her poor?"

"Red hair and freckles are quite unfashionable," she answered.

"Red hair?" Mairi exclaimed.

"Freckles?" Amanda echoed.

The stepsisters looked at each other and burst into giggles.

"Laughing at the less fortunate is unseemly," Celeste told them, but the giggling continued.

"Blaze Flambeau is *not* less fortunate," Ross insisted.

Dirk Stanley bobbed his head in agreement. "Miss Flambeau is quite lovely."

Celeste looked at Ross. "You realize that she and her sisters were born on the wrong side of the blanket?"

"Dinna repeat old scandals," the duke interjected.

"Inverary acknowledged his daughters," Ross told his stepmother, and reached for another cucumber sandwich.

Celeste gave him a haughty smile. "Even His Grace cannot erase Society's memory of Gabrielle Flambeau's suicide."

Ross choked on a bit of cucumber and coughed. "Her mother committed suicide?"

"Inverary buried the slut on his estate because consecrated ground was forbidden," Celeste added.

"Damn ye, Celeste, enough." The Duke of Kilchurn poured himself a whisky and gulped it down in one swig. "Gabrielle Flambeau was a countess and the mother of my best friend's daughters. Her death devastated Inverary, and I dinna want anyone"—the duke looked at each of them in turn—"anyone discussin' her tragic ending."

"Mairi and Amanda, do not gossip about this with your friends," Celeste ordered them.

Did his stepmother actually believe she could drop a bit of juicy gossip and the girls would never whisper it to their friends? At first opportunity, he would send the Duchess of Inverary a warning note that Celeste was spreading gossip. Even his stepmother feared Roxanne Campbell.

"In his younger days, Magnus Campbell was never known for controlling his desires," Celeste was saying to his father. "I heard Prince Rudolf Kazanov is Inverary's natural son."

"You heard correctly, Your Grace."

Everyone whirled toward the doorway. Prince Lykos Kazanov was standing there. Dodger looked ashen, mortified that the prince had overheard a slur on his family.

A pleasant smile pasted on his face, Prince Lykos sauntered across the drawing room. The coldness in his gaze belied the smile on his lips.

"Cousin Rudolf is an acknowledged Kazanov prince," Lykos told Celeste, "and, with all due respect, I urge your tongue to discretion."

The duchess's mottled complexion mirrored her discomfort. "I do apologize," she said. "Ross, make the introductions."

"Lykos, I present my father, the Duke of Kilchurn," Ross said, and then purposely omitted his stepmother. "Here are my sister Mairi and stepsister Amanda. Ye met Dirk last night at Inverary's."

"That must have been an interesting dinner," Celeste remarked. "Will you take tea with us?"

Prince Lykos assumed a disappointed expression. "I am expected elsewhere. Another time, perhaps?" Without waiting for a reply, he turned to Ross, "I would like a private word, my lord."

Ross nodded. "I was just leavin'."

Prince Lykos looked at Mairi and Amanda. "You must promise me a dance at the Jockey Club Ball."

Both girls bobbed their heads.

Ross ushered Lykos out of the drawing room. Descending the stairs to the foyer, Ross said, "I apologize for Celeste."

"With eight brothers and three sisters," Lykos replied, "I know how difficult a man's family can be."

"Eight brothers and three sisters? That's a healthy family."

"You would use the word *miraculous* if you knew my mother."

"What can I do for ye?" Ross asked, as they reached the foyer.

"I would purchase a horse," the prince answered.

"I'm leavin' for the Rowley Lodge," Ross told him. "Let's set an hour to meet here tomorrow, and I'll show ye my stock."

"You misunderstand me," Lykos said. "I want to purchase Juno."

"Dodger, did ye send my bags to the Rowley Lodge?" Ross asked the majordomo, stalling his answer.

"Yes, my lord."

"And did someone bring my horse around?"

"Yes, my lord."

Ross ushered Lykos outside, his mind a jumble of thoughts. Fingers of jealousy curled around his chest, their grip tightening. His only real competition, the prince had somehow spoken to Blaze this afternoon and learned about Juno. Did the Russian think to impress her by purchasing the mare?

"I canna sell ye Juno," Ross refused the prince's request.

"You have received a previous offer?" Lykos looked dismayed. Apparently, few people dared to refuse a prince.

Ross smiled and shrugged. "I'll let ye know if the deal falls through."

"May I ask the identity of the new owner?" Lykos asked him.

"Ye can ask," Ross replied, "but I willna reveal his name."

"Damn, I need to think of another gift for Miss Flambeau," Lykos said.

"Dinna ye think a prospective suitor's gift should be impersonal," Ross suggested. "She would probably appreciate pretty lace handkerchiefs."

"We Russians do things differently," Lykos said, "but I will follow your suggestion. Will you be joining us at Inverary's tomorrow?"

Ross managed a smile. "I wouldna miss tea with Blaze for all the rubles in Russia."

Raven Flambeau walked down the stairs to her father's second-floor office. She knew the reason for her summons and didn't need to rely on her psychic ability.

Constable Amadeus Black and Alexander Blake had arrived earlier and closeted themselves in her father's office to discuss the jockey's murder. They needed her psychic ability to help the investigation. Fortunately, the constable was less of a skeptic than her betrothed.

Raven paused outside the closed office door. She knew this meeting would temporarily change her relationship with Alexander, the man she'd known and loved her entire life.

Holding her left hand up, Raven stared at her engagement ring, a rare star ruby surrounded by diamonds. Legend said the star ruby would darken to warn its owner of impending danger. Either the legend was nonsense, or she had never been endangered.

Raven tapped on the door and then entered before getting her father's permission. He had sent for her, after all. She smiled at the three men waiting for her.

More than six feet tall, Constable Amadeus Black cut an imposing figure in his customary conservative black. A legend in London, the constable enjoyed a fierce reputation for catching the most cunning criminals.

"Good afternoon," Raven greeted them. "A pleasure to see you again, Constable Black."

"The pleasure is mine," Amadeus Black said, and gestured to the chair beside his.

"Hello, Brat." Alexander smiled, softening his teasing. "We require your special ability to generate clues."

"Do you now believe in my psychic ability?"

"I place my faith in logic," Alexander answered, "but I do not disbelieve the possibility of such things."

"We are making progress," Raven said, "and you are not a lost cause."

"I'm relieved to know there's hope for me."

Alexander leaned close and, lifting her hand to his lips, asked, "Do you always need the last word?"

She gave him a flirtatious smile. "Yes."

Alexander grinned at her.

"I hate to interrupt," the Duke of Inverary said, "but Charlie will not rest in peace until we discover his murderer."

"And others could be endangered." Constable Black held a brown leather wallet and a gold ring. "Charlie was carrying these possessions at the time of his death."

"Notice the Campbell boar's head insignia on the ring," the Duke of Inverary said. "I gave him the ring after he won me the Triple Crown."

"I need to know if the murder happened during the commission of a robbery," the constable said, "or if the villain's intention was murder."

Raven inspected the wallet and the ring without touching. "Was there money in the wallet?"

"Are you using logic?" Alexander asked her.

Raven gave him a sidelong smile. "Bad habits are contagious."

The constable's lips quirked into a smile. "The wallet was empty when the locals found the body."

"Charlie's death was deliberate," Raven said. "A robber would have taken the gold ring, not merely the money. Whoever killed Charlie wanted us to believe the crime was a random robbery."

"On the other hand, unloading a distinctive ring would be difficult," the constable said.

"Perhaps." Raven shifted her gaze to her

father. "Papa, I will sit alone near the hearth for this reading."

"You never needed to sit alone before," Alexander said.

"I have never attempted a reading with my father in the room." Raven stood and, taking only the gold ring, crossed the office. With her back to the three men, she sat in the chair in front of the dark hearth.

"I need absolute silence," she said, glancing over her shoulder.

Cupping the ring in her left hand, Raven placed her right hand over it. She closed her eyes, relaxing every muscle in her body.

And then it happened.

Fog rolled across her mind's eye and slowly dissipated into a heavenly setting. Stars dotting a night sky served as background for a crescent moon. Draped across the moon was a black and green plaid with yellow pinstripes. A small dagger, the hilt's insignia two laurel branches *orle*, lay on the plaid. And then the fog rolled in again and clouded the heavenly scene.

Raven opened her eyes and rose from the chair. Crossing the office, she handed the constable the ring.

"Do you need the wallet?" the constable asked her.

"No." Raven resumed her seat between Alexander and the constable.

"Did you see a face?" Alexander asked her.

Raven ignored his question. He should have learned by now that her visions appeared in symbols.

"I saw a heavenly setting," Raven told them.

"Thousands of glittering stars accompanied a crescent moon. A small dagger lay on top of a plaid blanket draped across the moon."

"How curious," the constable said.

"No faces?" Alexander sounded disappointed.

"Can you describe this blanket?" her father asked.

"It had black and green squares with yellow pinstripes."

"Good God, that's the MacArthur plaid," the duke exclaimed.

"MacArthur's horse finished second to yours in every race last season," Alexander said.

"Money is an excellent motivation for murder," the constable remarked.

The idea of Ross MacArthur as a suspect troubled Raven. He did not need the prize money a first place would have brought him, and no sane man killed for glory.

"I've known Ross since the day of his birth and cannot believe him capable of murder." The Duke of Inverary looked at his daughter. "Tell us about the dagger."

"It was small," Raven answered, "and its insignia was two laurel branches *orle*."

The duke leaned down to open the desk's bottom drawer. He produced a dagger, asking, "Did it look like this?"

Raven nodded. "The only difference is yours has a boar's head insignia."

"The two laurel branches indicate the MacArthurs," the duke told the constable, "but we Scots call this type of dagger a dirk. That means we should also consider Dirk Stanley a suspect."

"Dirk Stanley is MacArthur's stepbrother," Alexander told the constable.

"Could they have conspired?" Amadeus Black asked.

The Duke of Inverary chuckled. "Ross dislikes Dirk so there is no chance of conspiracy."

Raven doubted that Dirk Stanley was a murderer. She hadn't felt any negativity emanating from the earl. He seemed almost too eager to please.

"We need more information before suspecting either man," Amadeus Black said. "Spying, especially at social events, would gain us more insight."

"How do we do that?" Raven asked. "Only close friends exchange confidences."

"If Raven and Alexander quarrel in public," the constable said to her father, "then Raven can befriend Dirk Stanley."

"I can do that," Raven agreed, and peeked her betrothed's unhappy expression.

"Alex, you befriend Dirk's sister," the Duke of Inverary said. "Amanda Stanley is a lovely blonde."

"I'll do it." Alexander smiled at Raven's unhappy expression. "We can confer after social events."

Spying lost its appeal to Raven. She trusted Alexander, but not blondes.

"Argue at the Jockey Club Ball next week," the duke suggested. "Everyone will be attending."

"I doubt anyone will believe a serious rift," Alexander speculated. "Who will spy on MacArthur?"

"Trust me on this," the Duke of Inverary said with a smile. Then, "Tinker."

The door opened instantly to reveal the major-domo. "I was passing by when I—"

"Whatever you *accidentally* overheard must not be repeated," the duke said. "That includes my wife."

"I understand, Your Grace."

"Tell Blaze I must speak with her immediately," he instructed his man.

"Yes, Your Grace."

The Duke of Inverary looked at the others. "I want no interference dealing with my daughter."

Upstairs, Blaze sat alone on the chaise in front of the hearth in her bedchamber. She leaned back, closed her eyes, and focused on communicating with Pegasus.

Visualizing her father's stables, Blaze imagined herself standing at Pegasus's stall. She gazed into the filly's eyes, letting her love for the horse swell in her breast.

Love Peg. Love Peg. Love Peg.

No answer.

Love Peg. Love Peg. Love Peg.

No answer.

Love Peg. Love—

Out.

Out?

Blaze opened her eyes and giggled. Puddles sat in front of her, his tail swishing across the floor, and placed his paw on her leg.

Leaning close, Blaze hugged her mastiff. "Let's go out."

Puddles dashed across the chamber. Blaze followed him and opened the door.

Tinker stood there, his hand in the air to knock. "His Grace requires your presence in his office."

An official summons. What had she done now?

"Will you take Puddles outside?" Blaze asked him. When he hesitated, she added, "I will tell you everything later."

Tinker looked at the mastiff. "Come along, Master Puddles."

The majordomo and the dog hurried down the corridor in the direction of the servants' stairs. Blaze walked at a slower pace in the opposite direction and then descended the main staircase.

Without knocking, Blaze entered her father's office. "You wanted to see—" She stopped short at the sight that greeted her.

Her father sat behind his desk. Four chairs formed a semicircle around the front of the ducal desk. Raven, Alexander, and Constable Black occupied three chairs. One vacant chair sat between the constable and her sister.

This had the look of the Spanish Inquisition. Had her father somehow learned about her plans for The Craven? If so, what had Constable Black to do with it? Was he arresting her for conspiring to impersonate a jockey?

The Duke of Inverary beckoned her forward. "Sit there, daughter."

"We need your help with Charlie's murder investigation," Constable Black said without preamble. "We need a spy."

"My help?" His statement surprised Blaze, but subterfuge appealed to her sense of adventure. "I don't understand."

Constable Black looked at the duke. "Your Grace, I think you should explain."

"Raven gave us a reading," her father said. "Your

sister saw a MacArthur plaid and a Scottish dirk, making Ross MacArthur and Dirk Stanley our prime suspects."

"Ross MacArthur would never even step on an ant," Blaze leaped to his defense, her fingers crossed at the lie. "The bone sucker did it." She looked at her sister. "Did you see the disgusting way he scraped the duck's bone clean with his teeth?"

"Bone sucker?" the constable echoed in confusion.

Raven giggled, and Alexander Blake burst into laughter. The Duke of Inverary wore a satisfied smile.

"I don't give a fig about Dirk Stanley," the duke said, "but I need your help eliminating Ross as suspect."

"How do I spy on the marquis?" she asked him.

"Spend time with Ross," he advised her, "and he will soon become comfortable sharing his thoughts."

Blaze lowered her gaze to her hands, folded on her lap, and considered the matter. Spying gave her a good reason to pass time with the marquis. They already shared the secret of racing Pegasus. Other secrets would follow.

"James MacArthur is my best friend," the duke said, "and I would appreciate your eliminating his son as a suspect. Not only will I purchase Juno but will send her to the breeding barn with Zeus."

"I'll do it," Blaze agreed, "but Her Grace will object because she favors Prince Lykos."

Her father smiled. "I can handle my own wife."

Chapter Five

"Blast it, Blaze. What d'ye think yer doin'?"

Blaze slipped off Pegasus, catching a glimpse of Rooney's and Bender's smiles in the early morning light. She would not allow her status to be diminished in front of the others.

Ready for battle, Blaze advanced on the marquis. She wished he weren't so big. She felt like a kitten challenging a lion.

"What do you think I'm doing?" Blaze challenged him, her hands on her hips.

"Ye looked over yer shoulder," Ross snapped, glaring at her. "Any blockhead can remember to crouch low over the horse."

Blaze heard the muffled chuckles from the watching men. Blood rushed to her face. "Do not speak to me like that," she ordered, her finger jabbing his rock-solid chest.

The marquis stood his ground. "I'll speak to ye however I please."

"Who's in charge here?"

"I'm in charge," he told her.

"I own Pegasus which means—"

"Yer the jockey," Ross interrupted her, "and I'm the boss. If ye dinna want to win enough to follow my instructions, I'll sleep late in the mornin's."

Blaze dropped her gaze to the fog swirling around her ankles. The marquis had backed her into a corner.

She wanted to win. She needed to win. She could not win without him.

Blaze gave him a curt nod. "Tell me what I did wrong."

"I apologize for yellin' at ye," Ross said in a quiet tone, "but ye forgot to crouch low over yer horse."

"I wanted to see how far back Rooney and Bender were," Blaze said.

"Look with yer eyes, lass, not with yer head."

"In case you hadn't noticed, my lord, I do not have eyes on the back of my head."

Ross smiled at her sarcasm. "I did notice the location of yer bonny blue eyes, but there's a way to see behind ye without turnin' and breakin' pace."

"Enlighten me."

"Rooney, show her how to look back," Ross ordered. "Jeez, man, ye stink to high heaven."

The jockey grinned. "Nobody will come near me with the Stinking Billy in my pockets."

Ross gave Rooney a leg up on Pegasus and explained as the jockey demonstrated. "Yer crouchin' low over the horse for maximum speed. Yer head is down, yer eyes are lookin' straight ahead, and yer arms are up holdin' the reins. Are ye with me, lass?"

Blaze nodded. She already knew these things.

"If ye need to look back, drop yer head lower and

peek under yer arm," Ross explained. "Dinna raise yer head until ye pass the finish line." He turned to the jockey. "Show her on the track."

Crouching low over the horse, Rooney and Pegasus raced down track. He dropped his head and peeked under his right arm.

"Is that clear?" Ross asked her.

"Clearer than crystal."

"The expression is clearer than glass," he corrected her.

"Her Grace does not allow common glasses on her table," Blaze said, making him smile. "I left drinking from common glasses behind in Soho."

"Soho?"

"We lived in Soho until Papa acknowledged us," Blaze told him. "You did know that my parents never married?"

"I amna a complete blockhead."

Blaze gave him her sweetest smile. "Not a *complete* blockhead, no."

"Very funny. I'll give ye a leg up on Peg." Ross helped her mount and then ordered, "Show me the proper way to look behind ye."

"I'll demonstrate on track," she said, "after Peg passes through the hole."

Ross gestured the others to the start line. Her lips were moving in silent communication with her filly before reaching the line.

Blaze Flambeau was bonny and brave. No other lady of his acquaintance had the courage to race a thoroughbred. He admired her challenging his autocratic attitude and her good grace to stand down when she was wrong.

"Are you daydreaming, MacArthur?" Bender called.

"I was plannin' strategy. One, two, three, *go*." Ross watched Rooney and Bender gallop down track. "Go, lass."

Blaze and Pegasus gave chase, her lips still moving in silent chant. The filly flew through the hole between the horses. Several furlongs ahead of the two riders, Blaze dropped her head to peek under her right arm.

"Excellent," Ross said when she returned. "Do ye want to try yer distance communication?"

"I'm practicing from the house," Blaze answered. "I'll know Peg's ready when she answers my call."

"Dinna forget, lass, this scheme can only work at Newmarket," Ross warned her. "Epsom and Doncaster dinna have the same conditions."

"I haven't forgotten."

"I want to settle the plans for race day," Ross said, beckoning the trainer and the jockey. "Bender, ye escort Pegasus to the paddock and stay with the filly."

Ross turned to the jockey. "Rooney, ye weigh in with the saddle as usual. Afterwards, meet me on the far side of the training grounds. Ye'll switch places there."

Finally, Ross looked at Blaze. "Ye'll take Rooney's place in the paddock just before mountin' time. When the bell sounds, Bender will give ye a leg up and escort ye onto the track. From that moment, ye and Peg are on yer own. Will yer courage hold?"

Blaze felt a chill of excitement. "I fear nothing."

"If ye win," Ross said, "keep ridin' into the copse of trees where Rooney and ye can make the switch.

I'll get ye back to the winner's circle with no one the wiser."

Ross looked at the trainer and the jockey. "Any questions or concerns?"

"She'll need to drink my shot of whisky," Rooney said. "The boy brings me a shot to steady my nerves before mounting."

Ross looked at the trainer. "Bender, any concerns?"

"I have many concerns," the trainer said, "but you're the cause of all my worries."

"Bobby, ye need to enjoy the intrigue," Ross said, smiling, and gestured them off. "Blaze, I want ye to ride with me to the Rowley Mile so I can explain the track strategy."

Blaze yawned. "Can we go this afternoon?"

Ross shook his head. "No one will be millin' aboot at this hour."

Blaze glanced over her shoulder. Bender was already leading his horse toward the path to the stables. Rooney and Pegasus followed the trainer.

"Do you want me to walk?"

"We'll share my horse." Ross mounted first. "Put yer foot in the stirrup and climb up behind me."

"I'll topple off."

"Trust me, lass." Ross held his hand out. "I willna let ye fall."

Blaze placed her left foot in the stirrup. Grabbing his hand, she hoisted herself up and swung her right leg over the saddle.

"Wrap yer arms around me," he told her.

Blaze did as instructed, wrapping her arms around his chest, and blushed when she realized her breasts and belly were pressing against his back. Sitting this close was indecent and arousing.

She caught his mountain heather scent, mingling with oiled leather and musky horse. The heat of his body warmed her, and she could not resist the urge to lean her cheek against his back.

"Dinna fall asleep."

"I won't." Sleep had never been farther from her mind.

Leaving the Inverary practice track, they rode down Snailwell Road to Fordham Road. A private lane off Fordham would bring them to Newmarket Heath and the Rowley Mile.

The whole area was deserted, and Blaze suffered the uncanny feeling they were the only two people in the world. She knew, though, every stable and yard was a beehive of drowsy activity at that hour.

Daily chores were well underway. Boys were mucking out stalls, riders were saddling the horses for morning exercise, and stablehands were preparing breakfast for the horses.

Blaze decided this was an auspicious moment to begin spying. Engaging the marquis in casual conversation was the best way to discover information.

Guilt spread through her at the idea of spying. She knew the marquis could not have murdered Charlie. The bone sucker did it.

As agreed, she would ask questions. Reporting what she learned was an entirely different matter.

"Constable Black and Alexander Blake conferred with my father about the murder," Blaze said, hoping she sounded casual.

"Is that so?"

Blaze wished she could see his expression. On the other hand, she could feel his body respond. That arousing thought tinted her cheeks pink.

"Did you know Charlie?"

"Newmarket is a small town, lass."

No help there. Was he evading an answer or simply uninterested?

Blaze felt no tension in his body. She would try another angle. "What did you think about your horse placing second to my father's?"

"I thought my horse placed second."

"I meant, what did you feel?"

"Feel?" Ross echoed. "What d'ye mean?"

"Were you disappointed? Angry? Bitter?"

"I didna have any feelin's."

His lack of response frustrated her. Was he hiding something? Or was lack of emotion typical of men?

Blaze tried again. "Everyone feels something."

"If yer determined to play at thoroughbred racin', ye must keep a cool head."

"What do you mean?"

"Sometimes ye win," Ross told her. "Sometimes ye lose, and sometimes ye scratch yer horse."

"I don't understand *scratch*," Blaze admitted.

"It's good to hear ye dinna know everythin'," Ross teased her. "Scratch means ye drop yer horse out of the race for one reason or another."

They reached the Rowley Mile. The track was deserted, but Blaze knew that the scene would be alive with excited activity in less than a week.

"Pay attention," Ross said. "The spectator stands are on yer right."

Blaze rolled her eyes. "I have attended the races many times."

"Comin' on yer left are the judges' boxes," Ross said, ignoring her comment. "The last judge will wave the colors of whichever rider wins for the spectators who canna see."

Ross halted his horse when they neared the last part of the mile. "Ye need to quicken yer pace at this point before crossin' the Devil's Ditch. Ye can see the race ends uphill."

"Once Peg gets through the holes," Blaze said, "no one will catch her."

Ross nudged the horse down the Devil's Ditch and through the Running Gap. With Blaze clinging to him, they climbed the uphill side and rode across the clearing beyond the finish line.

"Bunbury Farm is on yer left," Ross said, "and Burwell is on yer right beyond that copse of trees. If ye win, ride down the path over there. Rooney and I will be waitin' just out of sight."

"I understand."

Ross glanced over his shoulder at her for the first time. "I admire yer determination and spunk."

"That's high praise coming from a Highlander."

He smiled at her.

She returned his smile.

"What will ye do with the coin ye win?"

"I'm saving to buy land for an animal refuge."

"God in heaven canna refuse such a worthy cause," Ross said. "Why dinna ye ask His Grace for the funds?"

"No practical businessman like my father would invest in a profitless project," Blaze answered, and then sighed. "God save the world from practical people."

"Do ye count me among the practical?"

"Have you considered selling me Juno?" she asked.

"Yes."

"And?"

Ross winked at her. "I havena made a decision."

Blaze studied her reflection in the cheval mirror. She wouldn't win any beauty contests, but her appearance would not induce vomiting or incite screams of terror.

Hopefully, her Nanny Smudge had been correct. A pleasing personality was better than beauty, which always faded in time.

Unfortunately, she had never been known for her sweet disposition. She had more in common with a cantankerous camel than a lap dog.

Blaze turned this way and that, studying herself from all possible angles. She wore a violet daygown with matching slippers and white stockings embroidered with butterflies.

After dressing like a jockey every morning, Blaze wanted to look pretty for the marquis. That realization created a melting sensation in the bottom of her belly. Whatever the reason, she wanted him to think her more appealing than the stepsister who'd been offered to him in marriage.

Blaze had brushed her fiery hair back, allowing it to cascade almost to her waist. The marquis liked her hair loose. Something was missing, though.

Crossing the chamber, Blaze yanked the highboy's

drawer open and reached inside for the jeweled, butterfly hair clasp that had once belonged to her mother. In fact, her mother was wearing the butterfly ornament when she'd posed for the portrait hanging in her father's drawing room.

Blaze lifted a length of blue ribbon off the bedside table and looked at the mastiff. Puddles raised his head, his eyes fixed on the ribbon, and then scurried behind the privacy screen.

"Come, Puddles."

Nothing.

"You must dress for our guests."

Nothing again.

"Do you want a cinnamon cookie?"

With his tail between his legs, Puddles appeared from behind the privacy screen and sat in front of her. Blaze attached the blue ribbon to his collar and tied it in a bow.

Cookie?

"Eat cookies later."

With a few minutes to spare, Blaze sat on the chaise to practice distance communication. She closed her eyes and forced her breathing to even. In her mind's eye, she pictured herself standing in front of her horse's stall.

Love Peg.

No answer.

Love Peg.

No answer.

Love Peg.

"Are you ready?"

Blaze glanced over her shoulder. Raven stood in the open doorway.

"Are you and Alex taking tea?" Blaze rose from the chaise.

"I am taking tea," her sister answered, "while Alex and the constable interview the tavern's customers the night of the murder."

"Where are Bliss, Sophia, and Serena?"

"The cowards have taken themselves into the village," Raven answered. "I suspect they will return after the bachelors have gone."

"The marquis knows nothing about the murder," Blaze told her. "Watch the bone sucker. I feel he may be involved."

Raven raised her left hand to wiggle her fingers in front of her sister's face. "My star ruby will warn me of danger."

"Come, Puddles." Blaze walked out of the bedchamber, asking, "How does the ruby do that? Do you hear the word *danger* in your mind?"

"Stones cannot speak," Raven said. "The ruby darkens to blood red."

"When I communicate with animals," Blaze said, "I hear words or see images in my mind."

With the mastiff between them, the sisters walked down the corridor to the main staircase. The drawing room was located on the second floor.

"Here you are, my darlings," the duchess greeted them from her chair near the hearth. "Blaze dear, violet whisper is a superb shade on you."

"I thought the gown was purple," Blaze said, sitting on the settee opposite her stepmother's chair.

The Duchess of Inverary dropped her gaze to Puddles, wagging his tail. "The dog does not belong at afternoon tea."

"Whoever marries me will also be marrying Puddles," Blaze told her. "If Puddles leaves, so do I."

"Then your dog must stay, of course."

"Sister, sit beside me," Blaze said.

"Raven, sit on the sofa," the duchess ordered. "One of the gentlemen may wish to sit on the settee."

"That's the reason I want Raven beside me."

"Yes, I know." The Duchess of Inverary gave her a serene smile. "I must warn you that some in Society may remember the details of your mother's tragic ending."

"Mother passed away five years ago," Raven said.

"Why would anyone mention it now?" Blaze asked, glancing at her mother's portrait.

"Society mamas envy my matchmaking successes," the duchess answered. "I did engineer royal husbands for Fancy and Belle. Anyway, if anyone references your mother's death, you will tell me the person's identity, and I will deal with her."

Blaze prayed no one would mention her mother's death. Doing so would be unhealthy for that person. Nanny Smudge had taught them to fight their own battles and she refused to relinquish that pleasure to her stepmother.

Puddles lifted his massive head and looked toward the door. *Cookie man come.*

Tinker walked into the drawing room. "The Marquis of Awe has arrived."

"I told ye, man, there's no need to announce me."

"I enjoy announcing guests."

Blaze smiled at the exchange. MacArthur looked breathtakingly handsome in his customed-tailored jacket, waistcoat, and trousers. She couldn't decide whether she preferred him dressed roughly for working with horses or the more sophisticated marquis.

She felt the butterflies winging and the melting sensation. Did the sight of him make her ill? Or was the cause something more dangerous . . . like desire? She'd never felt desire or even a fondness for any gentleman.

Ross MacArthur looked at her and caught her smile. He greeted the duchess first, nodded at Raven, and then sat on the settee beside Blaze.

The Duchess glanced in the direction of the empty doorway. "Tinker, you may begin serving."

"Yes, Your Grace," the majordomo answered from the hallway.

Ross turned to Blaze. "Ye look lovely like the butterfly in yer hair, but"—he reached down to remove the bow from the dog's collar—"but men dinna wear ribbons."

"I chose a blue ribbon."

Ross reached into his pocket to produce a napkin with three cinnamon cookies. He set the cookies on the floor for Puddles.

"You know the way to win my stepdaughter's regard," the duchess teased him.

"Bribery comes easily to us Highlanders," Ross said with a smile. "The lass willna care for any gentleman her dog dislikes."

Blaze would have spoken, but four footmen arrived at that moment. One carried a silver tea service while a second brought the tray with tea's accoutrements. The other two had trays of refreshments, one platter with dainty cucumber sandwiches and the other with tiny pastries.

The duchess gestured the footmen out and poured the tea herself, serving the marquis first and then the girls. "Sugar?" she asked. "Lemon?"

"I drink mine plain," Ross answered.

"So do I," Blaze said.

"What a happy coincidence," he teased her. "The best part is no meat, no fish, no poultry."

Tinker walked into the drawing room. "His Highness, Prince Lykos Kazanov."

The prince brushed past the majordomo to greet the duchess first, bowing over her hand. He acknowledged Ross with a nod and offered Blaze a package tied with a pink ribbon.

"I ventured into Newmarket yesterday," Lykos said, "and seeing this in a shop window, I thought of you."

"Thank you, Your Highness."

"Lykos, remember?"

Blaze blushed and cradled the gift on her lap. She didn't know what to do since no gentleman had ever given her a gift.

"Do you take sugar or lemon?" the duchess asked, pouring the prince his tea.

Prince Lykos sat in the highbacked chair beside the duchess's. "I take tea plain."

"The marquis and I drink ours plain, too." Blaze frowned as the words slipped from her lips. Even she realized how inane she sounded, exactly like those silly society maidens she scorned.

"The world would be bleak without sugar in my tea," Raven remarked.

"Dearest, open your gift." The Duchess of Inverary looked at the prince. "I adore surprise gifts."

"You adore all gifts," Blaze said, and untied the pink ribbon. Opening the wrapping, she saw three fine handkerchiefs trimmed in delicate lace and embroidered with tiny blue flowers. "How lovely."

"The blue flowers reminded me of your lovely blue eyes," Lykos said.

"I value your thinking of me more than the gift." Blaze set the package on the table and reached for a cucumber sandwich. Eating seemed easier than making small talk.

Thankfully, her stepmother excelled at meaningless babble. The duchess began an endless monologue about refreshments and decorations for the Jockey Club Ball.

Blaze bit into the cucumber sandwich and chewed slowly. Setting that aside, she lifted her teacup to sip the steaming brew and then wasted time dabbing her lips with the napkin.

Catching a movement in her peripheral vision, Blaze realized the marquis had lifted his arm to rest against the back of the settee behind her. What should she do? If she sat forward, he would be insulted. If she didn't, he would believe she wanted his arm there.

Blaze heated by several degrees, her complexion flushing in a mixture of embarrassment and confused consternation. She glanced sidelong at the marquis, but he was staring at the prince. Looking none too happy, the prince was returning the stare.

Lykos slid his gaze to hers. "How goes the training for The Craven?"

"Take my advice and wager on Pegasus." Blaze glanced at the marquis. "Did my father send you a note?"

"I havena received any note," Ross answered, "but I did move into the Rowley Lodge yesterday."

"You haven't sold Juno?"

"No, lass."

Tinker walked into the drawing room, announcing, "The Earl of Boston."

The blond, green-eyed earl crossed the room toward them. He carried a bouquet of yellow daisies, blue forget-me-nots, and baby's breath.

"I hope I'm not too late." Dirk Stanley sat beside Raven on the sofa. Glancing at his hands, he stood again and offered the bouquet to Blaze. "I happened by a flower shop in Newmarket, and the forget-me-nots reminded me of your blue eyes."

"Thank you, my lord."

"That makes two of ye," Ross said, lifting one of the lace-edged hankies. "His Highness thought the embroidered flowers looked like her bonny blue eyes."

Catching her sister's gaze, Blaze raised her brows in an unspoken question. In answer, Raven glanced at her betrothal ring and then gave an almost imperceptible shake of her head.

Blaze felt the marquis's gaze on her. Covering their silent communication, she lifted the bouquet to her nose and inhaled its fragrance.

Achoo. She sneezed and sneezed and sneezed.

Grabbing one of the lace-edged hankies, Blaze blew her nose in an unladylike honk. She met her stepmother's frown with an apologetic smile.

"Sometimes spring flowers make me sneeze," she said, blushing.

"Tinker," Ross called, lifting the bouquet out of her hand.

"Yes, my lord?" The majordomo materialized in an instant.

Ross held the bouquet out. "Put these in a vase." He smiled at Blaze, saying, "I dinna think those hankies were meant for noses."

"Nonsense," Prince Lykos spoke up. "The lady can use her gift however she chooses."

Embarrassment heated Blaze. What would their guests have thought if she'd used the sleeve of her gown to wipe her nose?

The Duchess of Inverary turned to the prince and the earl. "I do hope your respective families will arrive in time for the Jockey Club Ball."

"My father and stepmother arrived yesterday," Ross said.

"They've brought Mairi and Amanda," Dirk Stanley added, "and I know the Calders and the Gordons have arrived."

Raven turned to the earl. "I hope you will invite me to dance at the ball."

Dirk Stanley looked surprised and flattered. "What will the Marquis of Basildon think?"

"I haven't married Alexander yet," Raven said, her smile flirtatious.

"I'll dance with ye," Ross said. "I intend to dance with all the Flambeau sisters."

"You mean all the ladies," Blaze corrected him. "You partnered all the ladies at my sister's wedding."

Ross grinned at her. "I'm flattered ye noticed."

"You must dance with Amanda," Dirk said, "or she'll be crushed."

Amanda Stanley, Blaze frowned, the stepsister. She wondered if the other girl was pretty. Could Ross harbor an interest in her? Perhaps he'd refused marriage with the stepsister because he wasn't ready to marry.

"How goes the training for The Craven?" Dirk asked her.

"Very well, thank you."

"I wondered if you would care to watch the race with me," Dirk said, and then turned to Raven. "I would enjoy your company, too."

"I would enjoy sitting together," Raven said, and shifted her gaze to her sister.

"I am sorry," Blaze said, "but Ross has already invited me."

"I suppose that leaves me sitting with my brothers," Prince Lykos said, making everyone smile.

"How do you communicate with animals?" Dirk asked. "I cannot believe that possible."

"Give us a demonstration," Ross said.

"I would like to see it, too," Prince Lykos added.

"Come, Puddles," Blaze said, ignoring her stepmother's frown. When the dog sat at attention in front of her, she leaned close and stared into the mastiff's eyes. *Scare cookie man.*

No.

Her dog was no fool. *Scare flower man.*

Puddles stood and approached Dirk Stanley. The mastiff glared at the earl, curled his lips, and bared his fangs. His hackles raised, the dog growled in a low rumbling sound and drool dripped from both sides of his muzzle.

Dirk Stanley shrank back, his complexion paling. "Call him off."

Flower man good.

Puddles turned his head to look at Blaze, the drool swaying in the movement. *Cookie man good.*

"Come here," Blaze ordered the mastiff. When the dog circled the table to sit in front of her, she wiped his drool with a lace-edged hanky.

Ross MacArthur laughed out loud. When she looked at him, he dropped his eyes to the hanky in her hand.

"Oops." Blaze slid her gaze to the prince. "I am so sorry."

"I am glad you have found a use for the handkerchiefs instead of placing them out of sight in a drawer," Prince Lykos said, his tone amused. "Whenever your dog drools, you will think of me."

"You have made me a true believer," Dirk told her, "but I believe my Emperor will beat your filly."

"Scratch yer horse," Ross advised the other man, his hand on the settee dropping to Blaze's shoulder. "Ye've no chance of winnin' against Pegasus."

Dirk lifted his gaze from his stepbrother's offending hand. "What gift did you bring Miss Blaze?"

"Well, I didna bring her sneeze-inducin' flowers," Ross said, giving the other man an infuriating smile.

"You didn't bring her a token, did you?"

"I brought myself." Ross winked at Blaze. "My gift is waitin' outside."

"As usual, you needed an audience," Dirk said. "Very well, get your gift and make your presentation."

"I prefer to present my gift outside." Ross rose from the settee and offered Blaze his hand. "Come with me, lass."

Blaze placed her hand in his. She thought the marquis was merely polite, but he refused to relinquish her hand.

"I can hardly wait to see this," Dirk said.

Everyone stood and followed them downstairs. Blaze felt she was leading a parade. Standing in the foyer, Tinker opened the door for them.

"Where is this gift?" Dirk asked, scanning the deserted courtyard.

Ross whistled long and loud. From around the corner of the mansion walked an Inverary groomsman leading a chestnut thoroughbred.

"Juno." Blaze lifted her skirt and dashed across the courtyard toward the mare.

Ross smiled at her joy. She was the most amazing woman he'd ever met. He'd made her happy without squandering a fortune on diamonds and other expensive geegaws.

"You gave her that barren mare?" Dirk sneered.

"I gave her what she wanted."

Prince Lykos smiled at him. "Well done, MacArthur."

"Yer a good sport for a man who's losin'," Ross told the prince. "I couldna sell ye the horse and let ye grab my glory."

"I have not lost yet," Lykos said. "A world of difference lies between a thoroughbred and a betrothal ring."

The three men watched Blaze stroke the mare's neck and face, her lips moving in soothing words.

She gazed into the horse's eyes and, unexpectedly, lifted the reins out of the groom's hands. Then she headed in the stable's direction.

"Where are you going?" the duchess called. "You cannot abandon our guests."

"A smart man would accompany the lady to the stables," Lykos said.

"I dinna need advice aboot wooin' ladies."

Ross stepped away, his long strides easily catching Blaze. He lifted the reins out of her hands, and they walked down the path to the stables.

"Thank you for granting my wish," Blaze said, her blue gaze sparkling. "Pegasus and Juno will become great friends. Your impractical gesture will surprise my father."

"Is that a compliment?"

She nodded. "You are not beyond salvation."

Ross grinned at being labeled impractical. He could only gain by giving her Juno. After all, Inverary was the one housing and feeding a useless mare.

For the moment, Ross reminded himself. With any luck, he would soon be wasting money by housing and feeding his bride's useless mare.

Perhaps he could give her another useless pet instead of an expensive betrothal ring. No, the duchess would never allow that. As her husband, he would save a fortune not buying her furs for every evening gown.

"When Pegasus wins The Craven," Blaze told him, "my father promised to mate Juno and Zeus."

The duke's impracticality surprised Ross. Granted, Inverary must have thought winning beyond Pegasus, but there was always a chance.

"What if ye lose, lass?"

"Peg won't lose."

Ross admired her confidence. "I meant, what happens in the unlikely event that ye do lose?"

"I promised to marry the man of his choice."

Ross smiled at that. He loved no-lose situations.

By fair means or foul.

He would marry her if she won or lost. Of course, his bride's mood would be lighter if she won.

With Juno between them, Ross and Blaze entered the stable. The clumping of the mare's shoes sounded hollow on the straw-covered floorboards. Musky horse, grassy hay, and oiled leather scented the air.

"Put her in the stall beside Peg's," Blaze said, grabbing a woolen blanket to drape across the mare's back.

With that done, Blaze called to a stablehand, ordering, "Handle Juno with care. She will deliver champions for Inverary stables."

She stroked the mare's face and then gave her attention to Pegasus. "You can return to the house," she said. "I want to make mash for my horses."

"We'll make mash together," Ross said, removing his jacket and rolling his shirt sleeves up. "Fetch the bucket and a jug of water."

Without complaining about his issuing orders, Blaze set a bucket down and grabbed a jug. Ross watched her for a moment and wondered if she realized he was now in charge. He would not call her attention to that little fact, though. He wasn't a fool.

Ross poured bran and grain pellets into the bucket. Then he added molasses as well as apple and carrot chips the stablehand brought. When Blaze arrived with the water jug, he added water and stirred the concoction. Grabbing another bucket, he ladled half the mixture into it.

"I would never have imagined a marquis performing manual labor," Blaze said, carrying the buckets to her horses.

"I've mucked plenty of stables," Ross told her. "Workin' with horses isna for men who dinna want to dirty their hands."

"I cannot imagine my father making mash for his horses," Blaze said, leaving the stable and starting down the path.

"Inverary is an old man now." Ross shrugged into his jacket. "I'm certain our fathers dirtied their hands long before we were born."

Blaze looked at him. "I doubt my father was ever young."

"Come here, lass." Ross grabbed her hand and led her behind the trees lining the path. He smiled into her questioning gaze and gently drew her closer.

Blaze knew he was going to kiss her. And she was going to allow it.

His head dipped lower, his mouth inched closer, his breath mingled with hers. His lips were warm and firm, his kiss gently persuasive, his invitation subtle.

Accepting his invitation, Blaze pressed herself against him. Ross wrapped his arms around her body, and her hands slid up his chest to entwine his neck.

His mouth on hers sent delicious shivers down her spine. She sighed, surrendering to these new sensations.

The kiss deepened, demanding her response. She met his growing passion with equal fervor. The world faded away, leaving her alone in the universe with only this man.

Ross flicked his tongue across the crease of her lips, which parted, allowing him entrance to the sweetness of her mouth. She felt consumed but wanted more. Much more.

Breaking their kiss, Ross lifted his head and traced a finger down her hot cheek. He smiled at her dazed expression.

"I've been wantin' to do that since yesterday," he whispered, his voice husky.

His smile was sensuous, seductive, *smug*.

Blaze stomped on his booted foot, her slippers doing little damage. "I've been wanting to do *that* since you yelled at me this morning."

Ross laughed and dragged her into a sideways hug, ushering her onto the path again. "Ye'll never bore me, lass."

Chapter Six

"Are ye nervous?"

"No."

"Why are yer hands shakin'?" Ross asked her.

Blaze met his gaze, her expression deadpan. "I suffer the palsy?"

Ross grinned. "Yer a brave lass, Miss Blaze Flambeau."

Sitting in the phaeton, Blaze looked over his shoulder across Newmarket Heath. The Rowley Mile Track lay beyond the field, the grandstands rose at one end of the track, and the Jockey Club flag waved above all to signify race day. Even from this distance, Blaze saw the crowds who'd assembled for the season's opener.

"Ye resemble Rooney in that garb," Ross said, digging inside his leather satchel. "I wouldna recognize ye if I passed ye on the street."

Blaze wore the usual jockey attire. Her racing silk jacket in Campbell colors—green, black, blue—matched her cap. Her red hair was tucked inside. Breeches and lightweight riding boots completed the outfit. Goggles dangled around her neck, and fingerless leather gloves masked her feminine hands.

The binding over her breasts was constricting her breathing. The pale yellow gown worn beneath the breeches and jacket restricted movement somewhat, but the padding offered no protection in the event of a fall.

Ross produced a small packet of Stinking Billy attached to a leather cord. He placed the cord over her head.

"Pardon my touch." Ross slipped the packet and cord beneath her jacket.

"That smells worse than the dead," Blaze complained. "Peg will be sneezing instead of running."

Ross dipped a finger into another packet and smudged mud across her cheekbones. "Anyone seein' the smudges will believe yer Rooney."

"You have considered all angles," Blaze said. "I admire your sneakiness."

"Dinna forget to quicken the pace before the Devil's Ditch," Ross said, "and dinna walk like a girl."

"What do you mean?"

"Dinna wiggle yer butt."

Blaze blushed. "I do not wiggle."

"Jockeys swagger," he told her, "and they never blush."

"Only jockeys swagger?"

"Short men swagger in public to compensate for their lack of height."

Blaze glanced over his shoulder. "Here comes Rooney."

Both Ross and Blaze climbed out of the phaeton.

She watched in fascination as Rooney approached. The jockey looked like her.

"I told the guys I needed to piss," Rooney said, passing her the whip. "Are you certain?"

"I'll see you on the path." Blaze gave them a jaunty smile and walked away, her gait confident.

"Jeez, she's wigglin' her butt," Ross muttered.

The closer Blaze walked to the spectators, the louder the cacophony of sounds assaulting her ears. She passed groups of roughly dressed men entertaining themselves with cockfights and dicing. The animals' distressed cries made her heart ache with the unrequited need to rescue them. Maybe she couldn't save every animal, but she could speak to her father about persuading the Jockey Club to ban all violent entertainment between races.

"Hey, Rooney," the Stanley jockey called. "How did the piss come out?"

"Ye stink to high heaven," the MacArthur jockey added. "Did ye take a bath in it?"

"Give the drunk a break," the Inverary jockey said, eliciting the other men's laughter. "His Grace has him riding the balking filly."

Blaze kept walking, but an imp entered her soul. She lifted her arm in the air and gave them her middle finger. Behind her came the unmistakable sounds of scuffling and a voice warning, "Ye'll get tossed if ye go after him."

Poor Rooney. She should warn him those three had violent intentions. They would respect Rooney when he and the balking filly won the Triple Crown.

Blaze spied Bobby Bender and Pegasus at the far

end of the paddock. She raised her hand, greeting the trainer, and then stood in front of the filly.

Love Peg.

Me love.

Peg run?

Run, run, run.

"Are you certain you want to do this?" Bender asked, glancing around at the other trainers and jockeys. "It isn't too late to change your mind."

Blaze smiled, surprisingly calm as the moment neared. "We'll meet you in the winner's circle."

"Rooney?"

Blaze turned to see a stableboy, offering her a small glass. She lifted it out of his hand and gulped the whisky in one swig. The liquid burned a path to her stomach, making her cough and wheeze.

"The booze went down the wrong pipe," Bender told the boy.

The bell rang.

Bobby Bender gave her a leg up on Pegasus, and she passed him the whip. The trainer mounted his own horse, and together, they followed the line of jockeys and escorts riding toward the track.

The crowd roared with anticipation as the first horses came into view. They paraded down track in pairs toward the starting line like Noah's creatures marching toward the Ark.

"Good luck," Bender said, turning his horse away, leaving her and Pegasus.

Her breath caught in momentary panic. Nerves churned her stomach, and her pulses raced.

Blaze moved Pegasus into position at the starting line. She crouched low over her horse, her gaze on the official holding the flag. And then the flag dropped.

Peg run.

Run, run, run . . .

What had he done? Ross worried, standing on the path beyond the finish line. He wanted Blaze to win, but he also wanted her safe. No one knew better than he that racing horses could produce unexpected and sometimes fatal results. Some jockeys were known for their unscrupulous tricks, willing to do anything in an effort to win.

"They're off." Rooney sat on a thick tree limb, spyglass in hand.

"Call the race," Ross ordered.

"She made a clean start," Rooney told him. "Peg's seventh but moving up. Sweet Jesus."

"What happened?"

"Peg is flying," the jockey said. "She's sixth. Fifth, now. Oh, no."

"I'll kill ye, man."

"MacArthur and Wakefield horses made a hole to block her," Rooney called. "Aha, Peg slipped through the hole and is accelerating to catch the last two in front of her. Oh, shit."

"Rooney."

"Inverary and Stanley jockeys are blocking her," Rooney said, and then laughed. "Our girl's pushed through the hole, nearly toppling the two off their horses. She's free, clear, and gaining speed. Five lengths in front. Ten lengths, fifteen, twenty . . ."

The jockey whooped in glee and dropped from the tree limb. "Fuck me, she did it."

Ross heard the pounding hooves coming closer and closer. "Get ready," he ordered the jockey.

Blaze and Pegasus appeared on the path. "Peg won," she cried.

"We've no time for applause." Ross pulled her off Pegasus and, yanking the goggles over her head, tossed them to Rooney before giving him a leg up.

Rooney hooked the goggles over his head, letting them dangle from his neck. Then the jockey rode down the path to the field.

"Yer father will be lookin' for ye," Ross said, helping her remove the racing garb. "Dinna forget the Stinkin' Billy."

Grabbing a wet linen, Ross washed the grime from her face. He set a wide-brimmed bonnet on her head and wrapped a shawl around her shoulders.

"Keep the shawl around ye cuz we dinna want anyone noticin' yer flat titties," Ross said, making her blush.

After lifting her into the phaeton, Ross climbed in beside her and smiled. "Congratulations, lass. Ye've accomplished the impossible."

"*We* accomplished the impossible," Blaze corrected him.

Ross winked at her. "I like the sound of *we*."

Reaching the grandstands, Ross leaped out of the phaeton and tossed a coin to a track boy, ordering, "Take care of my horses." He grabbed Blaze's hand to escort her through the crowd to the winner's circle.

"Where's my daughter?" the Duke of Inverary was asking. "Blaze owns the filly."

Her father stood on one side of Pegasus and Bobby Bender on the other. Rooney sat on top of the filly.

"Go, lass," Ross said.

"You must come, too."

Ross smiled at that. He was definitely making progress with her, and soon the Lykos Kazanov threat would be a memory. He never doubted he could best the prince, though.

"Here's my daughter now," the Duke of Inverary said, putting his arm around her shoulders. He shook Ross's hand, saying, "You and Bender worked a miracle."

"Blaze deserves the honor," Ross said.

"The trainers and jockey get the accolades," the duke replied, "and the owner gets the money. Your parents are dining at Inverary House tonight. Come along, and we'll celebrate."

Blaze touched his hand, her smile pure sunshine. "Please, join the celebration."

Ross grinned at her. "I would love to celebrate with ye."

Was tonight's dinner a celebration or the opening battle of a war?

Dining with the Duchess of Kilchurn meant she needed to look her best. Emanating hostility, the MacArthur duchess hadn't bothered to mask her disapproval. The woman possessed a basilisk's deadly stare.

Blaze gave herself a final inspection in the cheval mirror. She wore a blush silk gown with a modestly scooped neckline, short puffed sleeves, and a scalloped flounce hem.

Her stepmother insisted bland colors provided the perfect background for her fiery hair. White and black provided the most striking starkness.

She needed jewels. Crossing to the highboy, Blaze opened the drawer and lifted her mother's jeweled butterfly hairclasp and its matching bracelet. She sensed the Kilchurn duchess had known and disliked Gabrielle Flambeau. Flaunting her mother's jewels appealed to Blaze.

Celebration or battle? Blaze was prepared for both. Her victory in the race had vanquished her worry, making her feel invincible, and she almost welcomed a fight with the MacArthur duchess.

Blaze would have preferred celebrating with her team, though. Ross, Rooney, Bender, and Pegasus deserved the honor and were more companionable than the witch.

Delaying the oncoming storm, Blaze sat on the chaise in front of the hearth. She had a few minutes to practice distance communication with her horse.

Closing her eyes, Blaze relaxed and took several deep breaths. She imagined herself staring into her filly's eyes.

Love Peg.

No answer.

Love Peg.

No answer.

Love Peg.

Me love.

Her eyes flew open. Had she imagined an answer?
Love Peg. Love Peg. Love Peg.
Me love. Me love. Me love.

Blaze laughed and bolted off the chaise, calling, "Puddles, I did—" The bedchamber was empty,
the mastiff preferring the kitchen during the
dinner hour.

Elated by her success, Blaze waltzed toward the
door. She couldn't wait to tell the marquis.

Blaze paused, her hand on the doorknob, as
doubts stepped from the shadows of her mind.
Should she tell the marquis or remain temporarily
silent?

One communication did not guarantee success.
She needed more practice, and the marquis would
insist Rooney ride Pegasus in the First Spring Race
three weeks hence.

Blaze decided on silence. She would continue
practicing and ride Pegasus in the next race. That
would give them six weeks before the Second
Spring Race.

With her decision made, Blaze left her bedchamber and walked down the corridor to the main staircase. She met the marquis on the second floor
landing.

MacArthur appeared the image of sleek sophis-
tication in his midnight blue, impeccably tailored
trousers and jacket. He grew more appealing each
time she saw him. Or was her imagination playing games because they shared the secret of Pegasus's win?

"Yer beauty shames those jeweled butterflies,"
Ross said, bowing over her hand.

Blaze blushed at his compliment, her smile flirtatious. "You are an outrageous flatterer, my lord."

"Ye mean partner in crime," Ross said, and winked at her. "Where's yer dog?"

"Puddles loiters in the kitchen during dinner."

He smiled at that. "I delayed my arrival to avoid Celeste as long as possible."

"So did I."

"Shall we show the old witch a united front?" Ross asked, offering her his arm.

"Our arriving together may irritate your stepmother," Blaze said, slipping her hand through the crook of his arm.

"I consider that an added benefit."

"And so do I."

Ross escorted her down the hallway. "This dinner could prove interesting."

"Forget interesting," Blaze said. "You hold the witch down while I drive a stake through her heart."

Ross grinned at her. "Yer very bloodthirsty, but I admire that trait."

Arm in arm, Ross and Blaze walked into the drawing room and strolled across the Persian carpet. Sipping sherry, the two older couples sat in front of the white marble hearth.

"Here comes the winning team," the Duke of Inverary said, drawing attention to them.

"They make a spectacular team," the Duchess of Inverary said. "Don't you agree, Celeste?"

Uh-oh. Her stepmother was baiting the witch.

Blaze looked at the two duchesses, the women's diamonds nearly blinding her. "Their brilliance dazzles the eye," she whispered, leaning close to the marquis. "Both are wearing every diamond they own."

Ross chuckled, a husky sound that conspired with his mountain heather scent to send the butterflies in her belly winging into flight. "I'm thankful they arena wearin' furs," he said, "lest ye recruit me to dig graves."

Blaze giggled, drawing different reactions from the two couples. Their fathers looked pleased, and her stepmother beamed her approval. The Duchess of Kilchurn's stare was positively venomous.

The Duke of Kilchurn stood and bowed over her hand. "Congratulations, my dear."

"Thank you, Your Grace, but your son deserves the honor," Blaze said. "Pegasus could not have won without his expertise."

"Call us James and Celeste," Kilchurn said, and looked at Ross. "Good job, son."

Blaze glanced at the Duchess of Kilchurn. The blonde gave her a stiff smile.

"Blaze is the image of Bedelia," Kilchurn said to her father.

"I fear we may hear Sainted Bedelia stories all evening," Celeste MacArthur said.

"I never tire of Bedelia's adventures," Roxanne Campbell said.

The Duke of Inverary passed Ross a glass of sherry. "Blaze, would you like a drop of sherry?"

"Winning The Craven will not change my dislike of spirits," she refused.

"Where are your other stepdaughters?" Celeste asked.

"Raven and Alexander are dining with his

grandfather, the Duke of Essex," her stepmother answered. "Bliss, Serena, and Sophia are dining with their married sisters. Both married Kazanov princes last year."

"You've done well by them," Celeste said. "Two princes and a future duke."

"I want everyone as happily married as I," the Duchess of Inverary said. "I heard several more Kazanov princes may be visiting within the year. Only Princes Lykos and Gunter have seen Prince Drako's and Princess Katerina's one-year-old son. Drako is the oldest of twelve, you know."

"Their son was born less than nine months after their marriage," the Duchess of Kilchurn said, her expression pinched.

Roxanne Campbell gave her a dimpled smile. "I say, all's well that ends well."

"Dearest, I believe Shakespeare said that first," the Duke of Inverary interjected.

His wife smiled at him. "Even the great bard could not manage two marriages of the decade within the same year."

"What a unique butterfly hair clasp and bracelet," Celeste said, drawing Blaze's attention. "Did Princess Katerina design them?"

Blaze gestured to Gabrielle Flambeau's portrait. "The butterflies belonged to my mother."

"I see." The Duchess of Kilchurn frowned in obvious disapproval.

Blaze clenched her hands into fists, her fingers itching to strike the woman. She wished society did not disapprove of ladies brawling.

"Gabrielle Flambeau was a lovely woman,"

the Duchess of Inverary said, smoothing over the awkward silence. "Here is Tinker, signaling us to dinner."

The Duchess of Inverary escorted the Duke of Kilchurn down the stairs to the dining room while the Duke of Inverary partnered his friend's wife. Ross and Blaze lagged behind the foursome.

"My stepmother definitely dislikes yours," Blaze whispered.

"Nobody likes Celeste except her children."

"Your father must love her."

"Celeste canna compare to my mother," Ross said. "I suspect my father harbors regrets."

The Duke and Duchess of Inverary took their usual seats at the ends of the mahogany table. The Duke of Kilchurn and his son sat on either side of their hostess. The Duchess of Kilchurn sat directly across the table from Blaze.

Standing near the sideboard, Tinker supervised the footmen. The majordomo served the wine to all but Blaze.

Dinner's first course arrived, tomato soup with a swirl of cream and chopped green herbs. Blaze felt relieved. No meat, no fish, no poultry.

Her father raised his wine glass in a toast. "Congratulations to Blaze, who believed in her horse when no one else did."

All raised their glasses in salute. Blaze lifted her glass of lemon barley water and saluted the marquis.

"You do not care for wine?" the Duchess of Kilchurn asked her.

"I dislike spirits, Celeste." Blaze smiled at the Duke of Kilchurn, who had invited her to use their first names. His wife, however, did not appear pleased by the informality.

"If you want to get along in Society," the Duchess of Kilchurn told her, "you must develop a taste for champagne."

"Society will accept me as I am," Blaze said, lifting her spoon to taste the soup, "for I will never change myself to please others."

"My dearest Blaze possesses an attitude that sets trends," Roxanne Campbell interjected.

"The girl is emulating you."

Her stepmother's dimpled smile appeared. "I like to think so."

Once they'd finished the soup, two footmen removed their bowls. Tinker gestured two other footmen to begin serving dinner's second course.

Blaze hoped duck did not appear on the evening's menu. If it did, she prayed the mother was not a bone sucker like her son. Instinct told her that the bone sucker had learned the disgusting habit from his mother.

Baked Dover sole appeared on the table. Asparagus gratin, dressed cucumbers, and mushroom caps stewed in butter accompanied the fish.

"Thank you," Blaze said, when the majordomo delivered her plate without fish.

Tinker gave her a conspiratorial smile. "You are very welcome, Miss Blaze."

"Did you wager on today's race?"

"I did," Tinker answered, "and my faith in your ability was handsomely rewarded."

Blaze smiled at the older man. "I made a small fortune, too."

"If you want to get along in Society," Celeste MacArthur spoke up, "you must never converse with servants. None of the Quality behaves so casually."

"In this household, we do converse with our employees," the Duchess of Inverary corrected the other woman. "We consider Tinker one of the family."

"How generous." Celeste turned her attention on Blaze again. "You do not care for fish?"

"The lass lives on fruits and vegetables and grains," Ross answered. "Eating meat, fish, and poultry gives her the hives."

Celeste MacArthur ignored her stepson. "Gentlemen do not marry finicky women."

The Duke of Inverary cleared his throat and changed the subject. "Ross, tell us how you broke Pegasus of the balking."

"Sorry, Yer Grace, but that's our secret." Ross gave Blaze a sidelong smile.

"Chadwick comes out of mourning this week," Celeste told the Duchess of Inverary. "I do hope you will include him in the Jockey Club Ball. Dirk and he own several thoroughbreds together."

"Of course, Chadwick must attend," Roxanne Campbell replied. "Chadwick is too handsome a widower to remain unmarried for long. We must find him an heiress."

Blaze had no idea to whom the women were referring. She arched a questioning brow at the marquis.

"Squire Chadwick Simmons is Celeste's son and Dirk's half-brother," Ross explained, reaching for his wine glass.

How many men had Celeste MacArthur managed

to marry? Blaze doubted her stepmother wanted a mere squire walking through her door. On the other hand, Chadwick was the Duke of Kilchurn's stepson.

The footmen served roasted beef accompanied by crispy, roasted potatoes and horseradish sauce. Tinker set a vegetable and bean pie in front of her.

Blaze glanced across the table and caught Celeste MacArthur watching her, an expression of hatred in her green gaze. In response, she gave the woman her most infuriatingly serene smile.

"Papa, those violent entertainments between races is shameful," Blaze said. "Could you persuade the Jockey Club to ban cockfights?"

"Yer daughter sounds like Bedelia," the Duke of Kilchurn said, smiling. "Bedelia frowned upon dicing and whatnot."

Celeste rolled her eyes. "I suppose this begins the Bedelia stories."

The Duke of Inverary gave his daughter an indulgent smile. "The cockfights keep the ruffians out of trouble."

"Scheduling more races with less time between them could solve that problem," Blaze suggested. "The owners will make more money if you add races."

"What an outstandin' idea," the Duke of Kilchurn said. "The Club should have thought of this long before now."

Duke Magnus nodded at his friend. "We'll float the idea at the next meeting."

"Papa, do you employ carpenters on staff?"

"Why do you ask?"

"I need a cart built to carry Pegasus to Epsom

Downs and Doncaster," Blaze answered. "Peg will arrive less tired than the other thoroughbreds."

"You are drunk with today's success," her father said, a smile on his lips. "We've always walked the horses from one track to another."

"Always does not mean forever," she argued.

"Do you approve of her owning a horse?" the Duchess of Kilchurn asked, looking down the table at her stepmother.

"I can see no harm in her hobby," Roxanne Campbell answered.

Her stepmother was defending her? That was akin to a miracle.

"The cart idea has merit," Ross was saying. "I'm goin' to investigate the possibility."

"The horses may require special training getting in and out of the cart," Magnus Campbell said, "but I suppose it could work."

"Papa?"

Her father looked at her, his dark gaze warning her to beware. "What now?"

"When will Juno be visiting the breeding barn?" Blaze heard the Duchess of Kilchurn gasp while Ross and his father chuckled.

"Blaze, darling, that particular topic is unseemly for the dinner table," her stepmother said.

"Apologies." Blaze glanced at their guests and then looked at her father. "Papa?"

"You don't trust me?" her father asked.

"I trust you," she answered, "but this is business."

"Business is discussed in the office." Her stepmother's voice held a warning note.

Blaze ignored her. "Papa?"

The Duke of Inverary set his fork on the plate. "As promised, Juno will visit the barn in a couple of days."

"Thank you, Papa." Blaze was silent for a long moment. Then she cleared her throat and added, "The owner customarily witnesses the . . . the . . . the deed."

The Duchess of Kilchurn gasped again. The Duchess of Inverary joined her this time.

"You will witness nothing," her father said, his tone brooking no disobedience. "Maidens do not belong there."

"I will act as the witness," Ross said, laughter lurking in his voice.

Blaze acquiesced with reluctance. "Very well, the marquis will represent me."

Ross leaned close, saying, "We'll forgo the drawing room in favor of visiting Pegasus."

Blaze looked at him and nodded. She would have agreed to almost anything to escape Celeste MacArthur's basilisk stare as well as her stepmother's disapproval.

Once dinner ended, the two older couples retired to the drawing room. Once they'd disappeared up the stairs, Ross said, "Let's take yer dog along for the walk."

"I'll get Puddles."

"Send a servant."

"Don't be silly." Blaze closed her eyes and pictured the mastiff in her mind. *Puddles, come foyer.* She opened her eyes. "He will be here in a moment."

Ross heard the thud of paws running down the stairs, and then the dog appeared. "You communicated long distance," he said, awed accusation in his voice.

"Yes, I did."

"What is the delay with Pegasus?"

Blaze shrugged, her cheeks pinkening. "I've known Puddles longer than Pegasus."

She's lying.

Ross stared at her for a long moment, reddening her complexion even more. God's balls, she was easier to read than an open book. The girl blushed whenever she lied or heard a sexual reference.

Why would Blaze lie? She must know Rooney and Pegasus needed days, if not weeks, of practicing together. He would pretend to believe her for a few days. After all, there were three weeks before the next race.

"The moon is full so we dinna need a lantern," Ross said, ushering her toward the door. "How long have ye known Puddles?"

Her blush began to fade. "I've owned Puddles for several years."

They stepped into a mild April evening and strolled down the path to the stables. The night shrouded them like a blanket, but slivers of moonlight guided their way. All was eerily silent except for an owl, hooting nearby as it readied for its nightly hunt.

"The team will take tomorrow off," Ross said, "unless ye connect with the filly."

"I will tell you the moment I connect with Peg."

Ross wished he could see her complexion more clearly. He'd wager his last shilling she was blushing.

"Tell me about your stepmother," Blaze said.

"Celeste Chadwick was a vicar's daughter who married a wealthy merchant." Ross knew Blaze had purposely changed the subject from distance communication. "She and Merchant Simmons had one son, Squire Chadwick Simmons. When he died—"

"What killed him?" Blaze interrupted.

"He stopped breathin'," Ross answered. "Then Celeste married the Earl of Boston and bore him two children, Dirk and Amanda."

"I suppose the earl stopped breathing, too."

Ross chuckled. "Celeste became a close acquaintance—I willna say true friend—of my mother. After my mother died, Celeste married my father and became a duchess."

"Celeste rose from obscure origins to titled greatness," Blaze said. "You've met Squire Chadwick Simmons?"

"Chad seems a decent sort," Ross told her. "His wife and baby did not survive the birthin'."

"How sad." Blaze was silent for a brief moment. "Your father should beware since Celeste has buried two husbands."

"She'll never harm my father," Ross said. "The title, the lands, and the money pass to me. My closest male kin, the Duke of Inverary, inherits if I die without issue."

Distant voices, an unusual occurrence at that hour, disturbed their conversation. The closer they got to the stables, the louder the voices sounded.

"Are the stablehands celebrating Peg's victory?" Blaze asked him.

"They would've gone into town," Ross answered.

A dozen lanterns lit the stableyard. The hands had congregated into small groups.

Something was wrong. And then Bobby Bender walked out of the filly's stable. Spying them, the trainer crossed the yard, but Blaze brushed past him to get to her horse, her dog two steps behind.

"We had an intruder," Bender said, "but he escaped."

Ross raised his brows. "Any damage?"

"Pegasus is fine," the trainer answered, "but her decisive win today angered someone."

"I want Peg guarded at all times," Ross instructed the man. "Only Rooney gives Peg her daily workout."

"Doesn't the Duke of Inverary own these stables?" Bender asked, his tone dry.

Ross glanced toward the stable's open doors. "Pegasus is my responsibility."

"As is the filly's owner," Bender said, smiling. "I'm on my way to alert His Grace."

Ross nodded and walked into the stable. The familiar scents of musky horse and sweet hay tickled his nose, and the light from lanterns cast eerie shadows on the walls.

Blaze was stroking the filly's face. Like sentinels, Rooney and Puddles stood beside her.

"Bender said Peg is fine," Ross told her.

Blaze looked at him. "Will you tell my parents I'm sleeping here?"

"Sorry, darlin', ye'll sleep in yer own bed."

"I'll sleep here," Rooney told her. "I've a cot in the last stall."

"Puddles will guard you."

"I want no one near this filly," Ross instructed the jockey. "Ye give her the daily workout."

Blaze crouched in front of her dog and stared into its eyes. When she stood, Puddles walked into the empty stall opposite the filly's and curled up on a bale of hay.

Rooney grinned. "I'll move my cot into the dog's stall."

"We'll meet for practice the day after tomorrow," Ross told him. "I've a feelin' Blaze will distance communicate by then."

Ross and Blaze left the stable and started down the path. Instead of returning to the house, they strolled across the lawns in the direction of the gazebo.

"Whoever stabbed Charlie wanted to hurt Peg," Blaze said, unable to keep the worry out of her voice.

"Dinna fret aboot the filly." Ross put his arm around her shoulders, drawing her closer. "If necessary, I'll sleep in the stable for the whole racin' season."

They climbed the gazebo's steps and sat on the bench, the same place they'd sat only a week earlier. When she didn't inch away from him, Ross mentally rubbed his hands together at the progress he'd made.

"Explain how ye came by this gift of yers," Ross said. "Why is this animal refuge so important to ye?"

"I was born cursed, not gifted," Blaze said, her soft voice tinged with bitterness. "I can make money by asking the horses which will win a race, but the downside overshadows my life."

Ross stared at her. "What d'ye mean?"

"I feel their suffering and hear their cries for help," Blaze answered, unable to keep the pain out of her voice. "Nanny Smudge took us on a picnic near a pond once. I heard distant cries for help and looked around. Two older boys were tossing a sack into the water. By the time Nanny Smudge pulled the sack from the water, the kitten inside had drowned."

Saddened by her story. Ross read the anguish in her expression and understood her dilemma. She had no choice in the matter. She needed to rescue animals or live with their agony.

"Whatever ye win in the racin' season," he said, "I'll match the funds and help ye build the refuge."

"Most people never consider God's creatures," Blaze said. "Why do you want to help?"

"I'm partial to red hair, freckles, and noble causes."

Ross leaned closer and tasted her lips in a chaste kiss. She wanted him, but innocence blinded her to that fact. By God, he wanted her.

For the first time in his life, Ross felt the urge to propose marriage but held his tongue. Inverary had warned him this daughter planned never to marry. If he offered for her, she would take flight like the jeweled butterfly she wore in her hair.

By fair means or foul, Ross reminded himself. The only way to get her to the altar was through his bed. He expected her to rant and rave, but that would change to purrs and sighs soon enough.

"I want ye in my bed," he told her, "and I intend to have ye."

His words sent Blaze surging to her feet. "I beg your pardon?"

"I want ye," he repeated, "and ye want me."

The marquis was a swine.

"How dare you speak to me like that," Blaze said, her hands balling into fists. "Just because my mother—"

"My desire has nothin' to do with yer mother," Ross interrupted, and rose from the bench to tower over her. "Raise those tiny fists to me, darlin', and ye'll be sorry."

"You deserve a good thrashing."

Ross gave her a lazy, thoroughly infuriating smile. "That doesna change the fact I'll see ye in my bed."

"I'll see you there when cocks lay eggs." Blaze whirled away, intending to leave.

"Let me explain the facts of life." Ross grabbed her arm to keep her from bolting. "I willna help ye win the Triple Crown if ye dinna visit my bed."

"You're blackmailing me?" Blaze snatched her arm out of his grasp and lifted her nose into the air. "The team no longer needs your help."

"Meet me here tomorrow night," Ross said, as if she hadn't spoken. "I dinna want anyone recognizin' ye so wear a hooded cloak."

"Dress warmly, my lord. You will be waiting a long time."

"If ye arena here, I'm reportin' ye to the Jockey Club," he threatened her. "The team will lose their jobs, and Peg will be stripped of today's win."

Wham! Blaze slapped him hard. So hard his head jerked to one side. So hard the palm of her hand stung.

Blaze flew down the gazebo's steps and stormed across the lawn toward the house. She knew the marquis was following her. She could feel his gaze on her back.

When she quickened her pace, Blaze heard his husky chuckle. She opened the door, and he leveled his parting shot at her.

"I'll see ye tomorrow night, darlin'."

Boom. Blaze slammed the door shut behind her.

Chapter Seven

Softer than a woman's inner thighs.

Alexander Blake, the Marquis of Basildon, relaxed in the soft leather chair and stretched his long legs out. He lifted the crystal tumbler to his lips and sipped the whisky, savoring the amber liquid, letting his warm tongue release its bold, full-bodied flavor. Highland whisky, no doubt.

He smiled at the man seated across the enormous oak desk and then took a drag on his cigar, the best money could buy. Life was good for his future father-in-law, the illustrious Duke of Inverary. Simple pleasures like Highland whisky and expensive cigars made life enjoyable.

"Don't mention our cigar smoking to my wife," Magnus Campbell said.

Suppressing the urge to burst into disrespectful laughter, Alexander gave the duke a lopsided grin. "My lips are forever locked."

"Roxie insists tobacco stinks," Inverary told him, "and she only allows smoking in the dining room after the ladies withdraw. And the billiard room, of course."

"Baron Shores should arrive soon," Alexander said, checking the time on his pocket watch. "I sent the summons from Amadeus Black."

"The constable is not present."

"Crazy Eddie doesn't know that," Alexander said. "I'll question the stablehands tomorrow because I promised Raven a trip into Newmarket today."

"The intruder proves Charlie's murder was deliberate," the Duke of Inverary said.

"Raven sensed the crime was murder-for-hire," Alexander reminded him. "Someone is desperate to win the Triple Crown."

The duke sipped his whisky and then took a drag on his cigar. "I didn't believe Pegasus could win," he said. "Rooney reeked worse than dung. I daresay, the stench will grow fouler if he wins the First Spring."

"Tell him to wash," Alexander suggested.

"Jockeys are superstitious fellows," Inverary told him, "and Rooney will not chance breaking the streak."

"Your racing season could prove pungent."

A knock on the door drew their attention. Tinker stepped inside, announcing, "Baron Shores has arrived." When the duke nodded, the majordomo gestured to someone in the hallway.

Baron Edward "Crazy Eddie" Shores walked into the office. Though expensively dressed, the baron did not commune with London's elite. At least, not in the best drawing rooms. He walked the fine line between providing vices for gentlemen and true criminal activity.

"Tightly, Tinker," called the duke, and the door clicked shut.

"Good afternoon, Your Grace." The baron looked at Alexander, adding, "I didn't do it, and I don't know anything."

"Relax, Eddie." The Duke of Inverary beckoned him forward, gesturing him to sit in the chair beside Alexander's. He poured a measure of whisky into a crystal tumbler and passed it to the baron.

"Thank you, Your Grace." The baron raised his glass in salute and sampled the whisky. "Superior quality."

The Duke of Inverary smiled. "Highland whisky, of course."

"Someone murdered His Grace's jockey a few weeks ago," Alexander said, "and last night an intruder tried to break into the winning horse's stable."

Baron Shores raised his right hand. "I swear I know nothing."

"I believe you," the duke said, passing him a cigar, "but we need information such as the names of men flaunting money around town or any other gossip. I will, of course, pay for your services."

Alexander regretted the Newmarket locale. If they had been in London, the constable's runners would have provided twenty-four hour surveillance of MacArthur and Stanley. Circumstances forced him to use the baron and his connections.

"I can do that favor for you," the baron was saying, pocketing the cigar. "Do you suspect anyone?"

"The villain is planting evidence against two gentlemen of impeccable reputation," Alexander answered. "We need you to watch MacArthur and hire a friend to watch the Earl of Boston."

"You suspect MacArthur?" the baron echoed in apparent surprise.

"We do *not* suspect MacArthur," the Duke of Inverary insisted, "but we need proof that Stanley and he are marked to take the fall."

"If I murdered a jockey," the baron said, "I'd plant false evidence, too."

The Duke of Inverary stood, signifying the end of the interview. "You can report to Alexander or me if you learn anything."

"You have a deal, Your Grace." Baron Shores shook his hand and then looked at Alexander. "If you need me, I am staying at the Rowley Lodge. Give Constable Black my regards."

"The constable will regret missing our meeting," Alexander replied.

Once the baron had gone, Alexander looked at the duke. "If Eddie knows nothing, then the usual criminal elements are not involved. That makes the investigation more difficult but not unsolvable."

"Thank you, Alex."

"You are welcome, Your Grace." Alexander shook the older man's hand and turned to leave. "Duty demands I escort my sweet betrothed to town."

While Alexander Blake and her father were meeting, Blaze marched down the corridor toward the drawing room in search of her stepmother. She hadn't slept well the previous night, her thoughts fixing on the marquis.

Ross MacArthur assumed a bastard was an easy mark. Like mother, like daughter. He would never consider blackmailing the saintly stepsister nor any other properly-born lady.

She would never surrender to him. If he squealed to the Jockey Club, she would even the score. Somehow.

The thought of losing her chance to win the Triple Crown stepped from the shadows of her mind and slowed her pace. Under normal circumstances, she would have told her father about the marquis. She hadn't done that, though.

Pegasus would forfeit yesterday's win, which meant returning the prize money and, perhaps, paying a fine equal to the amount she'd won on the wager. Both Bender and Rooney would lose their jobs. Her animal refuge would never be built, and the animals' sufferings would continue.

And then her father's image surfaced in her mind's eye. She could not face his expression of shocked disappointment at her flaunting society by jockeying Pegasus.

Perhaps she should reconsider her options. The marquis was a handsome man, and visiting his bed would not be a hardship. Afterwards, she could pretend it never happened.

Blaze walked into the drawing room. The duchess sat near the window and concentrated on needlework. Puddles lay at her feet, his eyes fixed on a plate of cookies beside her. Raven sat in the chair opposite her stepmother.

Crossing the room, Blaze dropped onto an upholstered chair. "Good afternoon," she greeted them.

"You are still ecstatic about yesterday's triumph,"

the duchess remarked. "I have never seen you in a good mood for two consecutive days."

"You exaggerate," Blaze said. "What are you sewing?"

"Darling, embroidery is not sewing," her stepmother corrected, and then gave the mastiff a cookie. "Your father adores the Campbell crest on his handkerchiefs."

Blaze smiled. "You are embroidering a boar's head on Papa's handkerchiefs?"

"I will never understand the reason the Campbells chose a boar," the duchess said. "A rose would have been prettier."

"Roses are English and the Campbells are Scots," Raven said, and then looked at Blaze. "Alex is taking me into Newmarket. Would you care to join us?"

"No, thank you." Blaze had too much thinking to do before eight o'clock. She looked at her stepmother. "Do you dislike Celeste MacArthur?"

"I cannot say I dislike the woman," the duchess answered, "but I cannot find anything about her to like."

Blaze and Raven exchanged smiles. The duchess was always circumspect in her words. Her dimpled smile appeared whenever she insulted someone.

"I need your advice on an important matter," Blaze said, earning a pleased smile from her stepmother.

The duchess offered the mastiff another cookie. "How can I help you, dear?"

"I want to know about"—her complexion reddened—"about sexual intimacy."

The Duchess of Inverary snapped her gaze from her needlework to her stepdaughter. For the first time since Blaze had met her stepmother, Roxanne Campbell lost her placid expression.

"Darling, there's no need to know certain facts until you marry," the duchess said, recovering her poise.

Blaze glanced at Raven, who was smiling. "I swear I need to know."

The Duchess of Inverary arched an auburn brow at her. "Have you decided to marry?"

"No."

"What is urgent about that knowledge?"

Blaze felt her frustration rising. This wasn't as easy as she had thought. "Are you going to share your knowledge or not?"

The duchess's dimpled smile appeared. "I will tell you everything when you give me a good reason."

If she lied, the duchess would become suspicious. If she told the outrageous truth, the duchess would believe she was joking.

"I am considering a sexual liaison," Blaze said, her cheeks pinkening. "You know, a love affair."

"Who is the unlucky gentleman?" the duchess asked, eliciting her sister's giggles.

"The Marquis of Awe has invited me into his bed," Blaze answered.

"How interesting." Her stepmother lifted her gaze from her embroidery to look at her. "My advice is trust the marquis to tutor you."

Was the unscrupulous blackmailer a well-known expert in sexual matters? "I may change my mind and choose Prince Lykos," Blaze said, hoping for an answer.

"My advice remains the same," the duchess said. "Trust the prince."

"Would you offer the same advice about Dirk Stanley?"

"In that event, darling, I would say you had incredibly poor taste in gentlemen."

Raven laughed. Blaze giggled, knowing when she'd been beaten, and then a thought occurred to her.

"If you consider the earl unworthy," she asked, "why did you offer him as a potential suitor?"

"There is no accounting for taste in this world," the duchess answered, "and your father would have supported you. Financially, I mean."

Blaze exchanged glances with her sister. "Do you mean the earl lacks funds?"

"Dirk Stanley lives on a modest income from his father's estate," her stepmother answered, "and his thoroughbreds do well, generally speaking. His mother spent most of the earl's inheritance putting herself out."

"What do you mean by putting herself out?" Raven asked her.

"A lady cannot put herself in the way of a wealthy duke unless she dresses a certain way and receives invitations to certain gatherings," the duchess explained. "Most titled widows enjoy esteemed families who find them another husband, but Celeste MacArthur was not born into the upper class."

Blaze nodded at her sister. "Ross told me Celeste was a vicar's daughter."

"How did you meet Papa?" Raven asked.

"I'd known Magnus for years," she answered. "In our younger days, your father was one of my suitors."

"Why didn't you marry him then?" Blaze asked.

"I married another gentleman." The duchess set her embroidery aside. "Magnus and I met again after I'd buried my second husband."

"You buried *two* husbands?" Raven echoed in surprise.

"Did they die from chronic nagging?" Blaze asked, making her sister giggle.

Her stepmother gave her an unamused look. "Do not be flippant."

Tinker walked into the drawing room, ending their conversation. "Prince Lykos Kazanov requests a word with Miss Blaze."

"The prince is welcome," the duchess said, sounding like a queen. "Send him up."

"Yes, Your Grace." Tinker stepped into the hallway and gestured to someone.

Prince Lykos walked into the drawing room and headed straight for her stepmother. "Forgive my unexpected but brief visit," he said, bowing over the duchess's hand, "for my brother is waiting in the coach."

Lykos turned around to greet the sisters and gave Blaze a devastating smile. "I wish to invite you to sup with me at the Jockey Club Ball. That is, if you are not otherwise engaged."

His invitation surprised her. Why shouldn't she accept? The marquis hadn't invited her to supper, only his bed.

"I would enjoy supping with you," Blaze said, a blush rising on her cheeks.

"Then I look forward to the ball," Lykos said. With a nod to the duchess, the prince quit the drawing room.

"Accepting the prince's invitation was a wise move and certain to irritate MacArthur," the duchess remarked. "Trust me, girls. Men want what is difficult to obtain."

A short time later, Tinker walked into the drawing room again. "The Earl of Boston wishes to speak with Miss Blaze."

"Send the earl in," the duchess said.

Again, Tinker stepped into the hall and gestured. The Earl of Boston walked into the room and bowed over the duchess's hand like a courtier kissing the queen's ring.

"Miss Blaze, I wondered if you would sup with me at the Jockey Club Ball," the earl said.

"I am sorry, but I am engaged for supper." Blaze assumed a disappointed expression, though she had no intention of sharing a meal with the bone sucker. Ever.

Dirk frowned. "Are you supping with my stepbrother?"

"Prince Lykos extended the invitation."

Oddly, the earl's expression brightened. Did Dirk see himself in competition with Ross?

"Will you save me a dance?"

"Of course, I will save you a dance." Blaze smiled at him. "Would you care for tea?"

"Thank you, no. I promised my sister a trip to Newmarket's sweet shop."

The earl turned away, intending to leave, but Raven stopped him. "My lord, I would enjoy supping with you."

He dropped his mouth open in surprise. And,

for the second time that day, the duchess lost her placid expression.

"What will Lord Blake say?"

"Alexander won't mind," Raven said, waving her hand.

"I will enjoy supping together," the earl said, and then quit the chamber.

The Duchess of Inverary stared hard at Raven, but her sister refused to look at her. The duchess's gaze narrowed, and she opened her mouth to speak.

"Raven." Alexander Blake walked into the drawing room, preventing the duchess's questions. "Are you ready?"

Blaze stood when her sister did. "I've changed my mind about joining you." Her sister would visit the sweet shop, and she wanted to see the stepsister offered to the marquis in marriage.

The ride to Newmarket was short. Blaze and Raven sat together in the coach and Alexander opposite them. The unseasonably warm, dry day had enticed many outside, either walking or riding.

"Have you begun spying on MacArthur?" Alexander asked.

"Ross did not murder Charlie," Blaze answered, "nor does he know anything about the murder. I believe Dirk Stanley is the villain."

Alexander winked at her. "I daresay, you believe him the culprit because he sucks on duck bones."

"My outburst did surprise him that night," Blaze said, and giggled. "Thankfully, Stepmama had the wisdom not to serve poultry when the MacArthurs dined with us."

"Since we decided to begin our spying at the

Jockey Club Ball," Raven said, changing the subject, "I invited Dirk Stanley to escort me to supper. A mild flirtation is more believable than an argument and less conspicuous."

"Do you think either Stanley will share information if there is no argument?" Blaze asked them.

Raven looked at Alexander. "Arguing in a crowded social gathering defies belief. We should merely imply to our targets that we are not in accord."

"Fine, you sup with Dirk," Alexander said, "while I speak with the sister. We can share information after the ball."

"Dirk and his sister will be visiting the sweet shop," Raven told him. "If we're there, he'll introduce her."

The driver halted the coach on High Street near the corner of Wellington Lane. Alexander climbed out first and then assisted Raven and Blaze.

The sweet shop had a red brick exterior, its sign painted white with yellow letters. A wide window contained an appetizing display of their confections.

Blaze smiled, her concerns forgotten for the moment. Staring at the candy display made her feel like a child again, but she knew the anticipation was sweeter than the candies.

"Don't drool, Freckles," Alexander teased her. "We can indulge ourselves inside."

"I can never decide what I want," Blaze said, following her sister into the shop. "If I order nougat, then I will be wishing for walnut creams."

"You may order both today," Alexander said.

The interior of the shop was a delicious confection, its white walls trimmed in cheerful yellow. Several white table and chairs had been set in the rear of the shop for patrons who could not wait to indulge.

Rows of glass jars containing sugary delights perched on white shelves. There were twists of barley sugar, Wellington sticks, and Nelson's balls. One long shelf had been reserved for lollipops in every color and flavor imaginable. Other shelves held various creams, fudges, truffles, and nougats.

"I would like buttercream truffles and orange creams," Raven told the man. "My sister would like nougats and walnut creams."

The proprietor grabbed a sheaf of paper and twisted it into a candy holder which he filled with orange creams and buttercream truffles. He did the same for the walnut creams and nougats. "Anything for you, my lord?"

"No, thank you." Alexander paid the proprietor and escorted them to a table in the rear of the shop.

Blaze reached inside her candy holder and selected a walnut cream. Nougats were her favorite so she saved those to eat last. Closing her eyes, she bit into the walnut cream and savored its sweetness on her tongue.

The shop door opened. Dirk Stanley and a blond woman entered the sweet shop.

Alexander rose from his chair, saying, "Wait here."

Blaze watched Alexander greeting the earl and his sister. Then he gestured in their direction.

"You should be supping with Alex at the ball," Blaze whispered, her gaze on the blonde.

"Effective spying means supping with the earl," Raven told her, looking clearly unhappy.

Alexander returned to the table, saying, "Your idea was a minor stroke of genius. They will join us."

Her walnut cream lost its taste.

Blaze recalled her nanny cautioning her to be careful with what she wished, and now she understood the wisdom in the words. She had wanted to glimpse the stepsister, but the blonde appeared lovely, the image of feminine perfection.

Blaze glanced at Raven. She would wager her last penny her sister was regretting supping with the earl.

Carrying candy holders, Dirk Stanley and his sister approached the table. The earl wore a warm smile of greeting, but the blonde possessed a cool stare.

Alexander stood at their approach. "Miss Amanda Stanley," he introduced the women, "I present Miss Blaze and Miss Raven Flambeau."

Blaze eyed the flawless blonde, comparing herself to her, and losing in the comparison. The blonde was everything she was not and a potential rival for the marquis's attentions.

Where had that surprising thought come? Was she developing a fondness for the marquis? Or, had she been developing a fondness for him before the louse decided to blackmail her?

Was she actually anticipating tonight? If so, she had more in common with her mother than she had thought.

"Miss Blaze's filly won The Craven yesterday," Dirk told his sister, and then looked at her. "I would love to know the secret of how you cured the filly's balking."

"The praise belongs to Ross," Blaze said. "Pegasus could never have won without his expertise."

"My stepbrother is a marquis," Amanda said, her smile chilly. "You should refer to him as Lord MacArthur."

Blaze looked the blonde straight in the eye. "*Ross* has insisted I use his given name."

"Did Pegasus tell you she would win?" Without waiting for a reply, Dirk turned to his sister. "Miss Blaze communicates with animals."

Amanda Stanley rolled her eyes at her brother. "I do not believe in such foolishness, and neither do you."

"She and her dog gave me a demonstration," Dirk said.

Blaze wished she hadn't done that. Well-bred young ladies did not perform animal tricks. The blonde would gossip about her around Newmarket, and Society would consider her freakish.

"If my stepsister and I call upon you," Amanda Stanley said, "will you give us a demonstration?"

"My sister does not perform for the curious," Raven said, imitating her stepmother's haughty tone.

"I never meant to imply—" Amanda Stanley broke off. "I am sorry."

An uncomfortable silence descended over the table.

"Lord Blake, I hope you do not mind my supping with Miss Raven at the ball," the earl said, filling the awkward void.

"Raven may sup with whomever amuses her," Alexander replied. "Of course, that means I will be supping alone. Unless, Miss Amanda agrees to sup with me."

"I would enjoy supping with you, my lord."

"Please, call me Alex."

Blaze glanced at Raven. Her sister's expression resembled a woman with a pin stuck in her unmentionables.

Needing comfort, Blaze bit into a piece of sticky, nut-filled nougat. Without thinking, she turned to her sister, saying, "Mother always insisted nougats tasted like French sunshine."

"Our mother passed away several years ago," Raven told the Stanleys.

"I am sorry for your loss," Dirk said.

"Our father suffered with heart problems and passed away many years ago," Amanda said. "How did your mother die?"

Mother slit her wrists, Blaze thought but said, "She stopped breathing."

"The ache of losing a loved one remains forever in our hearts," Amanda said, her green gaze warming on Alexander. "Sad emotions seem out of place in this cheery shop."

"Well said," Alexander complimented her. "My own parents are deceased, and I can vouch for the veracity of your sentiment."

"The day is fair," Dirk said. "Perhaps we could stroll down High Street."

"I am sorry," Raven said before Alexander could speak, "but we must decline."

"Our stepmother expects us home shortly." Blaze returned the blonde's cold gaze with a serene smile that would have made her stepmother proud.

Chapter Eight

Anxiety gripped her, making her heartbeat quicken and her breathing shallow.

Blaze gazed out her bedchamber window and considered what she would soon be doing. Visiting the marquis's bed could insure a safe haven for God's creatures, but she doubted God would approve of her rescue method.

Though born on the wrong side of the blanket, Blaze and her sisters had led sheltered lives as befitting a duke's daughters. She had never been alone with a gentleman before the marquis's tour of his stables and family estate.

Blaze turned away from the window and crossed the chamber to the bed. Drawing the coverlet back, she arranged the pillows in a vertical line and pulled the coverlet up. Anyone peering into the room would believe she slept.

With her hood cloak draped over her arm, Blaze pressed her ear against the door. No sounds of movement in the hallway. She opened the door and gasped.

"Are you going somewhere?" Raven stepped into the chamber. "I sensed something amiss."

"I'll tell you tomorrow."

Raven folded her arms across her chest and leaned against the door, blocking her escape. "Tell me now."

Blaze knew Raven would not budge until she answered her. "I jockeyed Pegasus in The Craven and now—"

"You did what?" her sister exclaimed.

"Shhh." Blaze placed a finger across her lips. "Peg balked at going through holes to get ahead but would do it when I rode her," she explained. "The marquis devised a plan for me to replace Rooney, giving us more training time. Now the louse is blackmailing me into his bed."

Raven arched a brow, the hint of a smile on her lips. "The marquis is determined to win your hand in marriage."

"He proposed an affair, not marriage," Blaze corrected her. "I cannot allow Rooney and Bender banned from racing, nor will I abandon my animal refuge. Rendezvousing with the devil is my only choice."

"We always have a choice," Raven said. "Would you consider visiting Dirk Stanley's bed?"

Blaze grimaced and shook her head. "I could never kiss a bone sucker."

"Would you consider visiting the prince's bed?"

Blaze shrugged. "I might consider it but would decide against it."

"Consider this evening your wedding night."

Raven opened the door and stepped into the hallway. "Use the servants' stairs."

Blaze walked down the hallway to the back stairs. She tried not to hurry lest she arouse the suspicion of anyone who chanced to see her. Reaching the ground level, she nearly collided with the major-domo.

"You never saw me, Tinker."

"Enjoy your evening, Miss Blaze." His lips twitched as if he would smile. "I will leave the back door unlocked."

Stepping into the night, Blaze wrapped her black cloak around herself and pulled its hood up. She would blend into the night if someone peered out a window.

Blaze walked at a brisk pace through the formal gardens and past the maze. Only the expanse of lawn separated her from the gazebo.

Lifting her skirts, Blaze sprinted across the lawn and flew up the steps. The gazebo was empty.

Had the marquis come and gone? What should she do?

"Yer late, darlin'."

Blaze whirled around, relief and anxiety mingling inside her. His husky voice sent the butterflies in her belly winging again.

"I thought you'd gone."

"I'd wait longer than five minutes for ye," Ross said. "Ten, at least."

Blaze knew he was teasing her. "I'm honored."

Ross traced a finger down her cheek and dipped his head to plant a brief kiss on her mouth.

"My coach is waitin' beyond the practice track on Snailwell Road."

Hand in hand, they hurried to the path leading to the practice track. Overhead, a full moon peeked through thin clouds to light their way.

"Your coachman will recognize me," Blaze said, struggling to keep pace with his long-legged stride, "and the gossip will ruin my reputation."

"Gossipin' would mean loss of his job," Ross assured her, taking smaller steps. "Yer reputation is safe."

Reaching the coach, Ross opened the door and helped her up. Then he climbed inside, choosing to sit on the opposite seat.

The trip to the Rowley Lodge was short and silent. Blaze could not see his eyes clearly in the dark coach but felt his gaze on her. Which made her even more nervous.

Uncertain of what to expect, Blaze felt awkward and shy. The marquis and she would soon lay naked in his bed, and he would explore her body. She wondered if brides felt like this on their wedding day.

"Do you think the intruder will return tonight?" Blaze asked, unable to tolerate the tense silence.

"He willna risk it," Ross answered, "but I guarantee he'll find another way to come at us."

The coach halted in front of the Rowley Lodge. The marquis climbed out and then helped her down.

"Most lodgers are drinkin' at the taverns along High Street," he said. "Keep yer hood up, though."

With his hand on the small of her back, Ross ushered her into the lodge's nearly deserted common room. A lone patron sat on the far side of the room near the hearth.

"Walk straight to the stairs," the marquis said. "Yer doin' fine."

Nerves made her stumble on the third stair. Her hood slipped off, revealing her red hair.

The marquis yanked it up in an instant. "He didna see yer face."

Unlocking his chamber's door, Ross held it open for her. Blaze hesitated, meeting his black gaze, and then stepped inside.

The moon shining through the window lit the room enough for Blaze to see while Ross lit a night candle. The room was larger and more comfortable than she had expected though far from the luxury of the great houses. There was a bureau with a washing basin, a chair, a free-standing closet, and a bedside table. Her gaze fixed on the bed.

Watching her, Ross realized this was their wedding night without benefit of a ceremony. He felt a twinge of guilt that his bride would pass her wedding night at the Rowley Lodge.

"Let me take yer cloak," he said.

"I prefer wearing it." She clutched her cloak tight and pointed at the bed. "Shall I lay there?"

Ross hid a smile at her innocence. The brave girl who'd jockeyed a thoroughbred feared being alone with a man. She was a virgin in need of coaxing and wooing. Thankfully, brides were only virgins once. He didn't think he had the patience to do this every night.

"I'll take yer cloak," Ross said, prying her hands

off the garment. "Sit over there." He refrained from using the word "bed" lest he frighten her even more.

Ross placed her cloak across a chair and looked at her. She sat stiffer than a corpse on the edge of the bed.

Removing his jacket, Ross placed it on top of her cloak. Then he poured a measure of whisky into two tumblers and sat beside her.

"I ken ye dinna like spirits," he said, "but one drink willna kill ye."

Blaze lifted the glass out of his hand, their fingers touching. She had never been so aware of another person in her life.

Ross touched his glass to hers. "To us, lass."

Blaze sipped her whisky and set it on the bedside table. Ross placed his glass beside hers.

"I don't know how to do this," she confessed to the opposite wall.

"I'll show ye."

Gently, Ross cupped her chin and turned her face toward his. He leaned close, his mouth touching hers in a tentative kiss. Her body was rigid, her blue eyes wide with fright.

"Close yer eyes," Ross murmured, his lips hovering above hers, his breath warm. "Relax, darlin', and enjoy the sensations."

His mouth captured hers, and his hand massaged the nape of her neck. He felt her body relaxing by slow degrees. She responded, pressing her mouth against his, and he deepened the kiss, inviting her to follow his lead.

Their kiss was long and languorous. His gentle touch, his mountain heather scent intoxicated her, sending her senses reeling. She returned his kiss with equal ardor, instinctively pressing her body against him.

Ross wrapped his arms around her, one palm pressed against the small of her back, the other holding her head steady. He flicked his tongue across the crease of her mouth, parting her lips, and slipped it inside to taste her incredible sweetness. Lifting his head, he gazed at her hauntingly lovely face and recognized the budding desire in her eyes.

His lips hovered above hers. "I love the taste of yer mouth"—his finger caressed the crease of her lips—"the arch of yer brow"—his finger traced its shape—"the curve of yer ears"—his finger circled an ear and slid across her cheek—"the silken feel of ye."

His whispered words soothed and excited her. She entwined her arms around his neck, drawing his head down, and kissed him.

"I love yer natural passion." His words ignited a heat in her lower regions and a throbbing between her legs.

Ross laid her back on the bed and hovered over her. Blaze drew him down and kissed him, her lips parting in invitation. His lips became the center of her universe, his strength making her feel secure. They were the only man and woman in the world, and she yearned for his possession.

Ross brushed his lips across her cheeks, making her smile. His lips traveled down the column of her delicate neck, planting a kiss at the base of her throat.

"I'm goin' to undress ye," he said, unbuttoning the back of her gown. He ran a finger down her delicate backbone.

Blaze sucked in her breath. A chill shook her body, but where he touched her burned.

Ross drew her gown down to her waist, her thighs, her ankles. The he pulled his shirt off and tossed it over his shoulder.

Blaze stared at his muscled chest with its mat of black hair. Lifting a hand, she caressed it with her palm. His hair was coarse, and his muscles rippled beneath her touch.

"Yer touch excites me," he whispered, "but I've been longin' to see yer breasts."

Ross pushed the straps of her chemise off her shoulders and slid the garment down, exposing her breasts. She wore stockings with garters, and her mane of red hair cascaded around her.

She was a pagan goddess. No woman had ever looked more enticing.

"Ye've perfect breasts and dusky pink nipples." Desire made his voice hoarse. "Ye canna imagine how long I've wanted to admire these beauties."

Her body trembled at his words, her thighs quivered, and the throbbing between her legs quickened. She felt wanton and powerful, his words an aphrodisiac to her senses.

Using one finger, Ross circled each breast, starting around the outside and spiraling closer and closer to the center. Then he touched the tip of each jutting nipple.

Blaze gasped in surprised pleasure. She liked his hands on her body.

"Yer nipples are sensitive." Ross dipped his head, and his tongue teased the tips of her nipples.

Blaze moaned in pleasure. She held his head

against her breasts, savoring his lips and tongue
on her.

And then he stopped.

Ross rose up on his elbows, planted a kiss on her
mouth, and left the bed. Clad only in black breeches,
he crossed the chamber to the bureau and poured a
measure of whisky into a glass. He belted it down in
one gulp, heedless of the sacrilege against the aged
amber liquid.

His damn conscience was bothering him. He had
never coerced a woman into his bed and refused to
start with his bride-to-be. She had come to the lodge
unwillingly, but she must remain willingly.

Besides his conscience, his peace of mind was in
jeopardy. Once they'd married, his bride would
remind him of blackmailing her each time they
argued. Forty years of listening to her toss that in
his face was not worth one night of misbegotten
pleasure.

"Is that all?" Blaze asked from the bed. "Did I do
something wrong?"

Ross heard the bewilderment in her voice. He set
the glass on the bureau and turned around. She
was holding the coverlet close to her breasts.

"Ye did nothin' wrong," he assured her. "If ye get
dressed, I'll take ye home."

"You're not blackmailing me?" she asked, her
confusion apparent.

"I want ye willin' or not at all."

"I worried all day for nothing?" She sounded irritated.

"I'm givin' ye a choice," Ross said. "Will ye stay
or go?"

Blaze frowned at this unexpected complication. His offer removed the only reason she could bed him without feeling guilty. Now the damn Scotsman was forcing her to admit her feelings for him, and that could lead to something she didn't want. Marriage. On the other hand, where was the danger in one night of pleasure?

And then she smiled at him. "Come to bed."

Ross needed no second invitation. He pulled his breeches off and crossed the chamber to the bed. Then he drew her to her knees and held her tight against his muscular frame. Their bodies touched from breast to thigh, his smoldering kiss possessive.

Laying her back on the bed, Ross sprinkled dozens of feathery-light kisses across her eyelids, temples, and throat before returning to her lips. Her lilac scent, her silken heat, her throaty purr aroused him like no other lover.

Blaze looped her arms around his neck and surrendered to his kiss, willing to follow wherever he would lead her. She savored the sensation of his powerful, naked frame pressing her down on the bed.

Ross kissed her hungrily, and she returned his kiss in kind. Melting against him, her young body awakened to a primal instinct to mate with him. A pulsing urgency spurred her on, demanding she become one with him.

"Yer wet for me," he murmured, "but I need to prepare ye."

Ross pushed one long finger inside her, her body instinctively shrinking back against the bed. Blaze felt a burning sensation as his finger pushed deeper.

He caressed her wet, silken interior and then inserted a second finger.

Blaze felt vulnerable to his desire. She had never imagined this sensation of being filled. And then he withdrew his fingers, leaving her empty and disappointed.

Spreading her thighs, Ross positioned himself but paused to capture her mouth in a soul-stealing kiss. He thrust forward in one powerful but kind movement, breaking her virgin's barrier.

Blaze gasped once and then lay still, slight panting her only movement. Ross remained motionless, allowing her to accustom herself to the feel of him inside her.

"Are ye with me lass?" He sounded breathless.

"Yes." And so did she.

He moved then, slowly at first and gradually increasing his tempo. Catching his rhythm, she moved with him, meeting his thrusts.

"Ross," she moaned, waves of throbbing pleasure washing over her.

He groaned and shuddered, his seed flooding her. Unable to move, he dropped his head against her breast.

Their labored breathing was the only sound in the room while they floated from the heights of paradise to the reality of the lodge. Recovering first, Ross rolled to the side, pulling her with him.

"Yer everythin' a man could want." Ross planted a kiss on the crown of her head. "Next time will be even better."

Surprised by his remark, Blaze lifted her gaze to his. "I wasn't planning on a next time."

"Yer plans have changed, darlin'." He gave her an easy smile.

Now Blaze understood the temptation her mother had faced with her father. Gabrielle had succumbed to a handsome face, an easy smile, and persuasive words from a charming aristocrat. A penniless countess who had escaped the French Terror, her mother had never stood a chance against her father's domineering personality or the security he offered.

Blaze had learned hard lessons from her mother's misery. She was not her mother. She refused to become her mother. Love would never enslave her as it had her mother.

"There will be no next time," Blaze said, sitting up. "I will not follow my mother's path."

"Yer in no danger of becomin' yer mother," Ross said. "Trust me on that."

Trust me? So whispered the Serpent to Eve in Paradise.

Ross traced a finger down her cheek to her throat and her breasts. His touch hardened her traitorous nipples.

"Ye want me, darlin'."

"Wanting does not mean having."

His black gaze narrowed on her. "Yer more stubborn than a mule."

"Thank you for the praise."

Ross laughed at that and pulled her down on his chest. "Let's argue aboot this tomorrow."

They cuddled in sated silence for a long time, neither needing to fill the void with conversation. Ross slid the palms of his hands across her shoulders and down her back. Blaze snuggled against him, enjoying his hands on her.

"I met your stepsister in Newmarket," Blaze said, watching his expression. "I don't like her, and she doesn't like me."

"Amanda isna a bad sort," Ross said, "but Celeste pushes the girl at me. I keep a room here at the lodge so the witch canna set a marriage trap for me."

His words heartened Blaze, lessening her concern with the blonde. "Amanda is exceptionally pretty."

"Any man who marries a woman because she's pretty deserves the misery comin' his way," Ross told her, looking at her upturned face. "Beauty, titles, and wealth can be lost in an instant."

"So you won't marry a pretty girl?" That left the field open for her if she harbored the notion to marry, which she did not.

"I'll marry a pretty lady if she meets my requirements," Ross answered. "I want a wife with a big heart who loves children and animals, and she must love me for myself. Not my title, my wealth, or my incredible beauty."

Blaze smiled at that. "You forgot bossiness, arrogance, and conceit."

"So I did." Ross winked at her and then changed the subject. "Here's my plan for the Jockey Club Ball. Save me the last dance of the evenin', the last dance before supper, and, of course, sup with me."

Uh-oh. "I am already engaged for supper," Blaze told him.

He did not look pleased. "Get yourself unengaged."

"I cannot accept Prince Lykos's invitation one day and reject him the next," she argued. "Society would frown on that bit of rudeness."

"I dinna give a damn aboot Society."

"My stepmother would not approve," Blaze said, "and I will not hurt the prince's feelings."

"Rejectin' his invitation willna kill the man," Ross said. "Sharin' supper isna a life-long commitment."

"That is precisely my point," she countered. "Next time invite me before the other two."

"Two? Who's the other one?"

"Thankfully, your stepbrother invited me after the prince."

"Ye wouldna consider suppin' with the bone sucker." Ross hooted with laughter at the idea. "Have it yer way, lass, but consider yourself engaged with me for supper at every ball henceforth."

"I will consider your invitation." His easy capitulation bothered Blaze. She did not trust easy capitulations from pig-headed men. The marquis was planning something.

"So when did ye distance connect with Pegasus?"

"Yesterday—" The word slipped past her lips before she could stifle it. "One connection does not guarantee success. If I ride in the next race, Rooney and Peg will practice for six weeks."

"That makes sense."

"It does?" His easy agreement surprised her.

"Ye'll jockey the First Spring," Ross said, "and Rooney will jockey the other races. Dinna try wheedlin' a third race out of me cuz I willna change my mind. If six weeks of practice doesna do the trick, Pegasus isna destined to win the big races."

Ross rolled Blaze onto her back. "I want ye again," he said, "but I willna abuse yer body tonight. Ye'll be sore enough without a second helpin'."

Blaze blushed at his words. Talking about doing was more embarrassing than the actual doing.

"Yer blushin' again." Ross smiled, amused by her sudden shyness, and rose from the bed. "I need to get ye home now."

The ride from the lodge to Snailwell Road was still short and silent. Ross sat beside her this time, though, and their silence was relaxed instead of tense.

When they stood outside her back door, Ross cupped her chin and dipped his head to plant a chaste kiss on her lips. "Pleasant dreams, darlin'. Dinna forget practice at dawn."

Ross waited until she bolted the door. Then he jogged to Snailwell Road where his man waited.

Climbing into the coach, Ross yawned and stretched his legs out. The evening had proven satisfying, his courtship progressing. The only glitch was that sneaky Russian who'd beaten him to the supper invitation. Her supping with the prince mattered little, though.

Blaze wanted him as much as he wanted her. Now he needed to persuade her into marriage.

The coach halted in front of the Rowley Lodge. Ross climbed out, calling to his man, "Tomorrow night, same time."

Ross walked into the lodge's common room, intending to seek his bed and enjoy the sleep of the sated. Blocking his path, Baron Edward Shores sat on the stairs but stood to confront him.

"Good evening, my lord," the baron greeted him.

Ross groaned inwardly. He wanted his bed, not conversation with Crazy Eddie Shores, a man who profited from other men's vices.

"I'm tired, Eddie," Ross said. "Let me pass."

"You do appear drained," the baron said, "but I beg a moment to offer you a deal."

"Speak yer piece and then step aside."

"Give me five hundred pounds a week," Eddie said, his voice low, "and I won't tell Inverary you're bedding his daughter."

"Here's the deal, Eddie." In a flash of movement, Ross grabbed the baron's throat and slammed him against the wall. "Keep yer mouth shut, and I'll let ye live. Agreed?"

When the suffocating baron managed a slight nod, Ross dropped his hold on him. "A pleasure doin' business with ye, Eddie."

Chapter Nine

She felt different.

Bedding the marquis made her feel feminine but somehow vulnerable. She could live with feminine, but vulnerable reminded her of her mother.

The marquis had taken her innocence, initiating her into womanhood. She hadn't planned to join those ranks until achieving her goals.

She was lying to herself. The truth was the marquis had taken nothing. She had given him her virginity, offering herself like a Christmas goose on the silver platter of his bed.

Losing her virginity was one of life's milestones. Blaze wished she could have crossed that threshold under different circumstances.

She wasn't doing as well as her mother. Gabrielle had bedded the man she loved, who'd loved her in return. *She'd* bedded a man who professed to wanting her.

Did she love the marquis? Or were her tender feelings a product of sharing intimacy and the secret of Pegasus?

If she did love the marquis, how could she hold his attention? Society was filled with dozens of hopeful maidens who wanted to marry a marquis, including the blond stepsister. And none of the hopefuls had made the mistake of sharing his bed.

Blaze wished she hadn't scoffed at the duchess's life lessons. After yesterday's questions, her stepmother would become suspicious if she sought her advice. The woman was no fool.

Drowsy from lack of sleep, Blaze sat on the edge of the bed and dragged the black breeches up her legs. Then she donned her riding boots and slipped her arms into the leather jerkin. Without bothering to look in the mirror, she plaited her hair into one thick braid and hid it beneath a cap.

Blaze yawned and stretched before rising from her perch on the bed. Late nights and early mornings did not produce an alert person.

Curiosity got the better of her, and Blaze peered at herself in the cheval mirror. She looked the same— flame-haired, freckle-faced, flat-chested.

Blaze crossed the bedchamber and opened the door a crack, peering up and down the hallway. Satisfied the household slept, she walked toward the back stairs and exited the mansion through the rear door.

Passing the formal gardens, Blaze veered to the right and trudged across the dew-covered lawn to the path. The closer she got to the practice track, the slower her pace became.

Blaze conjured Ross's image in her mind's eye and replayed their evening. Again she felt the warmth of

his smile, his hands and lips caressing her, his hard-
ness moving inside.

Her body heated and her legs weakened. Remi-
niscing burned her skin.

Seeing Ross at the track worried her. Casual conversation and nonchalant behavior eluded her.
Their shared intimacy should never have happened
without benefit of marriage.

She would pretend nothing happened. A true
gentleman would not refer to her downfall in any
way. Gawd, she would die of embarrassment if he
mentioned it.

Blaze reached the practice track, shrouded in
ground-hugging fog. The three men were waiting
for her.

Puddles barked in greeting and dashed toward
her, giving her a moment to compose herself
before facing the marquis. She gave her dog a hug
and then ordered, "Stay." The mastiff sat, but his
tail swished back and forth across the grass.

Unable to delay any longer, Blaze walked toward
the men. She viewed the marquis differently. He
wore the usual working clothes—riding breeches,
shirt, leather jerkin; she saw him naked—broad
shoulders, muscled chest, perfect buttocks. She
knew what the bulge in his breeches hid.

"Good morning," Blaze said, her cheeks pinkening, and walked past them to greet Pegasus.

She stroked the filly's face. *Love Peg.*

Me love.

Peg run?

Run, run, run.

"The lady has a surprise for us," Ross told the trainer and jockey.

Blaze walked to where the men stood. Avoiding the marquis's gaze, she wondered when he had taken charge of her filly, her goals, her life.

"Are ye ready, darlin'?" Ross asked her.

Blaze snapped her gaze to his and nodded. She wished he would refrain from casual endearments in front of others, which diminished her authority as the horse's owner.

Ross gave Rooney a leg up on Pegasus. Then he and Bender mounted their own horses.

"Give us a five-length lead," Ross instructed the jockey, "and we'll keep a hole between us."

At the start line, Ross called to Bender, "One, two, three—*go.*"

Ross and Bender spurred their horses into action. Swishing and thudding, their horses galloped down track. When they were fifty feet from the line, Rooney and Peg gave chase.

Blaze kept her gaze fixed on the filly. She chanted inside her mind, her lips moving with a repetitive thought.

Peg through hole. Peg through hole. Peg through—

Pegasus shot through the hole between the two horses. Success.

The three men slowed their horses. Smiling, they rode back to where she stood.

"I'm relieved," Bender said, dismounting. "I don't have the nerves for subterfuge."

"Peg's the fastest horse I've ever seen," Rooney said in obvious excitement. "I'll take good care of her out there and promise to ride her to victory. Pegasus will become legend."

"Blaze is jockeyin' in the First Spring," Ross told the men. "That gives Rooney and Peg six weeks to practice."

"I know you're disappointed," Blaze said to Rooney. "You will jockey all the other races, which includes the Classics. You will ride Peg into legend."

"Our luck held the first time," Bender argued, "but we'll get caught if we try again. Inverary will never believe I failed to recognize his daughter."

"I'll take the fall if that happens," Ross said.

"Do you think Inverary cares I was following your orders?" Bender asked. "His Grace pays my salary, not you."

"Yer the best in the business," Ross told him. "His Grace willna want to lose ye."

"Do you swear this is the last race she jockeys?" Bender asked.

Ross smiled at the trainer and raised his right hand. "I give ye my solemn word."

Bender nodded, his reluctance apparent. So did Rooney.

"Rain or shine, we'll practice each mornin'," Ross told them. "His Grace is hostin' the Jockey Club Ball tonight. I dinna want any guest slippin' into Peg's stable."

Rooney led Pegasus toward the path to the stables. Bender followed with his own horse.

"I thought ye wouldna show after last night," Ross said. "I should've known ye wouldna falter."

"Thank you for the compliment," Blaze told his

chest, her complexion reddening. "I prefer not speaking about *that*."

"Look into my eyes." When she did, Ross said, "Stop blushing. Only the guilty blush."

Blaze heard the smile in his voice. "Everyone blushes, but redheads are more susceptible."

"Men dinna blush."

"What hour does Juno visit the breeding barn?" Blaze asked him.

"Trust me," Ross said. "Even if yer father gave his permission, ye dinna want to witness this."

"The owner always witnesses the breeding," she countered. "My father is old-fashioned about maidenly sensibilities."

"I'll tell ye what happens," Ross said, "and I'll speak to yer father if ye still want to witness."

Blaze nodded. "Very well."

"Juno's tail will be bandaged so it doesna interfere with the matin'," Ross told her, "and she'll be teased to get her in the mood."

Blaze felt her face heat with embarrassment. She didn't stop him, though, because her duty as an owner required she know the procedure.

"They put soft boots on her back feet and a huge leather collar around her neck to protect her from Zeus's love bites," Ross continued. "One man holds her left front leg up so she canna kick her back legs."

When he paused, she said in a voice barely louder than a whisper, "Please continue." The marquis was smiling at her discomfort, which didn't sit well with her.

"After sniffin' Juno, Zeus will rear up and land

on her back," Ross said. "The consummation time is short, maybe three or four thrusts to—"

"*Enough.*"

"Do ye still want to witness the act?"

Blaze shook her head. "I trust you to represent me."

"Yer face is burnin'." Lowering his head, Ross planted a chaste kiss on her lips. "We'll leave the Ball after yer supper with the prince."

"I will not leave with you."

Ross mounted his horse. "Lyin' is a terrible sin, darlin'."

"Sex without marriage is a worse sin," Blaze countered.

"Will ye marry me, then?"

"If I accepted your proposal," she said, her smile inscrutable, "you'd fall off that horse."

Blaze walked away, her dog at her side. He was watching her. She could feel his gaze on her backside. Losing an inner struggle, she glanced over her shoulder.

He was smiling at her. "I'll see ye tonight, darlin'."

Her beauty would never inspire love poems.

Blaze stood in front of the cheval mirror for a final inspection before joining her sisters in the ballroom. If she wanted to hold the marquis's attention, she needed to outshine the blond stepsister and every other maiden angling to catch a future duke.

Her ice-blue gown had a squared neckline, fitted bodice, and off-the-shoulder sleeves. The gown's ankle-length skirt allowed a peek at her silk stockings embroidered with butterflies.

Blaze wore her coppery mane upswept, her mother's jeweled butterfly hair clasp holding her hair in place. Several loose tendrils of fire accentuated her slender neck. She wore her mother's gold choker and bracelet, both bearing jeweled butterflies, and carried a deep blue fan with a mother-of-pearl butterfly motif.

Blaze frowned at her reflection. Outshining the other unmarried hopefuls would surely prove impossible.

She needed blond hair.

She needed an ivory complexion.

She needed bigger breasts.

Attitude means everything, Blaze recalled her sister's advice.

Staring at her reflection, Blaze lifted her nose into the air to practice her superior attitude. Tonight, she was the queen. Her red hair had become the latest rage, maidens secretly pined for a sprinkling of freckles across their noses, and Society's fashionables considered big-breasted women vulgar cows.

Blaze spied her long, white gloves on the bed. She paused for a mere second and then left her bedchamber. Tonight she was setting the trends and refused to follow any archaic rule like wearing gloves indoors.

London's elite filled the ballroom, only death keeping the socialites from attending an Inverary function. A four piece orchestra—cornet, piano, violin, cello—played at the top of the ballroom and served as background for cultured conversations, muted laughter, and air kisses.

The ladies were gowned in a rainbow of colors.

Priceless gems sparkled on every woman's neck, arms, fingers, and ears. Their perfumes wafted through the ballroom, scenting the air like a lush garden.

The gentlemen appeared more elegant by lack of color. Their black and white evening attire provided a stark background for their ladies' flamboyant colors.

"Shall I announce you, Miss Blaze?" asked the Inverary majordomo.

"Only if you are contemplating leaving this life."

Tinker broke into a smile. "I believe your parents are standing at the far end of the ballroom."

"Thank you, Tinker."

Attitude, she reminded herself and took a deep, fortifying breath.

Blaze joined the milling throng and skirted the dance floor. Several guests congratulated her on her thoroughbred's victory. She acknowledged their good wishes with a smile.

Her sisters looked beautiful, of course. Ebony-haired women could wear any color. Raven wore soft pink. Bliss, her own twin, wore celestial blue. Serena and Sophia wore gowns in jonquil and violet whisper.

Catching the eye from a distance, the Duchess of Inverary wore a red gown and enough diamonds to blind a person. Diamond hair pins adorned her auburn hair, diamonds dangled from her earlobes, a gold and diamond collar circled her neck, and diamond rings sparkled on each finger.

"Where are your gloves?" the duchess asked.

"The gloves are lying across my bed," Blaze told her, and caught her father's smile.

"Well-bred women wear long gloves in the evening," her stepmother said. "You aren't completely dressed without gloves."

"Who made that rule?" Blaze countered. "The glove makers?"

Her father chuckled, earning a censorious glance from his wife. "Do not encourage her." She looked at Blaze, saying, "I'll send someone to fetch your gloves."

"No."

"I beg your pardon?"

"I intend to make bare arms the latest rage," Blaze told her.

"I hate these gloves," Raven said, peeling hers off.

"So do I."

"Me too."

"I don't like them either."

In turn each of her sisters voiced their dissent and removed their gloves. Raven collected the gloves and tossed them on a nearby table.

"Magnus, do something," the duchess said.

The Duke of Inverary was openly laughing at his daughters' insurrection. "Roxie, you always say my girls should set the trends. I believe they're learning from your example."

"How will they catch husbands if they don't wear gloves?" the duchess snapped.

"Catching a husband does not depend on young ladies wearing gloves," the duke replied, making his daughters laugh.

The duchess's dimpled smile appeared. "I

suppose one gloveless evening will not ruin anyone's reputation."

"Do you see Ross anywhere?" Blaze whispered to Raven.

Her sister scanned the crowded ballroom and shook her head. "Here comes trouble."

"Good evening, Your Graces," Celeste MacArthur greeted their group.

Blaze watched her father shake hands with Ross's father. Her gaze drifted to the two younger women with them, Amanda Stanley and a dark-haired beauty, Ross's sister.

"Good evening, Miss Blaze and Miss Raven," Dirk Stanley greeted them. "I present my brother, Squire Chadwick Simmons."

Tall and well-built, Squire Simmons was easily one of the handsomest men in the ballroom. Like his siblings and mother, he had blond hair and green eyes but seemed more masculine and self-assured than his brother.

"The Marquis of Awe," Tinker announced, instantly claiming her attention.

Dressed in formal attire, Ross MacArthur stood beside Tinker at the top of the stairs. His dark gaze scanned the ballroom until he found her.

And then he smiled.

She returned his smile.

Holding her gaze captive, Ross descended the stairs and walked toward her. Blaze felt her heartbeat quickening and the butterflies winging in the pit of her belly.

"Good evening, Miss Flambeau." Ross bowed over her hand, his smile boyishly charming.

"Good evening, my lord."

He offered her his hand. "May I have this dance?"

Blaze started to reach for his hand but—

"Sorry, MacArthur." Prince Lykos took her hand in his. "The lady promised me this dance."

The prince escorted her onto the dance floor, and she stepped into his arms. They swirled around and around the dance floor with the other couples, her gaze looking for the marquis each time they passed their group.

"Your dancing is much improved since your sister's wedding," Lykos said.

Blaze stepped on his foot. "Oops."

"I spoke too soon," the prince said, smiling. "You could excel at the waltz if you focus on your partner instead of MacArthur."

"I am sorry, Your Highness." Blaze blushed, mortified that he'd caught her interest in his rival.

"The marquis is watching us, not dancing," Lykos told her. "He appears unhappy about your dancing with me."

Prince Lykos returned her to her parents' group when the music ended. Before Ross could reach her, Prince Gunter claimed her next.

"I congratulate you on your horse's success," Gunter said, as they swirled in time with the other couples.

"The Marquis of Awe helped train her," Blaze told him. "Are you interested in thoroughbred racing?"

Prince Gunter smiled. "Gambling on the races interests me."

Alexander insisted on the next dance. "How is

your spying?" he asked, as soon as they walked onto
the dance floor.

"The marquis knows nothing," she answered.
"My sister regrets not supping with you."

That made him smile. Blaze had the feeling he
wanted Raven to worry about his supper with the
blonde.

Squire Simmons claimed her next dance. Blaze
wondered if she and the marquis would ever waltz
together.

"Congratulations on your filly's win," Chadwick
said, stepping onto the dance floor and taking her
into his arms.

"Are you interested in thoroughbred racing,"
Blaze asked, "or only gambling on the horses?"

"Dirk and I own Emperor and several other
horses together," the squire answered.

Blaze managed a polite smile but felt uneasy with
the man. "Horse racing is an expensive hobby," she
said. "My father gifted me with Pegasus."

"My late wife was the only child of a wealthy merchant," Chadwick told her, "and I inherited all that
was his."

"I'm sorry for your loss and for prying," Blaze said.

"There's no need to apologize."

Squire Simmons said all the right things and
smiled when he should, but his green eyes were
colder than his mother's. There was a definite cruelty
to his chiseled lips. The man probably envied his
younger brother's title.

When the music ended, Blaze returned to her
parents' group. The Duke of Kilchurn claimed her
before any young man.

"I would love to dance with you," the duke said, and escorted her onto the dance floor.

James MacArthur waltzed with grace and confidence. Dancing with her lover's father sapped her confidence, and she missed a step. Then she stepped on his foot.

"I'm sorry," the duke apologized. "I'm not very good at this."

Blaze gave him a rueful smile. "You aren't a very good liar, either."

The Duke of Kilchurn laughed and escorted her off the dance floor, leading her to his son. "This young swain has been waiting to claim a dance."

Ross offered her his hand. Blaze accepted the invitation, stepping onto the dance floor and into his arms.

The marquis moved with the ease and grace of a man who'd waltzed hundreds of times. Blaze moved with him, following his lead, focusing her attention on the man who held her in his arms.

"Yer dancin' has improved," Ross teased her.

"Prince Lykos said the same," Blaze told him, "and then I stepped on his foot."

Ross drew her closer. "Perhaps the fault belongs to Kazanov's poor lead, rather than yer dancin'."

"What a comforting thought," Blaze said. "I do tend to battle for the lead."

"I've noticed." Ross winked at her. "Have I told ye how beautiful ye look tonight?"

Blaze blushed at his compliment. "No."

"For the rest of my life I'll remember the way ye look tonight," Ross said, his voice husky.

"Our fathers are smiling at us," she whispered, "but your stepmother is displeased."

"How can ye tell?" he asked. "Celeste wears that forbiddin' expression more often than not."

"I can feel her deadly basilisk stare."

"Basilisk?" Ross laughed at that. The other couples cast curious looks in their direction as did the guests loitering around the dance floor.

"Why aren't you dancing with all the ladies?" Blaze asked him.

"Yer the only lady I want in my arms," Ross said. "We'll leave after supper."

"I cannot leave with you," she refused.

"We'll discuss yer objections after supper," Ross said, and returned her to her parents.

Blaze knew she was losing the battle. The marquis would never take *no* for an answer. She had never met a more arrogant, bossy, stubborn man.

"We must speak privately," Raven said, sidling up to her.

"Shall we visit the withdrawing room?" Blaze asked.

"Ladies may be resting there," Raven answered. "Let's get punch and then wander down the corridor."

Without a word to anyone, the sisters wended their way slowly around the perimeter of the ballroom toward the door. Refreshments were served in a room several doors down the corridor. There were tables and chairs positioned around the room and a long table laden with the crystal punch bowl, glasses, and light snacks.

Raven ladled punch into one crystal glass and handed it to Blaze. Then she filled a glass for herself.

Blaze sipped her punch. "Shall we sit at a table?"

"We cannot chance eavesdroppers or interruptions," Raven answered.

"This sounds serious." Blaze followed her sister out of the refreshment room, and they walked in the opposite direction from the ballroom. At the end of the hallway, they ducked into the servants' staircase.

"Look at my betrothal ring." Raven held her left hand out. The star ruby had darkened to blood red, signifying the owner was endangered. "The legend has proven true."

"Charlie's murderer is standing in our ballroom," Blaze whispered, and emptied her glass of punch. "We should tell Alex."

"He doesn't believe in hocus-pocus," Raven said. "I'll tell him after supper, and we'll make plans to review the guest list tomorrow."

"The ruby has narrowed the possible suspects," Blaze said. "Now we have only two hundred suspects instead of everyone in Newmarket."

"I sense Dirk knows nothing," Raven told her, "but Chadwick Simmons makes me uneasy. His lips are cruelly shaped."

"Celeste MacArthur makes me uneasy," Blaze said. "Her look is more deadly than a basilisk."

Raven giggled, which made Blaze laugh. By unspoken agreement, the sisters retraced their steps down the hallway. They reached the ballroom just as the guests were beginning to go down for supper.

Prince Lykos appeared and offered Blaze his arm. "Shall we go down, my lady?"

"I am merely a miss," she corrected him, slipping her arm through his.

The long, rectangular dining table held a variety of tempting fare. The guests would serve themselves and then find a table in the dining room or one of the smaller salons on the first floor.

"Tell me what appeals to you," the prince said, "and I will fill a plate."

Blaze strolled down the length of the table, seeing few dishes to encourage her appetite. There were slices of roasted beef and chicken, baked kippers from Argyll, poached salmon, and the potted dishes—chicken, ham, shrimp. None of which she planned to sample. Ever.

"I would like pickled gherkins, grilled mushrooms, and a scoop of potted cheese," Blaze said, and then pointed to a greyish pate. "What is that?"

"Beluga caviar," Lykos answered. "Beluga is a Russian delicacy."

"I'll try that, too."

The prince placed two small squares of black bread on her plate. Then he topped each with a dollop of caviar.

"I would love another glass of the punch," Blaze said.

"Where is this punch?"

Blaze pointed to the crystal bowl in the middle of the dining table. Lykos looked from the bowl to her and smiled. He passed her the plate and ladled the punch into a crystal glass.

"Let us sit over there." The prince ushered her toward a table and set the plate and the glass down. "Taste the Beluga and tell me your opinion."

Blaze lifted a piece of black bread and took a tiny bite. Though unimpressed by the taste, she smiled at the prince and nodded her approval. Russian delicacies were probably an acquired taste.

The Duke and Duchess of Inverary chose a nearby table. The duke nodded at Lykos and the duchess smiled. Blaze caught the irritated look her father gave her stepmother.

"Why is you-know-who supping with you-know-who?" Blaze heard her father ask.

Her stepmother waved her hand. "Strategy, dearest."

"Strategy, my arse," her father muttered.

Blaze struggled against the laughter bubbling up. She lifted her glass and sipped the punch.

"Tell me how MacArthur cured your filly of this balking problem," Prince Lykos said.

"I cannot divulge our secret," Blaze said, "but you should wager on Pegasus in the next race."

Prince Lykos inclined his head. "I will certainly follow your advice."

One floor above the dining room, Ross stood with his sister and waited for the last of the guests to go to supper. He did not want anyone eavesdropping on their conversation.

"Are we goin' to supper or not?" Mairi asked him.

"I want yer help," Ross told her. "I need ye to keep Prince Lykos busy while I lure Blaze away."

"Why do ye want the company of the redhaired, freckled, illegitimate daughter of a suicide?"

I love her, Ross thought, surprising himself. This

wasn't merely a competition to win the lady's hand in marriage. He could not imagine growing old with anyone else. And Blaze wanted him, even if she didn't know it yet.

Ross would never consider baring his heart to his sister or anyone else. "I intend to marry the lass."

"What aboot Amanda?" Mairi exclaimed. "She's been waitin' for ye to settle."

"I never encouraged Amanda or Celeste regardin' marriage," Ross said. "In fact, I moved to the Rowley Lodge so Celeste canna catch me in the marriage trap. If yer smart, ye'll bolt yer door in the event Dirk wants to trap ye in marriage."

"I've been lockin' my door since Da married Celeste," Mairi told him.

"I see ye share my intelligence," Ross said. "Listen carefully, sister. I'll only say this one time. If I ever hear ye speakin' ill of Blaze, I'll wash yer mouth out with soap."

"Are ye threatenin' me?" Mairi arched a dark brow at him. "Ye've a strange way of seekin' favors."

"I mean every word."

"Very well, I willna voice any disparagin' thoughts," Mairi said, turning toward the stairs. "And I'll help ye. Are ye comin'?"

"Thank ye, sister."

"Ye do know yer leavin' yer baby sister with a notorious ladies man."

"Lykos is a rake?" Ross couldn't keep the surprise from his voice.

"I wouldna go so far to name him a rake," Mairi replied, "but he enjoys the company of various women. The ladies call him the Wolf Prince, and

the peaheads would swoon at his feet if he smiled
at them."

When they entered the dining room, Ross felt as
if he'd walked into an opera's last act. Raven Flambeau was supping with his stepbrothers while
Alexander Blake supped with Amanda. The reason
for the shift in partners eluded him.

"They're sittin' over there," Ross said, his gaze on
Blaze and the prince.

"Are ye so hot for her ye'd make yerself a fool?"
Mairi placed a restraining hand on his arm. "Fix a
plate for me, and then we'll wander over there."

Ross grabbed a plate, asking, "What do ye want?"

"I'll take a slice of beef, a piece of the spinach
souffle, and two kippers."

With plate in hand, Ross escorted his sister to
Blaze's table. "Good evenin', Yer Highness," he
greeted the other man. "Do ye remember my sister,
Mairi?"

Prince Lykos stood and bowed over her hand. "I
could never forget a beautiful woman."

Mairi MacArthur inclined her head. "Are all
princes as smooth as ye?"

Lykos smiled. "Please join us."

"As a matter of fact," Ross said, setting his sister's
plate down and lifting Blaze's, "I need a private
word with Miss Flambeau. If ye dinna mind, that is."

"I do not mind if Mairi keeps me company."

Ross drew Blaze out of her chair, and his sister sat
in it. "I'll bring yer plate in case this takes longer
than I anticipate."

"What are you doing?" Blaze whispered.

"I'll tell ye in a minute." Ross noted the curious

gazes watching their exit and knew that tongues would be wagging in the morning. Thankfully, Blaze seemed oblivious to their audience.

"I dinna want anyone eavesdroppin'," Ross told her, "so we'll walk outside."

"What is the secret?" Blaze asked, when they reached the gazebo. "Has this to do with Pegasus?"

"I wanted to sup with ye."

Blaze rolled her eyes, but a smile flirted with the corners of her lips. "That was a sneaky trick."

"Thank ye for the praise." Ross grinned at her. "What are ye eatin'?"

"I chose gherkins, mushrooms, potted cheese, and Beluga caviar."

"Do ye know what Beluga caviar is?"

"Beluga is a Russian delicacy," she told him.

"What kind of delicacy?"

"I don't recall the prince telling me."

"Beluga is sturgeon roe," Ross informed her. "Sturgeon is a fish, and roe its unfertilized eggs."

An expression of horrified revulsion appeared on her face. Her hands flew to her throat. In desperation, she grabbed the crystal glass from his hand, gulping the punch in one long swig. Then she hiccupped.

"Are ye ill?"

"I needed the punch to wash the taste from my mouth."

Ross smiled and glided a finger down her cheek. "The punch is spiked with champagne."

Blaze giggled. "The punch tickled my throat going down."

"Champagne will do that." Ross stared at her upturned face, the invitation in her eyes.

Miss Blaze Flambeau was a delightful paradox. Innocence clung to her like a sensuous perfume, but she wasn't above getting her hands dirty or mucking stables. The Highland blood pumping through her veins was apparent in this Flambeau.

"I want to know the reason yer sister is suppin' with my stepbrothers," Ross said, "and Alexander Blake is suppin' with my stepsister."

"They're investigating Charlie's murder." The words slipped out before she could stop herself.

"Is Dirk a suspect?"

"Anyone who owns a thoroughbred is suspect."

"Am *I* suspect?"

"Do you own a thoroughbred?"

"Blast it, Blaze," Ross said. "I want to know what's happenin'."

"I know you are an innocent man," Blaze said, "but you must pretend to know nothing."

Ross narrowed his gaze on her.

"God gifted Raven with the ability to read events from holding objects," Blaze began.

Ross laughed in her face. "I apologize, darlin'. Finish yer story."

"Raven did a reading with Charlie's gold ring," Blaze continued. "She saw a night sky with a crescent moon. Draped across the moon was a MacArthur plaid and a dirk."

"That isna evidence, and ye havena answered my question aboot tonight's supper."

"Alex and Raven are spying," Blaze explained.

"Befriending the Stanleys may give them important information."

"Why isna anyone spyin' on me?"

Blaze leaned close and stood on tiptoes to whisper in his ear. "I am."

Ross turned his head and captured her lips in a lingering kiss. "I didna realize bein' investigated could feel so good."

She gave him a coy smile. "Neither did I."

"If I could see yer bedchamber," Ross said in a husky voice, "I could imagine ye there when I'm lyin' in my lonely bed at night."

She brushed her lips across his cheek. "Only look?"

"Well, I'd love to touch."

"Are all aristocrats as smooth as you?" Blaze asked, echoing his sister's words.

"Sorry, darlin' I'm the best of the lot."

Blaze offered him her hand. "We'll use the servants' stairs."

No one saw them scoot up the back stairs. The staff was busy in the kitchens, serving supper, or assisting the guests' coachmen in the front courtyard.

Ross bolted the bedchamber door. He turned around slowly and smiled at her.

Blaze walked into his embrace, molding her body to his, drawing his head down to kiss him. She poured all of her passion into that single stirring kiss.

He unbuttoned the back of her gown, making his way from neckline to waist. Parting the sides, he caressed her delicate backbone with a finger.

Blaze purred at the sensation. A delicious chill danced down her spine, her body heated, and her nipples hardened in arousal.

Pushing the gown down, Ross let it pool at her feet while his warm lips touched the side of her throat. "Let's go to bed," he said, his voice hoarse with need.

Without embarrassment, Blaze crossed the chamber to the bed. She wore her lace and silk chemise, silk stockings, garters, and satin slippers.

Ross lifted the ice-blue gown off the floor and, following her across the room, tossed it onto the chaise near the hearth. When he faced her, desire gleamed in his dark eyes.

Holding her gaze captive, Ross undressed slowly. He removed his jacket and waistcoat, placing both on the chaise. Next were his cravat, shirt, and trousers.

Naked, Ross crossed the room and knelt in front of her. He slid his hands up her legs, pushing the silk and lace chemise up to reveal her thighs. After removing her garter, he rolled her stocking down her leg slowly. Then he did the same for her other leg.

Ross slid her chemise off her body and, pushing her down on the bed, lay on top of her. Blaze liked his hands on her body and his weight pressing her down.

He kissed her cheeks, eyelids, temples. Then his lips drifted down her throat.

Kneeling again, Ross cupped her breasts and whispered, "I love yer nipples."

He dipped his head to lick and suck one pink-tipped peak and then the other. She wrapped her arms around him, holding his head against her breasts, savoring the throbbing in her lower regions.

His lips burned a trail from her breasts to her belly and beyond. He buried his face against the coppery curls at the juncture of her thighs.

Blaze rose up in alarm. "What are you doing?"

"Trust me." Ross flashed her a smile, gently pressing her back on the bed.

"So said the Serpent to Eve in Paradise," she murmured.

He kissed her inner thighs, his lips moving toward the center of her womanhood. When his tongue touched her swollen nub, Blaze arched against him and cried out as waves of pleasure surged through her.

Ross stood then, drawing her closer to the edge of the bed. He positioned himself, saying, "Wrap yer legs around my body."

When she did, he thrust into her and—

Someone knocked on the door.

Blaze opened her eyes. Ross winked at her and withdrew from her moist heat.

Again came the knocking. "Are you there, Blaze?" The voice belonged to her stepmother.

"One moment," Blaze called, placing a finger across her lips. She pointed at his clothing and the privacy screen in the corner. Blaze donned her robe while he gathered his garments and crossed the room.

Blaze threw the bolt and opened the door a crack. "What is it?"

"What took you so long?" the duchess asked her.

"I was sleeping." Blaze feigned a yawn.

"Why is your door locked?"

"We have guests in the house."

"Why did you leave the Ball?"

"The punch made me dizzy," Blaze said, irritation tingeing her voice. "Are you practicing for the Spanish Inquisition?"

"Darling, you are so amusing." Her stepmother gave her a feline smile. "Your father wants to speak with Ross MacArthur. Have you seen him?"

Blaze dropped her gaze to her bedrobe and then looked at her stepmother. "Apparently not."

"The marquis and you disappeared during supper."

Blaze heard the suspicion in her stepmother's voice and pasted a serene smile on her face. "Shall I check under the bed?"

"No, thank you, darling." The duchess's dimpled smile appeared. "You have told me what I wanted to know."

Chapter Ten

Three weeks of sensual nights at the Rowley Lodge and dawn practice at the track were ruining her health. She'd been queasy, tired, and cranky for the past week. She hoped the late nights and early mornings were making her feel poorly, the alternative too scandalous to consider.

"Ye dinna look well," Ross said. "Rooney can jockey Pegasus today."

"It's too late to switch places." Blaze recognized the concern in his dark eyes. "I'm tired but well enough to ride."

Ross and Blaze sat inside his closed phaeton on the practice field at Newmarket Heath, as they'd done three weeks earlier.

The Rowley Mile lay beyond the heath, the grandstands rising near the start line. Waving in the gentle breeze, the Jockey Club flag beckoned Newmarket's inhabitants to the races.

Gamblers, aristocrats, horse people, and country gentry mingled together near the grandstands. The second race of the season offered the public a chance to watch a filly make history by beating the colts a second time.

Blaze wore the same jockey attire. Her racing silk jacket sported the green, black, and blue Campbell colors. Her mane of red hair was hidden beneath the jacket's matching cap. Light-weight riding boots covered the bottom of her breeches. Goggles dangled around her neck, and fingerless leather gloves covered her hands.

Digging in his leather satchel, Ross produced the packet of Stinking Billy and passed it to her. Blaze placed the cord over her head and slipped both beneath her jacket.

The stench assaulted her. Her hands flew to her throat, and she gagged dryly.

"Are ye ill?"

Blaze waved her hand. "I'm fine, momentary revulsion to the Stinking Billy."

"Could ye swagger a bit on the way to the paddock?" Ross slashed mud streaks across her cheekbones. "I caught ye wigglin' last time."

"Here comes Rooney," Blaze said, and they climbed out of the phaeton.

Rooney grinned and passed her the whip. "Good luck."

"I'll see you on the path." Blaze gave them a thumbs up and started across the heath.

The closer Blaze walked to the spectators, the louder the noise. The cacophony of sounds—conversations, laughter, shouted oaths—could make a healthy body wish for deafness.

The groups of roughly dressed men were still entertaining themselves with cockfights. She needed to remind her father to speak with the Jockey Club about that.

"Here's ya drink, guv." The boy offered her a shot of whisky.

Without breaking stride, Blaze lifted the glass out of his hand. She tossed it down in one gulp and shuddered, the amber liquid burning a trail to her stomach.

The three jockeys who'd heckled Rooney at the last race appeared sullen. Looking straight ahead, Blaze walked past them.

"Hey, will ya look at that," one jockey said, his voice loud.

"Rooney wiggles like a girl," a second jockey said, making his friends laugh.

"He'll be using his winnings to buy a new gown," the third said.

The three losers wanted to get a rise out of Rooney so the officials would toss him out of the race. What would Rooney do at the insult to his manhood?

Blaze lifted her hand and again gave them her middle finger. She and Peg would make them eat dirt.

Arriving at the paddock, Blaze spied Bender at the far side. She raised her hand in greeting but walked to Pegasus first. *Love Peg.*

Me love.

Peg run?

Run, run, run.

Turning to the trainer, Blaze passed him the empty

shot glass. Bender looked around and then pocketed the glass.

"Rooney?" The boy who'd delivered her whisky the last race stood there, offering her a shot glass. "Here's ya whisky."

Blaze shifted her gaze to the trainer and saw his surprised expression. To his credit, Bender recovered his composure, saying, "The other boy brought the whisky."

"I always bring Rooney his whisky," the lad said. "There's no other boy."

"My mistake," Bender said, offering her the shot glass, "I was thinking of something else."

Blaze gulped the whisky down and passed the boy the empty glass. If she hadn't been poisoned, she would definitely be drunk.

"Don't race today," Bender said, his voice low. "Someone could have slipped you poison."

"I'm already dead if someone fed me poison," Blaze said, her placid expression masking her fear. "Pegasus will win the race before I expire."

"MacArthur is correct," Bender said. "You're too damn stubborn."

"Thank you for the compliment."

The bell sounded. Bender gave her a leg up on Pegasus and then mounted his own horse.

"Cheer up." Blaze passed him the whip. "I will be sitting in the grandstands the next time Peg races."

They left the paddock in pairs, jockeys on the thoroughbreds with their escorts. The crowd cheered as the first thoroughbreds appeared on the track.

"Pegasus," someone shouted when the filly walked onto the track. The excited crowd began chanting the filly's name.

"Peg is the crowd's favorite," Bender remarked.

"I won't make any money if everyone bets on her," Blaze said, making the trainer smile.

The two horses in front of her suddenly blurred into four, making her queasy and disoriented. If she quit now, they'd be in trouble. She needed to hang on and let Peg fly to the finish.

"Good luck," Bender said, and turned his horse away.

Blaze moved Pegasus into position at the start line. She crouched low, her gaze on the official holding the flag. Seeing two flags didn't matter as long as she saw them drop.

And then the Jockey Club official dropped the flag.

Peg run.

Run, run, run. Peg bolted off the start line to take the lead.

"Faster, faster, faster," Blaze whispered.

And Peg flew like the mythical winged horse. The filly increased her lead, racing against herself, leaving the others behind.

Blaze felt the world spinning out of her control. Determined to stay seated and win, she slumped forward and clung to the filly's neck.

Ross stood on the path in the copse of trees beyond the finish line. "Call the race," he shouted to the jockey.

"They're off." With spyglass raised, Rooney sat on a tree limb. "Sweet Jesus, our girls are in the lead. No holes blocking them. Peg gaining speed. Ten lengths in front. Fifteen, twenty . . ." The jockey looked down at him, his face ashen and his expression stricken. "Blaze is slumped over Peg's neck."

Ross didn't need to hear more. He ran down the path, the jockey two steps behind him.

Bursting into the clearing, Ross saw Peg crossing the finish line first. The official waved the Campbell colors, and he heard a roar of approval from the grandstands.

Peg slowed gradually and stopped near Ross. Blaze lay slumped over the filly's neck. Her eyes were closed, her lips were moving in silent chant, and her knuckles were white from holding the filly so tight.

"I'm here, lass." Ross gently lifted her off the filly and lay her on the grass.

Blaze opened her eyes, whispering, "Whisky drugged." And then she lost consciousness.

Three hours later, Ross paced back and forth across the Inverary drawing room. Reaching the front, he pushed the drapes aside to look out the window at the courtyard. Then he turned and crossed the room to stare at the portrait of Gabrielle Flambeau.

He should have listened to Bender. He should never have allowed her to jockey Pegasus. He should have known she would be targeted.

The Duchess of Inverary had promised to report on Blaze's condition but hadn't appeared yet. The Duke of Inverary and his own father were meeting with the members of the Jockey Club.

"Sit down, MacArthur. You are tiring us."

Ross paused in his pacing and looked at Prince Lykos Kazanov, sitting on the sofa. Grim-faced, Bobby Bender and Rooney sat in high-backed chairs.

The Duke of Inverary and the Duke of Kilchurn appeared in the drawing room doorway. Bender, Rooney, and even Prince Lykos stood when the older men walked into the room.

Without a word or a glance at them, the Duke of Inverary accepted the glass of whisky his old friend passed him. The duke prolonged their misery by sipping his whisky before speaking.

"Peg's win stands," the duke told them. "Apparently, the rules do not include a ban on female jockeys." He looked at Ross. "That oversight has now been corrected." Next the duke turned to the trainer and the jockey. "The Club forgives your transgressions in this affair, assuming you had no choice but obey the marquis's order. You are still in my employ and will leave now."

Bender and Rooney hurried out of the drawing room before he changed his mind. If the duke dismissed them, no one would hire them after this fiasco.

"Your membership has not been revoked," the Duke of Inverary told Ross, "but the Club considers you a troublemaker and will be watching." He drained his whisky and set the glass on a table. "I am going upstairs to confer with Dr. Elliott and my wife about my daughter's health and will return to tell you the news." At that, the duke quit the chamber.

"Do ye have a brain in yer head? How could ye behave so irresponsibly?" The Duke of Kilchurn rounded on his son as soon as his friend disappeared out the door. "Ye've embarrassed me and, more important, endangered my friend's daughter. She could have been killed, not to mention the damage ye've done to her reputation."

Ross remained silent, knowing he deserved worse than a dressing down. His father should have shown more discretion than rebuke him in front of the prince, but he didn't think pointing that out would lighten his father's mood.

"Well? Do ye have nothin' to say?"

"Yer correct, Father." Ross met his gaze. "I used poor judgment."

"*Poor judgment?* Ye nearly caused a catastrophe." His father walked away, though, silenced by his son's remorse.

A short time later, the Duke and Duchess walked into the drawing room. "Magnus, calm yourself," the duchess was saying.

Inverary poured himself a whisky and didn't bother to sip. He committed the ultimate sacrilege by belting the whisky down in a single gulp.

Ross feared the worst. How could he live with himself if Blaze died?

"My daughter is awake and as well as can be

expected," Inverary told them. "Dr. Elliott believes she'd been slipped a sedative but will recover."

"The news is good," Ross said, every muscle in his body relaxing.

"You have relieved my mind," Lykos echoed the sentiment.

"There is more, however." The duke paused a moment and then added, "I trust whatever I say will not be repeated."

"Magnus, you need not involve His Highness in this," the duchess said.

"His Highness was supping with Blaze at the Ball," the duke argued, "and he's been visiting on a regular basis."

"I can vouch for his behavior," the duchess said. "You will create a scandal."

The Duke of Inverary rounded on his wife. "In case you hadn't noticed, Roxie, Ross and Blaze already created the scandal."

"I assure Your Graces," Lykos spoke up, "I will keep your confidence."

The Duke of Inverary stared at Ross, making him squirm mentally. He looked at Lykos for a long moment before shifting his gaze to Ross again.

"Who impregnated my daughter?"

Ross dropped his mouth open and tried to get his mind around what the duke had asked. He was going to be a father?

"I will marry Blaze," Prince Lykos said.

"I'll marry her," Ross growled. "She's carryin' my heir."

"Blaze refused to name the father, and I needed

to be certain before accusing Ross." The Duke of Inverary offered the prince his hand. "I thank you for your offer."

Lykos shook the duke's hand. "You can depend on my discretion." The prince nodded at the Duke of Kilchurn and grinned at Ross. "I congratulate your impending fatherhood." And then he left the drawing room.

"I hope your powers of persuasion are as sharp as your powers of seduction," Inverary told Ross. "Blaze refuses to marry, but if she doesn't, I will kill you."

"Don't be so dramatic," the duchess said. "Of course, they'll marry. Blaze will view the situation differently once she's rested. Five years from now, we will enjoy a merry chuckle about this affair. I mean, situation."

"I may not live that long," the duke replied. "My daughters are digging me an early grave. Would that I had sired all sons."

"Sons give us gray hair, too," the Duke of Kilchurn told his friend.

"I'll speak with Blaze now," Ross said.

"You will speak with her when I allow it," the duke told him. "Tomorrow is soon enough."

"I will return in the mornin'." Ross crossed the drawing room to leave. Behind him, he heard Inverary saying to his father, "Let's toast our sharing grandchildren."

With Puddles at her feet, Blaze sat in a corner of the drawing room and stared at her mother's portrait. She'd never known her mother the way she appeared in the portrait—incredibly young, sensuously innocent, surprisingly happy. The woman she'd known had been broken by losing her family in the Terror, loving a man unable to marry her, and giving birth to seven illegitimate daughters.

Gabrielle Flambeau had been a countess, but Society shunned women who broke the rules. Society was less stringent when a gentleman sinned, averting their collective gazes and pretending ignorance.

Life was unfair. Women were either wives or mistresses. Only men were allowed to be more than husbands and lovers.

Now Blaze understood that Gabrielle drank to dull the pain. She wished she'd been kinder to her mother. Why did understanding come too late? She'd give her right leg to reverse time and relive those days. Would her mother still live if she'd been kinder?

Her thoughts turned to the marquis. Ross would soon be arriving to propose marriage. What else could he do? He was unmarried, and their fathers were best friends. Refusing to marry her meant ruining a lifelong friendship.

She needed to consider what was best for her baby. She recalled her own childhood and her yearning for a father. She did not want her child labeled a bastard, nor would a son thank her for tossing his birthright away.

When the marquis proposed marriage, she would give him one chance to escape. If he did not

take it, then so be it. She didn't relish the thought
of living with a husband who did not love her, but
she would make the sacrifice for her babe. What
else could she do?

Puddles lifted his head. *Man come.*

Ross MacArthur stood in the doorway and flashed
her a smile. His heart wrenched at the sadness in her
smile. She seemed so alone and small, much too delicate to carry his child.

"How are ye feelin' today?" Ross sat beside her on
the settee.

"I'm completely recovered."

"Ye gave me a scare," he said. "I should've known
the villain would target ye before the race."

"What's done is past," she assured him. "I'm relieved Pegasus wasn't harmed. Did you hear the
crowd chanting her name?"

"I dinna want to discuss Pegasus or racin'," Ross
told her. "What's done isna past. We'll soon become
parents and must discuss the future."

Blaze looked at him through enormous blue eyes,
and Ross felt himself falling under her spell. He
forgot himself when she looked at him, the urge to
kiss her banishing rational thought.

Puddles whined, breaking the moment. The mastiff lifted his paw.

"I nearly forgot ye." Ross reached into his pocket.
He unfolded a napkin and gave the dog a cinnamon cookie.

Ross slipped his arm around Blaze's shoulders
and drew her against his body. "We'll marry as soon
as possible."

"Are you asking or telling?"

Oops, he'd forgotten the crankiness of pregnant women. "I meant, will ye do me the honor of becomin' my wife?"

"You don't need to marry me because I'm pregnant," Blaze said, offering him the escape route. "My father never married my mother."

"Yer father was a fool," Ross said, "but dinna repeat that. I *want* to marry ye if ye'll have me."

"Yes, I will marry you."

"Ye willna regret this." Ross lowered his head and kissed her. "I'll never let ye down."

"I believe you and will never let you down," Blaze promised him. "I need a tiny favor."

"I'll give ye anythin' within my power."

"The mornings sicken me. I want to schedule Peg's track practice later in the day."

"That's an enormous favor," Ross teased her, "but I can manage it."

He'd won her hand in marriage. Now he needed to win her love. *By fair means or foul.*

Alexander Blake sat inside his grandfather's coach, his destination Inverary House. Constable Black was indefinitely detained in London, and Alexander dreaded giving the Duke of Inverary the bad news.

Without any hard evidence, this horse-racing business was becoming complicated. The villain had left no clues, and no witnesses had stepped forward.

After yesterday's fiasco at the track, Alexander

scratched MacArthur's name off his list of possible suspects. MacArthur would not help Blaze and then drug her.

Alexander grinned, thinking of Blaze Flambeau disguised as a jockey and riding her filly into horse-racing history, His future sister-in-law was an Original, and he hoped her luck held for the rest of the season.

The coach halted in the Inverary House court-yard. Alexander climbed out and walked toward the house.

The majordomo opened the door. "Welcome, Lord Blake."

"Thank you, Tinker." Alexander walked into the foyer. "His Grace is expecting me."

"His Grace will need to wait," Tinker said. "Miss Raven wants to speak with you before the meeting. She's waiting in the garden."

Alexander gave him a puzzled smile. "This sounds serious."

"A life-or-death emergency, I'm sure."

Alexander made his way through the mansion to the garden door. Stepping outside, he paused to inhale the mingling scents of lilacs and wisteria.

Nearest the mansion were flowerbeds and shrubs. An Elizabethan maze created from clipped hedges stood beyond, and Alexander made a mental note to get lost with Raven in the maze.

Manicured lawns carpeted the grounds. In the distance, the gazebo perched at the edge of the woodland. Even from this distance, he saw Raven pacing back and forth.

Alexander had a bad feeling. Why did Raven need to speak with him so far from the house? Was she angry? Or did she expect his anger?

"Hello, Brat." Alexander climbed the gazebo's steps. "If we were any farther from the house, we'd be speaking in London."

He smiled, admiring her fresh beauty, especially her courtesan lips. She would become his wife in a few short weeks, and then he could taste those lips whenever he wanted.

Raven fidgeted with her betrothal ring. "We must postpone our wedding."

"Last summer you refused a Christmas wedding because you wanted June," Alexander reminded her, annoyance tingeing his voice. "Now you want to postpone our June wedding?"

"I do not want to postpone our wedding," she said, "but my sister's need is greater."

"I don't understand."

"Blaze is pregnant," Raven told him, "so I offered her our arrangements. My stepmother cannot plan two weddings at the same time."

Alexander stared at her for a long moment. He understood her reasoning, but she hadn't consulted him to make postponing their wedding a joint decision. If their roles were reversed, she would be livid.

"You offered without consulting me?" It was a statement, not a question.

Raven ignored his irritation. "We can plan a festive Christmas wedding."

"No."

She looked surprised. "October?"

"No."

"August?"

"I refuse to make plans that will be canceled," Alexander said.

Raven stepped back a pace as if she'd been struck. Her complexion paled, and her bottom lip trembled.

"You're breaking our engagement?"

"We need a longer engagement," Alexander said, his gaze softening on her. "You need time to settle this marriage matter in your mind."

"What about His Grace?"

"My grandfather will survive." Alexander turned to leave. "I am meeting your father and cannot linger to discuss this."

And then Alexander walked away, one of the hardest things he'd ever done. He refused to look over his shoulder lest he catch her weeping. Or hexing him with incantations.

Raven didn't mind postponing their wedding but worried that he'd changed his mind about marrying her. Let her worry for once. Suffering was good for the soul.

Reaching the duke's office, Alexander shook his hand and sat in a leather chair in front of the oak desk. "I apologize, Your Grace, but Constable Black is needed in London. He will come to Newmarket as soon as possible."

"You have been working with the constable for several years," the duke said. "I have confidence in your ability."

"I appreciate that."

The door opened, drawing their attention. Blaze peeked into the office.

"Come inside," the duke said, beckoning her. "Alex wants to ask you about yesterday."

"Tell me what happened," Alex said, when she sat in the chair beside his.

"Rooney takes a whisky shot to calm his nerves before a race," Blaze told him. "At The Craven, a boy delivered the whisky to the paddock. Yesterday, I was crossing the heath when a boy approached me and handed me the glass of whisky."

"Can you describe the boy?"

"He was small," she answered, "and his hair was brown."

"Hundreds of boys in Newmarket fit that description," the duke remarked.

"I would recognize him if I saw him again."

"Too bad there isn't an object for Raven to read," Alexander said.

"There might be an object," Blaze said, smiling. "I lifted the whisky glass out of the boy's hand without stopping and gulped it on the way to the paddock. I passed the empty glass to Bender, who pocketed it."

"Tinker," the Duke of Inverary called.

"Yes, Your Grace?" The majordomo opened the door and stepped inside. "I was just passing by when—"

"Send a footman to Bender," the duke interrupted. "I want the empty whisky glass Blaze handed him, if he still has it."

"I understand, Your Grace."

"With all the excitement yesterday," the duke said, "Bender may have forgotten the glass in his pocket."

"I hope so." Alexander looked at Blaze. "Congratulations on your filly's win and best wishes on your impending marriage."

"I apologize for using your arrangements."

"Don't worry about that," Alexander said. "Raven needs more time. We've decided to wait a while before planning another wedding."

"My wife will never approve," the Duke of Inverary said. "Roxie will believe you're breaking the engagement."

"With all due respect, Her Grace should complain to Raven."

A short time later, Tinker rushed into the room. He carried an empty whisky glass.

"Send Raven here."

"Yes, Your Grace."

Meanwhile, Raven sat alone in the drawing room and thought about Alexander. Of course, she wanted to marry him. She had loved him forever and could not imagine life without him.

Her sister's need for the wedding arrangements had disappointed her, too. Did Alex recognize her sisterly sacrifice? No, he mistrusted her motives.

Did Alex's attitude have anything to do with the blonde? Amanda Stanley knew nothing, and neither did her brother. Their spying would end now, or Alex would regret it.

"Miss Raven," Tinker called, walking into the

drawing room. "His Grace requires your presence in his office."

"Thank you, Tinker." Raven walked down the corridor and knocked on the door. She entered without waiting for permission. Her father sat behind his desk. Blaze and Alex sat in leather chairs.

"This held the drugged whisky," Alexander said, standing when she entered the room. "I need a reading."

Raven arched a brow at him. "You believe in my hocus-pocus?"

"Constable Black and I believe in anything that solves a crime," Alexander said. "Your hocus-pocus cannot be used in court but can provide clues."

Raven lifted the glass out of his hand without touching his fingers, which made him smile. She crossed the room to sit alone in front of the dark hearth. She held the glass in her left hand and placed her right hand over it. Closing her eyes, she relaxed her body.

And then it happened.

Fog rolled across her mind's eyes and then dissipated slowly. The familiar vision of the heavenly night sky appeared. There were the crescent moon, the MacArthur plaid, and the dirk.

That vision faded away, replaced by another. A candle, its wick standing tall in its center, transformed into a blond gentleman passing a boy the whisky glass. She tried to see the man's face, but it was a candlewick. And then the fog rolled in again, obstructing her view.

Raven stood and returned to the others, setting the whisky glass on her father's desk. Then she sat beside her sister.

"I saw the heavenly night sky again," Raven told them. "The MacArthur plaid and the dirk were still there. That vision faded into a candle, its wick tall in the center. Then the candle changed into a man handing the glass to the boy."

"A candle became a man?" Alexander sounded skeptical, which did not sit well with her.

Raven stared at him. "That is what I said."

"Can you describe the man?"

"He was tall and blond."

"I told you the bone sucker did it," Blaze said. "Nobody listens to me."

The Duke of Inverary chuckled at his daughter. Even Alexander and Raven exchanged smiles.

"Did you notice his face?"

"He had no face."

Alexander ran a hand through his hair. "Did you see anything where his face should have been?"

"His face was a candlewick."

"This will give me nightmares," Alexander muttered. "I wish you heard voices instead of seeing these symbolic visions."

"Only crazy people hear voices," Raven said.

"You forgot Joan of Arc," Blaze reminded her sister. "She wasn't crazy."

Raven looked at her. "That point is debatable."

"What do you think a faceless man means?" Alexander asked Raven.

His question surprised her. "You want my opinion?"

Alexander nodded.

Raven placed a finger across her lips. "He's invisible."

"An invisible man?" Alexander echoed, sarcasm tingeing his voice.

"Someone who feels overlooked is invisible."

Alexander grinned. "That is a logical point."

A knock on the door drew their attention. Tinker stepped into the office, saying, "Excuse me, Your Grace. Baron Shores requests an interview. He has something you want."

The Duke of Inverary looked at Alexander, who shrugged and nodded. The duke gestured the majordomo who, in turn, beckoned someone in the hallway.

"I brought you a gift," Crazy Eddie said, stepping into the room. With the baron was a scrawny, dark-haired boy.

"That's the boy," Blaze and Raven exclaimed in unison.

"How did you find him?" Alexander asked.

"I ain't guilty of nothing," Eddie said. "I happened to see Jack here pass whisky to a jockey. Later, I heard the gossip and went looking for him."

The Duke of Inverary beckoned the boy forward and pointed to the empty chair. "Sit here, son."

"Mind your manners," Eddie warned the boy. "These men are a duke and a marquis. If you aren't honest, they'll know and send you to the gallows."

"Your name is Jack?" the duke asked.

"Yes, Your Grace."

The duke pointed at Blaze. "You delivered whisky to that woman."

"She didn't look like a girl."

"The lady disguised herself as a jockey," Alexander said.

"I bet on Pegasus and made a few pounds," Jack told her.

"Congratulations." Blaze rounded on her father. "Does the Jockey Club approve of children gambling?"

The Duke of Inverary ignored her. "Describe the man who gave you the whisky."

Jack shrugged. "Dunno."

"What color was his hair?" Alexander asked.

"Dark brown."

"Could you recognize him if you saw him again?"

"I suppose so."

"How old are you?" the duke asked.

"Fourteen."

"You're small for fourteen," the duke said. "Do you like horses?"

Jack bobbed his head.

"How would you like to train for a jockey?"

Jack bobbed his head again.

"Give this to your parents." The Duke of Inverary passed him a gold sovereign. "The baron will take you home to pack your belongings. Then he will deliver you to my trainer. The baron will collect you each morning to wander Newmarket looking for the man. Once we catch him, you'll begin training."

"Jack is our only witness," Alexander told the baron. "You must protect him."

"You're asking me to be a child minder?"

"I'm telling, not asking," Alexander said. "Or would you prefer Constable Black investigating those parties at your London home?"

"I'll do it," Eddie said. "Come on, Jack. Let's fetch your belongings."

The baron and the boy left the duke's office.

"The boy saw brown hair." Alexander looked at Raven. "How can a man be blond and dark-haired?"

"Have you ever heard of wigs?" Raven countered.

Alexander smiled. "How logical of you."

"Our problem is this," she said. "Is the wig blond or dark?"

"What do you think, Brat?"

"The man is blond but disguised himself with the brown wig."

"Mark my words," Blaze said. "The bone sucker did it."

Chapter Eleven

She would never recommend motherhood to anyone. Except her worst enemy.

Feeling sorry for herself, Blaze sat on the edge of the bed and slipped into her ankle boots. Her recent morning routine—dry toast and dry gags—disgusted her. She should have known the marquis's baby would give her problems. Like father, like son.

All her dreams and goals had evaporated like mist beneath the noonday sun. Why? The marquis had desired her in his bed. She'd gone along with the idea without realizing the high price.

Blaze slid her hand to her belly. Destiny demanded payment, her cost seeming larger than his.

And then Blaze smiled. What she wanted was still within her grasp. She held the ace card, the marquis's heir growing inside her.

They would be signing the betrothal contract that night. She would suggest—no, insist—on revisions. No revisions, no marriage, no legal heir.

Blaze felt much better. She grabbed a shawl

and draped it around her shoulders. Humming a spritely tune, she crossed the chamber and opened the door.

Raven stood there, her fist in the air.

"Are you going to hit me?" Blaze asked her.

"I want to watch Pegasus and you practice."

"Come along, then."

Raven fell into step beside Blaze. They walked down the servants' stairs to the garden door.

Nature had come alive on that first day of May. Yellow daffodils and forsythia bowed to pink azaleas. Lilac bushes were laden with perfumed purple blossoms, and pesky yellow dandelions dotted the grass carpet beyond the formal garden.

"I'm sorry for causing you and Alex trouble," Blaze said, starting down the path to the practice field.

Raven touched her shoulder. "The blame lies with Alex, not you."

"He is refusing to plan another wedding."

Raven waved her hand, dismissing that with confidence. "Alexander will see the situation my way eventually."

"What if—?"

"If he walks away from our betrothal," Raven said, "Alexander will crawl back on his belly and grovel for my forgiveness."

Blaze smiled at that. "Somehow, I cannot see Alex crawling and groveling."

"No crawling or groveling means no wedding," Raven said. "There are other men in the world."

The sisters reached the end of the path. The usual morning fog covering the track had evaporated hours earlier.

Standing with Bender and Rooney, Ross smiled at Blaze. The three men watched them approach.

Greeting the men with a nod, Blaze headed straight for Pegasus. She stroked the filly's face. *Love Peg.*

Me love.

When she returned to the others, Ross touched her cheek. "The later hour suits ye?"

"I feel well." Blaze blushed at the reference to her condition, wondering if the trainer and the jockey had heard the news. "Raven wants to watch us practice."

Ross gave Rooney a leg up on Pegasus. Then he and Bender mounted their horses.

"Give us a five length lead down track," Ross told Rooney. "We'll keep a hole between us."

The jockey nodded.

"Rooney." Blaze held her hand out, and he passed her the whip.

At the start line, Ross called, "One, two, three—*go.*"

Bender and Ross spurred their horses into action, galloping down track. Rooney and Pegasus gave chase.

Blaze began her silent chant. *Peg through hole. Peg through hole. Peg—*

Pegasus shot through the hole between Ross and Bender.

Blaze relaxed, confident of their success. Rooney would ride her filly to victory. Pegasus would become legend, Rooney would permanently quit drinking spirits, and she would build her animal sanctuary. The future was sunshine and blue skies, no clouds on the horizon.

Pegasus would never see the inside of the breeding barn, though. She would never put her filly through that humiliating experience. Sadly, the magic and legend would die with the filly.

"Touch Peg," Blaze said to her sister. "Let me know if she'll win the Second Spring."

"I cannot see into the future," Raven said.

"Touch her," Blaze persisted, "and tell me your impression."

"I can't promise anything."

Blaze led Raven to the white Arabian and stroked the filly's face. "Peg, my sister wants to touch you."

Pegasus stood perfectly still, as if she understood. Raven closed her eyes and placed the palms of her hands on the filly's face.

Blaze watched her sister's placid expression become a frown that disappeared as quickly as it had come. Raven dropped her hands and opened her eyes.

"What is it?" Blaze asked her. "You sensed something."

"Pegasus will win the Second Spring," Raven said, patting her shoulder.

The touch felt more like consolation than congratulation. Her sister wasn't telling her everything.

"What about the Triple Crown?" Blaze asked her.

"I did not sense her winning," Raven said, "but I did not sense her losing, either."

"How puzzling." Blaze recalled Ross's words. Sometimes you win, sometimes you lose, and sometimes your horse gets scratched. Why would Pegasus be scratched from a race?

"Only God knows all things in advance," Raven

said. "Perhaps Pegasus needs to win the Second Spring before I can sense her luck in the next race."

"That could be it," Blaze said, expression clearing. "You'll need to travel with us to Epsom Derby and the St. Leger in September."

"Jeez, she'll be worryin' from now until September," Ross said, "and worryin' isna good for the babe." He smiled at her reddening complexion. "I knew I could make ye blush."

"Company has come calling," Bender said, drawing their attention.

Blaze turned around. Dirk Stanley, the Earl of Boston, and his half-brother, Squire Simmons, sauntered toward them. Both men were green-eyed and blond, but the squire was taller and more muscular.

"Good to see ye, Chad." Ross shook the squire's hand.

Blaze looked from Dirk to Chadwick. They could have been twins except for the squire's height and more masculine physique.

She thought the resemblance uncanny but supposed Celeste's children looked like her. Both of her own parents had dark hair, but she had inherited Aunt Bedelia's red.

"That is the near-legendary Pegasus," Squire Simmons said, and then looked at her. "This is the filly's notorious jockey."

"All of Newmarket is gossiping about Pegasus," Dirk said. "I've never seen this much excitement over a horse."

"We may need to wager on Pegasus instead of Emperor," Chad said, smiling.

"All of Newmarket will be wagerin' on the filly," Ross said. "Ye willna make much money."

"Being a long-shot is more lucrative," Blaze said.

"That's the price of fame for ye," Ross told her, "but ye can take heart, darlin', the owner gets the prize money." He looked at his stepbrothers. "If ye dinna mind, we prefer private practices."

"We wanted to watch her run," Dirk said, sounding disappointed.

"Come along, brother," Chad said, turning to leave. "We can use our time putting Emperor through his paces."

Ross watched them disappear down the path that led to Snailwell Road. Then he gestured to the trainer and jockey.

"We'll meet tomorrow," Ross said. "I dinna trust them not to watch."

Bender and Rooney led the horses toward the stable path. Ross mounted his own horse, saying, "I'll see ye tonight." Then he turned his horse away, heading for the Snailwell Road path.

"Look," Raven exclaimed, holding her left hand out. Her star ruby had changed colors, darkening to blood red, warning her of danger.

Blaze looked her sister in the eye. "I told you the bone sucker did it."

Hours later, Blaze stood alone in her bedchamber and prepared herself for winning the revisions she wanted on the betrothal contract. She wore a violet whisper gown, its neckline modestly scooped, and her mother's jeweled butterfly hair clasp.

Looking good meant feeling good, giving her the confidence to demand what she wanted. Since this moment would never come again, she would haggle until the marquis surrendered.

Blaze left her bedchamber and walked down the stairs to her father's office on the second floor. She tapped on the door and then peered inside.

"Here she is." Sitting behind his desk, the Duke of Inverary beckoned her forward.

Ross and the Duke of Kilchurn sat in leather chairs in front of the enormous oak desk. Both father and son stood when she entered.

Three leather chairs had been set in a row. Ross assisted her into the vacant middle chair.

"Ye look lovely in purple," he said, and sat in the chair on her right.

"I'm wearing violet whisper, not purple," she corrected him.

"I apologize for my inaccuracy," Ross said, smiling. "Violet whispers and purple shouts?"

"I don't know if purple shouts," Blaze said, "because my stepmother forbids me to wear that shade."

"Listen, daughter," the Duke of Inverary said, parchment and quill in hand. "We don't need to waste time. The contract is standard with a generous monthly allowance. You sign and then Ross will sign."

Blaze folded her hands on her lap, signaling she wasn't ready to sign. She gave Ross a sidelong smile and then told her father, "I require revisions."

"Revisions?" Ross echoed.

Her father smiled. The Duke of Kilchurn chuckled.

"I require certain stipulations added," she told him.

Ross relaxed in his chair, stretching his long legs out. His expression said he found her amusing. Cute.

Blaze arched a copper brow at him. The marquis failed to realize that petite women despised cute. She would set him straight about that after she'd won her stipulations.

"Tell yer father what ye require," Ross said, gesturing to the duke. "I'll agree or not."

Blaze inclined her head. "What is mine I keep," she told her father. "Horses, money, whatever else I value."

"Whatever else ye value is too vague," Ross said. "Name what ye value at this moment."

"I retain ownership and control of my horse, pets, money, and my mother's jewels."

Ross nodded once. "I agree."

The Duke of Inverary lifted the quill and inserted the revision.

"I am allowed to build and control my animal refuge."

Again, Ross nodded at her father. His easy agreement boosted her confidence.

"The financial interests shared with my sisters pass only to my daughters," Blaze said. "If I die without daughters, my interests revert to my sisters and their daughters minus an invested amount, its capital gains sufficient to support my animal refuge."

Ross chuckled, his expression screaming *cute* again. "What interests do ye and yer sisters share?"

His condescending tone annoyed Blaze, and she

could not control the urge to best him. "We own the Seven Doves Company."

"Seven Doves Company?" Ross echoed. "Is that the company pauperin' Douglas Gordon in a price war?"

When she nodded, Ross shouted with laughter. Seven females were winning a price war against his friend. "I canna wait to tell Dougie he's bein' bested by females."

Blaze looked at her father. "My next stipulation is Ross is forbidden to pass that information to the Marquis of Huntly."

The Duke of Kilchurn chuckled, drawing her attention. "James MacArthur is also forbidden to tell Douglas Gordon anything."

The Duke of Kilchurn was smiling, as was her father. Even Ross had a smile flirting with his lips. Three smiling Highlanders boded ill.

Blaze placed a finger across her lips as she considered weaknesses in her demand. Highlanders could find a loophole the size of a grain of sand.

"Both are forbidden to tell a third party who will give Douglas Gordon the information," Blaze added.

"How can I look my friend in the face when I know the owners of the company stealin' his money?" Ross countered.

"The Seven Doves is not stealing his money," Blaze said, "and Bliss does not twist his arm to learn his secrets. If the Marquis of Huntly cannot keep his own counsel, then he deserves to lose his money."

"The lass is correct," the Duke of Kilchurn agreed with her. "Dougie wouldna be losin' the price war if he wasna tryin' to impress her sister with his financial prowess."

Ross gestured to the Duke of Inverary. "Give her what she wants." He looked at her. "Tell me the reason only daughters can inherit yer Seven Doves interests."

"Women need their own money," Blaze told him. "No daughter of mine will depend upon a man for food, clothing, and shelter."

"What's wrong with us men?" he asked.

"How many days can you spare to listen?" she answered, making all three men smile.

"Ye've met yer match," the Duke of Kilchurn told his son. "I can hear the crockery crashing."

"Papa, what is my pin money?"

"Ross gives you one thousand pounds per month."

Blaze smiled, pleased with the amount. One thousand pounds was nine hundred more than she received now.

"Why should I share?" Ross asked, smiling. "She isna sharin' with me."

"Nobody is forcing you to share with me." Blaze stood, ready to leave, and looked him in the eye. "No monthly pin money, no marriage, no legitimate heir."

The Duke of Inverary and the Duke of Kilchurn hooted with laughter. "She's got ye there," Kilchurn told his son.

"I'm teasin' ye," Ross said, grabbing her hand. "What's mine is yers, unlike a certain selfish individual who will remain nameless."

"I will take the quill now." Blaze sat in her chair

again and signed her name. Then she passed the quill to Ross.

"If Peg loses the Second Spring or the Epsom Derby," Ross said, "we'll leave early for the Highlands instead of waitin' for August."

"Why are we going to the Highlands?" Blaze asked.

"Newly-married couples need time away from others," Ross answered.

"What if Hercules wins the Derby?" Blaze asked. "You'll miss the 2000 Guineas Race."

"My father was racin' thoroughbreds before I was born," Ross said. "He knows what to do."

Ross reached in his pocket and produced a small velvet-covered box. Opening its lid, he took the ring and slipped it onto the third finger of her left hand. A solitaire diamond topped a channel-set platinum band of diamonds.

"This was my mother's wedding ring," Ross told her. "I thought ye could wear this until yer betrothal ring is finished. If the notion appeals to ye, I would be pleased if we used my mother's ring for yer wedding band."

"You honor me with your mother's ring," Blaze said, looking from the diamonds to his black eyes. "I will cherish it always."

Ross leaned close and planted a chaste kiss on her lips. "Yer blushin', lass."

"We need a toast." The Duke of Inverary set three crystal tumblers on his desk and poured a measure of whisky into each. "This has been aged eighteen years."

Ross raised his glass. "I salute my bride, only a bit older than the whisky." He sipped the amber liquid and then set the tumbler on the desk. "I've another gift for ye, but we must go outside."

The four stood and left the office, stopping at the drawing room to show her stepmother and Celeste MacArthur the betrothal ring. "What an exquisite ring," the Duchess of Inverary gushed. "Don't you agree, Celeste?"

"Yes." Celeste MacArthur looked like she'd sucked a lemon.

"The ring belonged to Ross's mother," Blaze told them. "I'm wearing it until my betrothal ring is finished, and then I'll wear this as my wedding ring."

"Family heirlooms carry more meaning," the duchess said. "I love diamonds almost as much as my husband."

"Thank you for that, dearest," the Duke of Inverary said, smiling. "I've always wondered which of us—diamonds or me—you loved best."

"Magnus, you are a rare jewel among men."

Ross escorted Blaze out of the drawing room. They walked down the stairs to the foyer.

"Congratulations, my lord," Tinker said, opening the door. "Best wishes, Miss Blaze."

"Thank you, Tinker."

"Brace yerself." Ross placed the palm of his hand on her back and ushered her outside.

A Campbell groom held the reins of a donkey. Wearing a puzzled smile, Blaze approached the animal.

The brown donkey had long ears and an erect mane. A dark stripe ran along its back, and another crossed over the shoulders. Dark stripes banded its legs.

"I want ye to meet yer animal sanctuary's first guest," Ross said. "I caught two boys beatin' the beast and knew ye'd want me to rescue him."

The donkey stood statue-still, allowing Blaze to stroke its head. "You poor, poor donkey," she cooed.

"I named him Beau."

Blaze smiled. "I like Beau."

"Beau is his nickname," Ross said. "His full name is Flambeau."

"Flambeau?" she echoed.

"His stubbornness reminded me of ye." Unexpectedly, Beau erupted into braying hee-haws. "What did he say?"

Blaze looked at him, her expression deadpan. "Beau said hee-haw."

Pegasus was poised to gallop into horse-racing legend, the filly that flew as fast as mythology's winged horse. Excitement grew in Newmarket each passing day, and the Jockey Club basked in the filly's glory.

Blaze could not suppress her own excitement. Winning the Second Spring meant Pegasus would run in the Epsom Derby, the first of the Classic Races.

Race day dawned sunny, nary a cloud marring a brilliant blue sky. A fast track, no rain interfering with legends.

All classes of people crowded the grandstands and surrounding areas, maneuvering for the best place to see the race. The spectators were unusually noisy, extreme agitation raising voices.

Blaze loved the track's scents. Ladies' perfumes and musky horses mingled with hay and dung.

"Dinna fret," Ross said, escorting her across the paddock. "Yer sister predicted Pegasus would win."

Blaze greeted Pegasus in the usual way. *Love Peg. Me love.*

Peg run?

Run, run, run.

"I'll connect with Peg," Blaze told Rooney, "but if you can take the early lead, no one will catch you."

The bell rang, and Bender gave Rooney a leg up on Pegasus. The jockey passed her the whip, saying, "I'll see you in the winner's circle."

Ross and Blaze walked in the direction of the grandstands. Instead of going to the Duke of Inverary's reserved area, they stood near the start line. Only a wooden fence separated them from the horses.

The crowd cheered as the first thoroughbreds appeared on the track. Rooney and Pegasus came into view, and the grandstands reverberated with shouts, whistles, and chants.

Blaze ignored the pandemonium. She kept her gaze on the official holding the flag. And then the flag dropped.

Peg run.

Run, run, run.

Pegasus and Rooney bolted off the start line to take the early lead, and Blaze knew no horse could catch her. Pegasus lengthened her lead, racing against herself, galloping into legend.

The filly led by fifteen lengths at the half-way

mark. Her pace increased. The three-quarter point saw her lead at twenty-five lengths.

And then the filly connected with Blaze, slamming into her consciousness.

Run, run, run. Hurt, hurt, hurt. Run—

"Stop the race," Blaze shouted, already moving to enter the track. "Rooney, stop running."

Ross looked at her. She was yanking her hand out of his grasp, but he pulled her back. "What're ye doin'?"

Desperate to reach her horse, Blaze smashed her fist into his cheek. Striking hard. Hard enough to snap his head to the side. Hard enough to loosen his hold.

Blaze slipped through the track gate. She ran down the Rowley Mile after the thoroughbreds.

Wrapping his mind around what was happening wasted several seconds. Screaming like a madwoman, his bride-to-be was chasing the thoroughbreds down the Rowley Mile.

And then he understood.

Ross leaped over the fence and chased her. Reaching her side, he grabbed her hand and ran with her.

The last judge raised the Campbell colors, signifying the filly's win. The crowd in the grandstands cheered and then gradually quieted. Seeing the Marquis of Awe and the Duke of Inverary's daughter running down the track shocked them into silence.

Ross was almost dragging Blaze by the time they reached the Devil's Ditch. The two raced down the incline and struggled up the other side.

Pegasus lay on her side. With tears streaming down his face, Rooney knelt beside the fallen horse.

"No!" Blaze fell to her knees beside the struggling filly.

"Tell Peg to lie still." Ross watched Blaze lean closer, her lips moving silently, and the filly calmed.

"I dunno what happened," Rooney said, a sob catching in his throat. "We crossed the finish line first, and then she dropped."

Crouching beside Blaze, Ross scanned the growing crowd around the filly. The Duke of Inverary and Bobby Bender managed to cut through the throng.

Bender knelt beside Pegasus and gingerly examined her for any obvious injuries. He looked over his shoulder at the duke. "She broke both front carpal joints."

"What is that?" Blaze asked.

"Pegasus broke both front knees," Ross answered.

"You can fix them, Bender," Blaze said. "Can't you? People break their legs all the time."

Bender turned his head away. The trainer's throat was bobbing as the man tried to swallow raw emotion before speaking.

"Bender?"

Ross heard the fear in Blaze's voice.

The trainer looked at the Duke of Inverary. "We need to put her down."

"Pegasus is *not* dying today," Blaze told them, a river of tears streaming down her cheeks. "Bender, I demand you fix her." She looked at her father. "Papa, we don't put people down."

The Duke of Inverary cleared his throat. "Pegasus

cannot stand on broken knees, and lying down will kill her slowly."

"We'll make a body sling to hoist her up," Blaze said in desperation. "That will keep her standing and her front legs off the floor until they mend."

The Duke of Inverary shifted his gaze to Ross, his eyes pleading for help.

"Ye love Pegasus and dinna want her to suffer," Ross said, his tone gentle, his arm around her. "Do ye love Peg enough to let her go?"

Blaze bowed her head and sobbed, a gut-wrenching howl of pain that Ross hoped never to hear again. He'd never seen a body wracked with sobs, but he did now.

A Jockey Club official handed the Duke of Inverary a pistol. The duke shook his head and passed the pistol to the trainer.

His expression grim, Bender moved around to the filly's head. He looked at Ross and nodded.

In a flash of movement, Ross lifted Blaze away from the horse and backed away. He held her tight, her face pressed against his chest. Her body jerked at the sound of the pistol shot.

Blaze broke free and dropped to her knees beside the dead filly. She stroked her horse and wept.

Ross knelt beside her and prayed he would never witness such misery again. He put a comforting arm around her shoulders but said nothing. There was nothing to say. No words could console her.

The Duke of Inverary cleared his throat. "Come away, Blaze. Let the workers dispose—"

Ross leveled a deadly look on his future father-in-law, silencing him. "Let her grieve, Yer Grace."

The Duke of Inverary nodded and walked away. Bobby Bender handed the official the pistol and followed his employer.

Hours passed, the sun never pausing its westward journey to mourn the filly's untimely death. The curious onlookers faded away, leaving the woman to grieve in privacy. The grandstand emptied, the day's remaining races postponed.

Only Blaze, Ross, and Rooney knelt beside the fallen horse. Eventually, the horse grew cold and the tears were spent.

"Blaze?" Ross thought she might have cried herself to sleep. "We need to leave Pegasus and let the staff—"

Ross winced when she looked at him. Her eyes had swollen into slits. She held her hand out and stood with his assistance.

"Burn Pegasus." A steely determination had entered her voice. "No man or animal will feed on her flesh."

"I'll give the staff yer instructions," Ross said.

"Burn Pegasus now."

Ross studied her grim expression and knew Blaze would never budge until the filly was ashes. He crossed the short distance to the waiting Jockey Club staff. "Miss Flambeau wants her horse burned. Fetch whatever ye need."

"My lord, we always—"

"Always doesna mean this time," Ross interrupted, passing each worker a gold sovereign. "Miss Flambeau willna leave until it's done."

"As you wish, my lord."

Within twenty minutes, kindling covered Pegasus. Ross lit a torch and tossed it on the filly.

Blaze watched Pegasus burn. Fresh tears streamed down her cheeks, but the heart-wrenching sobs were silenced. She refused a handkerchief when the stench of burning horseflesh permeated the area.

"Raven was right," Blaze murmured. "Pegasus won the race."

Chapter Twelve

She had never imagined or even wanted a wedding day.

On the first day of June, Blaze stood in the back of St. Agnes Church and prepared to marry the Marquis of Awe. The guests were seated, the groom awaited, and two violins were playing in the choir loft.

Blaze felt like a princess in a cream-colored satin gown adorned with hundreds of seed pearls. The form-fitting bodice had a squared neckline and a dropped waist. The long sleeves formed a bell shape at her wrist. She carried a bouquet of fragrant orange blossoms. Much to her stepmother's chagrin, the fashionable bride ended there.

Blaze had insisted she was who she was. She'd already created two scandals, jockeying a thoroughbred and chasing the thoroughbreds down the length of the Rowley Mile. Creating a flurry of gossip seemed insignificant.

Refusing a veil, Blaze had left her head uncovered, her fiery mane cascading down her back almost to her waist. The duchess had loaned her a jeweled tiara.

"You sired seven lovely daughters," the Duchess of Inverary told her husband, "but their taste in fashionable coiffeur leaves much to be desired."

"Roxie, my daughters are setting the trends," the Duke of Inverary teased her.

The duchess's dimpled smile appeared. "I suppose the coming year will see an abundance of brides leaving their hair loose and wearing tiaras." She turned to the four unmarried Flambeau sisters. "Come, my darlings. The guests are waiting for our entrance."

The Duchess of Inverary led her charges down the aisle. Like a queen, the duchess nodded at family, friends, and foes.

Only Raven lingered behind. "Something borrowed?"

Blaze pointed to her tiara.

"Something blue?"

Blaze lifted one side of the gown to show her blue garter.

"Something old?"

Blaze slid one of her sleeves up to show their mother's butterfly bracelet.

"Something new?"

Blaze held her right hand out showing her betrothal ring, a butterfly created with diamonds, emeralds, rubies, and sapphires. Ross had commissioned the betrothal ring, and she would wear his mother's wedding band as her own.

"You have been wanting to ask me a question," Raven said. "The answer is I sensed Peg's win, not her death. I would have warned you if I had known."

"Thank you."

Raven turned away to follow her stepmother and sisters to the front pew.

Gazing down the aisle, Blaze noted the seated guests and the white flowers decorating the front of the church. Flickering candles cast dancing shadows on the walls and sunbeams streamed through two stained-glass windows.

God did not dwell in this house of worship. Why would He hide inside four walls when He could walk the earth and enjoy His wondrous creations?

"God isn't here," Blaze whispered.

"I know," her father said, "but please do not mention that to the clergy."

"Papa?"

"We'll speak later," the duke said, looping her hand through the crook of his arm. "Ross is fidgeting like a ten-year-old at the altar."

Blaze giggled at that, and two hundred guests turned in unison to look over their shoulders at her. Her father started forward, forcing her to step with him.

Elevating her status seemed incredibly easy. One moment she was an illegitimate miss, albeit acknowledged. A few words magically transformed her into a marquise and a future duchess.

Only one tiny thing marred the short ceremony. Blaze could feel the witch's basilisk stare on her back. A confrontation seemed inevitable.

Smiling, Ross turned to her at the end of the ceremony. He lifted her hands to his lips, his gaze telling her that all would be well.

"Are ye ready to begin yer life as my wife?" he

whispered, leaning close to plant a chaste kiss on her lips.

"Do you think you will survive having me as your wife?"

"I'll take my chances."

Less than an hour later, Ross and Blaze walked into the Inverary ballroom. Beneath her step-mother's supervision, the ballroom had been decorated for their wedding reception. Musicians played at the opposite side of the rectangular room. Round tables had been positioned around a small dance floor. Garlands of blue and white forget-me-nots adorned the hall while vases of white roses served as centerpieces for each table.

Wisely, the Duchess of Inverary had planned a reception menu with no meat or poultry served on bones. The main courses consisted of beef and chicken slices as well as poached salmon with caper sauce. Beluga caviar was kept out of the bride's sight.

Blaze ate baked eggs without the ham, calf's liver salad without the calf's liver, and a spinach and nettle souffle prepared especially for her. Her husband ate what she ate. Not one morsel of beef, chicken, or salmon passed his lips.

"Eat whatever you want," Blaze whispered against his ear.

Ross turned his head and planted a kiss on her lips. "I want to eat ye, darlin', but we've created enough scandals."

Blaze blushed. "I adore my butterfly ring and will

always cherish your mother's wedding band. When our son marries, he will give it to his bride."

"That's an outstandin' idea." Ross kissed her again. "My mother would have adored ye."

Blaze smiled at that. She wished the son would adore her. He'd married her because of their baby, and now she needed to win his love.

Loving a man was dangerous, though. When a woman gave her heart to a man, she lost her peace of mind.

The Duke of Inverary approached them and looked at Ross. "Take good care of my daughter."

"Yes, Yer Grace, I was plannin' to do that."

"Juno is breeding," the duke told Blaze, "and I'm giving Rooney the nod to ride Thor in the Derby."

"I hope Rooney continues abstaining from spirits." After her father walked away, Blaze glanced at her husband. "You wanted to sell Juno to the knackers."

Ross lifted her hand to his lips. "I admit ye were right aboot Juno."

"Taking Beau with us to Scotland would be right," Blaze said. "We're taking Puddles."

"Beau is a donkey," Ross said, "and Puddles is a dog."

"How incredibly observant."

"If we were travelin' by land," Ross said, "takin' Beau would be fine, but we're takin' the Kazanov ship to Oban. Beau wouldna feel comfortable on a ship. Juno and Beau will be safe at the Inverary stables."

"Where else would they be?"

"The vows we spoke made ye a MacArthur," Ross answered. "We'll be livin' at MacArthur House."

"You will need to hire a food taster to protect me from Celeste," Blaze said.

Ross laughed in her face. "Shall we dance?"

"Whirling around the dance floor will make me regurgitate my dinner." Blaze lifted her bouquet of orange blossoms. "I want to visit my mother's grave."

Ross stood when she did. "Shall I walk with ye?"

Blaze did not want him to know her mother had been buried in unhallowed ground. "I like visiting her alone."

"I understand." Ross nodded, though he could not mask his momentary hurt.

Blaze circled the dance floor, heading for the door. She felt guilty not taking her husband with her, but he would have known her mother had taken her own life.

Leaving the ballroom, Blaze nearly bumped into her sister. Raven lifted her hand. The star ruby had darkened, warning of danger.

Blaze looked from the ring to her sister's face. "The murderer is a wedding guest?"

Raven nodded. "I'm going to find Alex and insist we review the guest list, especially the men with blond hair."

Leaving her sister, Blaze ducked into the withdrawing room and was relieved to find it deserted. When Celeste MacArthur walked in a moment later, she suffered the uncanny feeling the woman had followed her.

"Ross would have married Amanda," Celeste said, "if you hadn't spread your legs and trapped him with a pregnancy."

Let the confrontations begin, Blaze thought, steeling herself for combat.

Blaze knew frustrated ambition incited Celeste to lash out at her. Refusing to rise to the bait would frustrate the woman even more.

Blaze gave her a serene smile. "Ross told me he wasn't interested in Amanda."

"My stepson did not want to hurt your feelings." Celeste returned the serene smile with one of her own.

And Blaze realized the MacArthur duchess was experienced in the art of insult. How fortunate for her that her own stepmother, a master of the insult, had tutored her and her sisters.

"My *husband*"—Blaze placed special emphasis on the word—"moved to Rowley Lodge to prevent falling into your marriage trap."

The older woman faltered for the briefest moment but recovered herself. "Remember, little girl, the marriage vows last only 'till death us do part.' Ross may be free sooner than you think."

Blaze arched a copper brow at the woman. "Are you threatening me?"

"Life is uncertain."

"Indeed, life *is* uncertain." Blaze smiled, wanting her to think she was amused. "Women of your advanced age should beware."

"You are a bastard and—"

"I am also a bitch," Blaze interrupted, satisfied with the woman's surprised expression. "Underestimating me could prove unfortunate for a vicar's daughter. Strange, how rumors spread when one least expects it."

"How true." Celeste regained her composure again. "Like someone's mother being a suicide."

Blaze managed to keep her expression placid, a lesson learned from her stepmother. "Or a woman murdering her first two husbands."

"Spread that rumor," Celeste said, stepping toward her, "and you will regret it."

Blaze stood her ground. "You don't frighten me."

"Oh, what a heartwarming sight. You are becoming better acquainted," the Duchess of Inverary said, walking across the withdrawing room. "Blaze dear, I thought you might be ill."

"I feel wonderful," Blaze said, smiling at her stepmother, "but poor Celeste may need your help. She's developed a chronic pain in her arse." With those parting words, she swept out of the withdrawing room.

Leaving the mansion by the rear door, Blaze walked slowly through the formal gardens. The first skirmish in her war with her stepmother-in-law had left her emotionally drained. She knew one thing for certain. The woman was dangerous and highly sensitive about being thought a murderer. Which meant she had probably murdered her husbands, but Blaze doubted anyone would believe her without proof. Her own husband would not thank her for upsetting his father.

Blaze crossed the wide expanse of lawns and circled the gazebo. Then she took the less-traveled path to a small clearing. The tiny area contained two gravestones and a bench.

"Papa?" She had never seen her father here.

The Duke of Inverary glanced over his shoulder

and beckoned her forward. "I'm visiting your mother."

Blaze placed her orange blossom bouquet between the gravestones. One read: GABRIELLE FLAMBEAU, BELOVED OF MAGNUS CAMPBELL, DUKE OF INVERARY. The second gravestone read: JANE SMUDGE, DEVOTED FRIEND.

"I'm sorry I've disappointed you," Blaze said, sitting beside him.

"Calling you daughter makes me proud," the duke told her, putting an arm around her shoulder. "You believed in Pegasus when no one else did, you proved bold and brave by jockeying the filly, and you demonstrated true love running down the Rowley Mile trying to stop the race."

Blaze blushed. "The gossipmongers will feed on that for a long time."

"Do not forget your husband believed in you and stood beside you every step of the way," the duke said. "I gave you Pegasus to teach you a lesson about the horse-racing business, but I was the one who learned a lesson."

"I don't understand, Papa."

"You shamed me into remembering what I had forgotten," her father told her. "Horse racing takes heart and means more than making a profit."

Blaze nodded in understanding and then asked the question she'd harbored inside for a long time. "Why did you bury Nanny Smudge here?"

"Smudge requested I bury her beside Gabrielle," he answered. "She'd taken care of your mother all those years and didn't want her to rest alone."

Blaze raised a hand to cover her mouth and struggled against the aching emotion. Two teardrops rolled down her cheeks, but her father brushed them aside.

"Smudge described you perfectly," her father told her. "Your tough exterior hides a tender heart, more sensitive than any of your sisters." He paused a moment and then added, "Do not worry about your mother and Smudge. The clergy could not refuse blessing Smudge, and the promise of a generous donation persuaded him to bless Gabrielle."

A noise behind them drew their attention. Ross stood there. "I apologize for interruptin' but I was worried aboot Blaze."

The Duke of Inverary rose from the bench and gestured to it. "Sit here, son, and enjoy a few quiet moments with your bride. Roxie will be wondering where I'm hiding."

"I don't think so," Blaze said, her lips turning up in a smile. "I left her calming Celeste in the withdrawing room."

"Is Celeste ill?" her father asked.

"Celeste discovered a chronic pain in the arse had married into the MacArthur family," Blaze answered, making them laugh. "She was expecting meekness but got me."

When the duke started down the path toward the mansion, Ross sat beside her on the bench and put his arm around her. "Like all bullies, Celeste will leave ye alone if ye stand yer ground."

"I bullied Celeste." Blaze gave him a sidelong glance, adding, "I threatened her in the withdrawing room."

He was smiling at her. "That's my girl."

"I threatened to spread a rumor that she was a vicar's daughter and a murderess."

His smile became a chuckle.

"She did bury two husbands and improve her finances each time she married."

His chuckle grew into a laugh.

"I wouldn't be surprised if Celeste murdered Charlie and drugged me," Blaze said. "She is the bone sucker's mother, after all."

"Yer the most amazin' woman I've ever met," Ross told her. "What would Celeste gain?"

"I'll let you know when I figure that out," Blaze said, noting his gaze on the gravestones. "Shall we return inside?"

"I'm yer husband now," Ross said, and gestured to the gravestones. "I want to know everythin'. Ye can start with Jane Smudge if ye want."

Blaze felt a sinking sensation in her belly. Nothing but the whole sorry tale would satisfy her husband, and then she would see either pity or disgust in his eyes.

Ross cupped her chin and waited for her to meet his gaze. "Trust me."

"Nanny Smudge lived with my mother before I was born," Blaze began. "My father had sent her to care for my mother during her first pregnancy, and Nanny Smudge stayed with us until she died."

"So Nanny Smudge helped yer mother care for her daughters," Ross said.

Blaze gave him a rueful smile. "Gabrielle helped Nanny Smudge care for us."

"Tell me aboot yer mother."

She had no escape. Her husband needed to know the truth.

Blaze looked at him through eyes blurring with tears. "I killed my mother."

Ross stared at her, his expression registering disbelief. "A woman who holds funerals for furs would never harm anyone."

"I wish I could reverse time and correct my mistakes," Blaze said.

"Livin' with regrets means yer human," Ross said.

"My mother suffered from the drinking sickness," Blaze told him, "but now I know she drank to dull her pain. One day I grabbed the glass out of her hand, smashed it on the floor, and wished her dead."

And Ross knew what she was going to tell him. His heart wrenched at the guilt she'd carried for years.

"Later, I returned to apologize," she said, "but my wish had come true. My words had driven my mother to cut her wrists with the shards of glass."

"Her death wasna yer fault," Ross said, holding her close. "Yer mother wanted to escape her pain and wouldna want ye to feel guilty."

"My wishing her dead killed her," Blaze said.

"If yer guilty of killin' yer mother," Ross said, "then I'm guilty, too."

"What do you mean?'

"I rode early every mornin'," Ross told her, "and the groom always had my horse saddled and waitin'. One mornin' I slept late, and my mother got to the stables first. She took my horse instead of her own.

"When the horse came home without her, we went searchin' and found her near the stone wall she always jumped. She'd fallen off my horse goin' over the wall and broken her neck."

"You did not wish her dead," Blaze said. "Perhaps she would have fallen if she rode her own horse."

"That doesna make me feel less guilty. I've always thought—" He shrugged, sorry he'd mentioned this on his wedding day. "What I always thought doesna change the outcome."

Blaze recognized remembered pain in his black eyes. "What did you think?"

"I thought her death was no accident," Ross answered. "I found a wire nearby and couldna shake the feelin' someone had strung it across her usual route. All of Newmarket knew my mother was a daredevil on horses and loved jumpin' fences and walls."

"Did you tell anyone?"

"The authorities called it an accident," Ross said, "and hunches dinna matter in a court of law. If there is a murderer, God will reveal him in His own good time."

"The bone sucker's mother did it," Blaze said.

Ross smiled at her. "How do ye figure that, wife?"

"Celeste Chadwick Simmons Stanley MacArthur buries a spouse when she finds a wealthier candidate," Blaze answered. "What would prevent her from eliminating a rival?"

"I canna believe that."

"I called her a murderess in the withdrawing room," Blaze said, "and she threatened me. Why is she so sensitive about that word?"

"Let's set that aside for today," Ross said, no longer amused. "We'll keep an eye on her when we return from the Highlands?"

"I've missed our evenings at the Rowley Lodge." Blaze reached up to trace his lips with a finger. "Will you kiss me now?"

"I thought ye'd never ask."

Raven searched the ballroom for Alexander but couldn't locate him. The card room, the billiard room, and her father's office were deserted.

Returning to the ballroom, Raven spied three Kazanov princes standing together and approached them. "I apologize for interrupting," she said, "but I misplaced my fiancé—Alexander Blake—and wondered if you'd seen him."

"We have not seen Blake," Prince Lykos said, "but I will walk with you to find him."

Raven smiled. "That is unnecessary."

Prince Lykos returned her smile. "I would much prefer walking with a beautiful woman to speaking with my brothers."

Arm in arm, the two circled the perimeter of the dance floor. Leaving the ballroom, they walked downstairs.

"Have you seen the Marquis of Basildon?" Prince Lykos asked a passing footman.

"I did see him, Your Highness," the footman answered. "I believe he was walking in the direction of the garden door. Shall I fetch him for you?"

"No, thank you. The lady and I will walk outside."

Prince Lykos and Raven walked toward the rear of the mansion and down one flight. They exited the garden door and strolled through the formal gardens.

Both stopped short when they spied Alexander standing near the maze. He was kissing Amanda Stanley.

Raven backed away without saying a word. She and the prince returned to the mansion.

"If you will excuse me, Your Highness," Raven said when they reached the foyer, "I will retire now."

"You will not retire now," Lykos said. "You will return with me to the ballroom."

Raven acquiesced with a nod but wished she could escape to her chamber. The humiliation and betrayal of her fiancé kissing another woman seemed too much to endure.

"Appearances can be deceptive," Lykos said, climbing the stairs beside her.

"I am not delusional, Your Highness."

Lykos smiled at that. "The marquis may have a plausible explanation for what we saw."

"I may be young, Your Highness, but I am no fool."

"Call me Lykos," he said, "and dance with me."

Something in his voice made her step onto the dance floor without argument. Swirling in his arms, Raven saw that Alexander and Amanda had returned to the ballroom.

"Do not look in his direction," Lykos ordered. "I will do for you what I did for your sister."

"What is that?"

"Your stepmother enlisted my aid in matching MacArthur and Blaze," Lykos told her. "Her Grace knows the challenge of competition whets a man's desire. Need I say more?"

"I accept your offer of assistance," Raven said. "I do hope the Marquis of Basildon enjoys groveling."

Prince Lykos laughed, drawing curious glances from other dancing couples and several sideline onlookers. "When we waltz past Blake," the prince said, "pretend you are enjoying yourself."

"I *am* enjoying myself." Raven gave the prince a flirtatious smile. When they swirled by her frowning fiancé, she wiggled her fingers at him.

"Look at that hill."

Sitting beside her, Ross chuckled. "That's a mountain, not a hill."

"What's the difference?" Blaze asked, dragging her gaze from the passing scenery to look at him.

"The difference is size," Ross answered. "Like a ship and a boat."

"Ships and boats float," Blaze said, "while mountains and hills stand tall. I can see no difference."

"Would you prefer sailing across the ocean in a ship or a boat?"

"I would prefer not sailing across the ocean at all."

Blaze peered out the coach window. The Highlands of Scotland was a land of lonely majesty with white-capped peaks, green glens, and blue lochs.

"What do you think, Puddles?" The mastiff barked.

"What did he say?" Ross asked her.

Blaze looked at him, her expression deadpan. "Puddles said arf-arf."

"I should have seen that comin'," Ross said, smiling. "In my great-grandfather's time, a coach couldna take us to Loch Awe because there were no roads."

"How did they get home?" Blaze asked him.

"They rode their horses."

"How did they know where they were going?"

"The clan members knew every nook and cranny and stone on their lands," Ross answered. "Most passed their entire lives on clan lands and never left home except to fight wars."

"I lived my entire life in London and never traveled farther than Newmarket."

"Ye'll soon see Ben Cruachan risin' behind Kilchurn Castle," Ross said.

Blaze glanced over her shoulder at him. "Ben who?"

"Yer incorrigible." Ross leaned close and kissed her. "There's Ben Cruachan and Kilchurn."

Backed by a mountain, a castle in ruins stood on a finger of land extending into the loch. A roaring stream raced down the mountain cove behind the castle.

"Kilchurn House is there." Ross pointed to the manor a short distance away. "My father visits in autumn after the St. Leger and leaves before the first snow falls. We keep a full household of servants, though."

Their coach halted in front of the manor. Ross climbed out first and turned to help Blaze. Puddles leaped out after her.

Several footmen hurried out of the manor to unload their bags. A tall man standing outside the front door appeared to be in charge.

"Welcome home, my lord," the man said. "Ye've had a long ride."

"We sailed to Oban and borrowed the coaches from a friend," Ross said. "We'll be returnin' to Newmarket the same way." He caught Blaze's hand in his. "Darlin', this is Donal. Donal, I present my wife, Inverary's daughter."

"I'm pleased to meet ye." Donal smiled at Ross. "Congratulations on catchin' such a bonny wife. Did ye resort to kidnappin'?"

Ross laughed and Blaze smiled. Then they followed Donal inside where a pudgy, middle-aged woman waited for them.

"Blaze, this is Donal's wife Ina," Ross introduced them. "Ina, I present my wife, Inverary's daughter."

"I'm pleased to meet ye, Lady MacArthur," the woman greeted her. "Whatever ye need, ye've only to ask and it's yers."

"Thank you, Ina." Blaze glanced around.

The foyer was smaller than those in London and Newmarket, but only the incredibly wealthy could afford Italian marble. On the right a winding staircase climbed to the upper floor, where a dark-haired child and two young women stood on the landing.

"Papa!" The little girl dashed down the stairs.

Ross laughed and scooped her into his arms. The girl wrapped her arms around his neck and planted a smacking kiss on his cheek.

Blaze stared in surprise at father and daughter. Nobody had mentioned a child.

Anger replaced surprise. Her husband should have warned her about his daughter.

Ross set his daughter on the floor. Holding her hand, he urged her forward. "Wife, I present my daughter Kyra," he introduced them. "Kyra, Lady Blaze is yer new stepmother."

The girl looked at her through her father's dark eyes. "What's a stepmother?"

Blaze crouched down eye-level with the girl and gave her a reassuring smile. "A stepmother is like a fairy godmother," she said, "and fairy godmothers always take care of their little girls."

The warm words encouraged the girl to inch closer. "What do I call ye?"

"Ye'll call her Lady—"

"She asked me the question," Blaze interrupted her husband, a definite lack of warmth in her blue eyes. She smiled at Kyra and drew her closer. "What do you want to call me?"

"Well . . ." The girl's black eyes were so familiar and the look in them heartbreakingly hopeful.

"You can tell me," Blaze encouraged her.

"Well, I always wanted a Mama like other children," Kyra said, her voice a shy whisper. A simple request, easily granted.

"Kyra," Ross began.

"Be quiet," Blaze ordered him, and then heard the muffled chuckles. She hugged the girl, saying, "You may call me Mama if I can tell people you're my little girl."

Kyra smiled and nodded and threw her arms around Blaze to give her a hug. "Who's that?"

Blaze looked over her shoulder. Puddles sat at attention, his tail swishing back and forth. The mastiff stepped closer.

"Puddles is my magical dog," Blaze told the girl, and watched her dark eyes widen at the word *magical*. "Kyra, I present Puddles. Puddles, this is my little girl, Kyra."

When the mastiff raised its paw, Blaze said, "Puddles wants to shake your hand."

Kyra giggled and shook the mastiff's paw.

Blaze stared into her dog's eyes. *Guard Kyra.*
Yes. Cookie?

Blaze stood and looked at Ina. "Do you have
cookies?"

The woman smiled at the abrupt question. "We
always keep cookies in the kitchen."

"Do you have any cinnamon cookies?" Blaze
heard her husband's chuckle.

"Puddles loves cinnamon cookies," Ross said,
"but he'll settle for anythin'."

"I want to feed Puddles the cookies," Kyra said.

Ina looked from Ross to Blaze. "Is it safe to bring
the dog to the kitchen?"

"Puddles is the most gentle dog in the world,"
Blaze answered, "and he adores kitchens. Don't
make any sudden moves toward Kyra because he'll
want to guard her."

"Nanny Morag and Nanny Jean will supervise ye
in the kitchen," Ross told his daughter. "Dinna let
Puddles slobber yer fingers when ye feed him."

"Come, Puddles." The mastiff trotted down the
hallway beside Kyra and Ina.

"These are Kyra's nannies, Morag and Jean," Ross
introduced the two young women.

"I'm pleased to meet you," Blaze said, and the
two young women curtseyed. "I prefer no curtsies,
please."

"Travelin' must have wearied ye," Ross said, ushering her up the stairs. "Ye can rest a while before
supper, and tomorrow I'll show ye around. How
does that sound?"

Blaze smiled and nodded and then turned to

Donal. "If Puddles gets too bothersome, you can bring him to our chamber."

Ross escorted Blaze up the stairs and down a hallway. He opened a door on the loch side of the mansion.

The bedchamber was large, its focal point an enormous, four-poster, curtained bed. A velvet bedspread, the blue of a Highland sky, matched the bed curtains. A Persian carpet in shades of blue with gold and cream covered the hardwood floors. Arched windows overlooked Loch Awe.

"Well, have ye nothin' to say?"

Blaze rounded on him. "How dare you!"

Chapter Thirteen

"How dare you show me such disrespect," Blaze said, trying without success to control her temper. "You should have told me about your daughter before we married."

"I didna intend any disrespect," Ross said, "but knowin' aboot Kyra wasna goin' to change anythin'."

Her husband sounded so reasonable, which fueled her anger. Blaze recalled her stepmother's teaching; hot anger should be served cold.

Turning her back, Blaze walked away and counted to twenty. Then she added another ten for good measure.

"You had no idea how I would react," Blaze said, looking at him. "You risked your daughter's feelings by surprising me."

"I knew ye'd rise to the occasion."

Did her husband believe a compliment would appease her? If so, he did not know her very well.

"You should have mentioned her existence."

Ross shoved his hands into his trouser pockets. "I couldna find the right time."

"People *make* time," Blaze said. "They don't find it. Besides, how could you leave your daughter here while you waltzed like a bachelor around Newmarket and London?"

"I *was* a bachelor." Ross looked away, muttering, "Someone should have warned me I was marryin' a nag."

Blaze narrowed her gaze on him. "How do you think I feel discovering I married a blockhead?"

"Wait a minute, wife."

"You wait a minute, husband," Blaze said, poking her finger into his chest to emphasize every word. "Is Kyra a bastard?"

"No."

That gave her pause. "Her mother is deceased?"

"Do I look like a bigamist?" Ross gestured to the chaise in front of the hearth. "Sit and we'll discuss this. *Please.*"

Blaze crossed the chamber and sat on the chaise. Ross followed and dropped down beside her.

"Kyra lives here from April through September because I'm busy followin' the thoroughbreds," Ross told her. "Durin' the season, my stepmother is in residence in Newmarket."

Blaze looked him in the eye. "What has Celeste to do with this?"

"Celeste has been unkind to Kyra," Ross answered. "Janet, Kyra's mother, was a maid in my father's employ. When she fell pregnant, I married her, and Celeste considers my daughter flawed by common blood."

If she disliked the woman before, Blaze hated the

witch at this moment. No one should be unkind to defenseless children and animals.

"No aristocratic blood runs through that woman's veins," Blaze remarked. "How did your wife die?"

"Janet sickened and died a few weeks after deliverin' Kyra," he answered.

"I am sorry for your loss."

"My daughter lost more than I did."

"Where and when did Janet die?" Blaze asked.

"Why do ye want to know?" Ross returned the question.

"Idle curiosity, I suppose."

"Janet died at Kilchurn House," Ross told her. "Kyra's birthday is September so Janet would have passed in October."

Blaze was silent for a long moment. She could not understand the reason her parents had failed to mention his previous marriage and the child. Unless—

"Do my parents know you're a widower with a child?" she asked him.

"I doubt it," Ross answered, shrugging. "Few people knew I had married."

Blaze arched a copper brow at him. "Why is that?" She could not keep the suspicion out of her voice.

"Janet did not want to step into Society," Ross told her. "She felt out of place and preferred to remain in the Highlands. My stepmother didna help matters by demeanin' her."

"I will nap for an hour or two." Blaze felt tired and wanted to sit alone to ponder what she'd learned.

"Give a shout if ye need anythin'." Ross stood and left the bedchamber.

Blaze dragged a chair across the chamber to the window. She sat and, gazing at loch's blue water, considered her circumstances.

She had never wanted to marry, and now she was married to a man who did not love her. Ross had married her for the same reason he'd married Janet, pregnancy.

There was nothing to be done for that. Moaning and sulking would not change the facts.

Ross should have warned her about his daughter, but he hadn't bothered. There was nothing to be done for that, either.

Counting her blessings seemed a good idea. She enjoyed a loving, supportive family. She could forge a family with her baby and Kyra. The girl was heartbreakingly hungry for a mother's love. She could understand that, having been heartbreakingly hungry for a father's love during her childhood.

Though he had supported them in style, she and her sisters had yearned for their father's attention. Too bad he'd waited until they had grown before publicly acknowledging them and moving them into his household.

Blaze suspected her stepmother had something to do with that. Her stepmother could be a pain in the arse, but the duchess had a big heart and no children of her own to lavish with love.

Pegasus had died, but Juno was breeding. The mare would deliver a champion. Not as special as Peg, perhaps, but a champion nevertheless.

The purses from Pegasus's three wins combined with her profits from the Seven Doves Company would give her enough wealth to build her animal sanctuary. Dogs and cats could live anywhere, but horses required land. Loch Awe appeared to be a good place to house retired thoroughbreds.

She had more blessings than most. Her husband could keep his love. She did not need it.

Her only problem was Celeste MacArthur, a malicious witch with no heart. The woman and her circumstances niggled at her brain. Celeste had married three times, each union increasing her wealth, and buried two husbands. Ross's mother had suffered a fatal accident, and his wife had sickened and died during October when the Duchess of Kilchurn was in residence.

Something smelled rotten in the MacArthur family. Was she the only one with a nose for evil? Blaze wished she could consult Raven.

Hours later, Blaze left the bedchamber and walked downstairs to the foyer. She found the dining room off the main corridor without any problem.

The dining room whispered wealth. Persian carpets covered the oak floors. Portraits and artwork decorated the red walls. The oak dining table seated twenty, a crystal and gold chandelier hanging over it.

Sitting at the head of the table, Ross stood when she walked into the room. He crossed the chamber and escorted her to the chair on his right.

Accompanied by Ina, two footmen carried covered serving platters into the room and set them on the sidetable. Donal served them glasses of wine.

"My wife doesna drink spirits," Ross told his man.

Blaze noted the portrait in a position of honor over the hearth. The woman had ebony hair, dark eyes, full lips, and rose-kissed cheeks on an ivory complexion. The artist had captured the gleam of mischief in the dark eyes, and the woman's inscrutable smile hinted that she was privy to an amusing secret.

"Is that your mother?" Blaze asked her husband.

Ross nodded. "Kyra MacArthur, my mother."

"She was an exceptionally beautiful woman. Where is her namesake?"

"Kyra is suppin' in her chamber," Ross answered. "I didna think ye'd want her suppin' with us. Celeste never—"

"Did I say I didn't want her?" Blaze asked him.

"No, but—"

"Do I look like Celeste?"

Ross grinned. "No."

Blaze stood and looked down at him. "Do not move from that chair."

Turning to leave, Blaze caught Donal and Ina exchanging smiling glances. She marched out of the dining room and climbed the stairs to the second floor. Then she began opening doors looking for the girl. Finally, she found the chamber at the end of the hallway.

Kyra sat at a small table eating a lonely supper of chicken slices and vegetable medley. Her nannies were sitting with her.

"Little girls eat supper with their mamas," Blaze said, crouching beside Kyra. She stood and pointed at Nanny Morag. "You carry the plate." She looked at Nanny Jean. "You carry everything else."

Blaze held her hand out to her stepdaughter. "You come with me."

Holding hands, Blaze and Kyra walked downstairs to the dining room. The nannies walked behind them. Lying outside the dining room door, the mastiff was whining for entrance.

When the footman opened the door, Blaze said, "Come, Puddles."

"Come, Puddles," Kyra echoed.

The small parade marched into the dining room. Ross smiled when they entered, but his wife ignored him.

Blaze escorted Kyra to the table and seated her on her father's left. The nannies set the plate and cup on the table.

"Eat your supper now," Blaze instructed them. "I'll bring Kyra upstairs later."

"Do ye want the dog in here?" Ina asked.

"Puddles goes where I go."

"Puddles didna eat in Inverary's dinin' room," Ross said.

"He ate in the dining room when no guests were present," Blaze told him. "Besides, that room belonged to Her Grace, and this room belongs to me."

Ross cocked a brow. "Celeste may argue that point."

"Celeste can argue all she wants," Blaze said, "but I will win the battle."

Blaze looked at Kyra and frowned. The girl was chin level with the table top. "She needs something to sit on."

Glancing at Donal and Ina, Blaze asked, "Do you have a Bible with both testaments?"

Ross burst into laughter which made Kyra giggle. He gestured to the footman who left the dining room.

"It's not sacrilegious," Blaze said. "God's bounty will be wasted if she can't reach the table."

Ross grinned. "If ye say so, wife."

"I do say so." Blaze smiled, adding, "I wouldn't invite the local vicar to supper while Kyra was sitting on the Bible."

The footman returned to the dining room. "Shakespeare was thicker than the Bible."

"Shakespeare will do." Ross lifted his daughter while the footman set the Shakespeare volume on the chair. The he set his daughter down again and pushed the chair closer to the table.

"Does that feel better?" Blaze asked her.

Kyra nodded.

Donal set a platter on the table. "Ina made yer favorite."

"Ah, jeez. I forgot to tell ye," Ross said. "My wife doesna eat meat, fish, or poultry."

"She's got the gift, then?"

Blaze looked at the woman. Ina sounded as if she believed in communing with animals.

"D'ye believe in such thin's?" Ross asked the older woman.

"Ye've lived too long in England," Ina answered, and shifted her gaze to Blaze. "What can I serve ye?"

"I'll take porridge tonight."

"I'll take porridge tonight, too," Kyra said.

"You eat what's on your plate," Blaze ordered her stepdaughter, and then looked at her husband's favorite meal. "What is that?"

"Haggis."

"I've never heard of haggis."

"Ye dice the heart, liver, and lungs of a sheep and

mix with suet, onions, oatmeal, and seasonin's."
Ross smiled at her stricken expression. "Then ye
boil the mixture in the animal's stomach."

Blaze flushed in distress. One hand covered her
mouth, the other flew to her throat. Her stomach
churned with nausea.

"Do ye want me to eat porridge, too?" Ross asked
her.

"Eat what you want but never suck bones in my
presence or inform me of disgusting recipes," Blaze
answered. "If I ask, tell me I don't want to know."

Ross looked at his daughter. "Do ye think ye'd
like a brother or sister?"

Kyra nodded and speared a piece of chicken.

"Come the new year, Mama Blaze will be givin' us
a baby," Ross said.

"Are we gettin' a brother or sister?"

"Which do ye want?"

"Both."

Blaze was blushing. She did not relish people
counting the months on their fingers from their
wedding day to the baby's birth day.

Changing the subject, Blaze told the little girl,
"Puddles's job is to eat anything that falls on the
floor."

Kyra tossed a piece of chicken and looked down.
"Ah, jeez, Puddles ate the meat."

Ross and Blaze looked at each other and laughed.
"You need to guard your words around children,"
she warned him.

"Mama, do ye know stories?"

"I know hundreds of stories," Blaze answered. "I'll
tell you about the princess and the frog tonight."

"Papa, do ye know stories?"

"Your papa doesn't know stories because men know nothing," Blaze answered for her husband, and heard muffled laughter near the sideboard.

"Papa, listen to Mama," Kyra said, "and ye'll know a story."

"That's good thinkin'," Ross praised her. "Tell us the story, Mama."

"You don't want to wait until bedtime?" Blaze asked the girl.

"We want the story now," Ross answered. "Kyra?"

The little girl nodded. "I want one now and one later."

"Once upon a time in a faraway country," Blaze began, "lived a queen and her three princesses. The queen was very sick and needed water from the Well of Good Health or she would die.

"The oldest princess left the castle and followed the path through the woods. Arriving at the Well of Good Health, the princess found the water guarded by a big, ugly frog. The princess ran back to the castle without the water.

"The second princess grabbed a bucket and followed the path through the woods to the special well. The ugly frog frightened her, too, and she returned home without the water.

"The youngest princess grabbed the bucket, walked through the woods to the well, and met the frog. The princess told the frog she needed his water to save her mother's life. The frog agreed to give her the water if she would marry him.

"So the princess promised to marry the frog and

filled the bucket with the healing water. She returned to the castle in time to save her mother's life."

Kyra started clapping. Ross smiled and clapped, too.

"Later that night, the princess went to bed. A voice awakened her, calling to open the castle's door. The princess went downstairs and pulled the door open. There stood the frog who reminded her of her promise.

"Lifting the frog into her hand, the princess carried it upstairs to her bedchamber and set it on the rug. She would marry him in the morning, but the frog said he would be dead by then. Would she give him a kiss?

"The princess lifted the frog into her hand again and kissed him *on the lips.* A miracle happened then. The frog became a handsome prince. He married the princess, and they lived happily ever after."

Kyra clapped her hands together. So did her father.

"Would ye fetch water for Mama Blaze if she needed it?" Ross asked his daughter.

Kyra considered his question. "We'll send Ina."

Later, Ross and Blaze delivered Kyra to her nannies. Blaze told the story of the princess and the pea. Then husband and wife sought their own chamber.

"I apologize for keepin' Kyra a secret," Ross said. "I should have told ye aboot her."

Blaze looked at him and considered what advice her stepmother would give her. She would be married to her husband for a long, long time. Passing the next forty years arguing was not an appealing thought.

Her stepmother would tell her that most men ignored what was unpleasant until it bit them. Her husband had delayed telling her about his daughter until he could not ignore it any longer. She supposed her husband was a normal man.

"We'll start fresh in the morning," Blaze said.

"D'ye think we could start fresh tonight?"

She gave him a flirtatious smile. "I might be persuaded."

"Sit on the bed, darlin'. I've a gift for ye." Ross rummaged in his satchel and produced a rectangular leather case. "Open it."

Blaze lifted the box's lid. On a bed of black velvet lay a link belt. Created in diamonds and gold, the links formed butterflies.

"I've never seen a belt like this," Blaze said, lifting her gaze to his. "I thank you."

"I told the designer ye were an Original and cherished yer mother's butterfly jewels," Ross told her. "She created this piece specially for ye."

"The belt must have cost a small fortune."

"It cost a large fortune." Ross winked at her. "I figured I'll be savin' a mountain of money through the years by not buyin' furs to match yer gowns."

"Hand me my bag." Blaze reached into her satchel, produced a small leather case, and passed it to him.

Ross sat beside her and lifted the box's lid. Inside lay gold cufflinks shaped like a horse's head. The eyes were rubies and its collar diamond-studded.

"I canna wait to wear them." Ross kissed her cheek.

"I told the designer you loved horses," Blaze said, "and she created them specially for you."

"Let's go to bed."

They stood and faced each other. Blaze pointed to her gown's buttons. Ross obliged her with a kiss and wrapping his arms around her body to unfasten her gown.

Holding her gaze captive, Ross pulled his shirt over his head and tossed it aside. Blaze giggled and let her gown drop to the floor, pooling at her feet.

He responded by dropping his trousers and kicking them aside. She answered him by sliding the straps of her chemise off her shoulders, letting the silk and lace garment flutter down to cover her gown, leaving her clad only in stockings and garters.

"You're drooling," she whispered.

Lifting the diamond butterfly belt off the bed, Ross wrapped it around her naked waist. "Ye look like a goddess."

By unspoken agreement, they stepped closer. Her softness teased the hard muscular planes of his body. Ross kissed her as if he'd never let her go, pouring his desire into that soul-stealing kiss, They stood as one, the candlelight casting a single shadow on the wall.

Scooping her into his arms, Ross gently placed her on the bed. He gazed at her hauntingly lovely face to her swollen breasts and dusky nipples. Lower his gaze traveled to her slightly rounded belly, proof that his seed grew inside her.

She held her arms out to him, but he dropped to his knees on the floor. Cupping her buttocks to hold her steady, he slashed his tongue into the moist crease between her thighs.

Blaze cried out and melted against him. Waves of pleasure surged through her body, carrying her to carnal paradise.

Ross stood and set her on the edge of the bed. Positioning himself between her thighs, he plunged deep inside her.

Slowly, Ross withdrew and then eased forward again and again and again. Rekindling her desire, he thrust deep and grinded himself against her heat.

With mingling cries, they exploded together and then floated back to earth from their shared paradise. He fell to the side, taking her with him, and cradled her against his body.

Husband and wife enjoyed the sleep of the sated.

Blaze breezed into the dining room the next morning. She'd expected to breakfast alone but found her husband and daughter there.

"We tried to wait for ye," Ross said, "but Kyra got hungry."

"You didn't need to wait." Blaze looked over the morning fare.

The barley bannocks appeared griddled to perfection, light and greaseless. The scones and butter looked delicious as did her stepdaughter's oatmeal porridge. She could live without her husband's fried sausage, though.

Ina walked into the dining room and set a mug beside her plate. "Drinkin' Old Man's Milk every mornin' will be good for the babe."

Blaze glanced at her husband. "What is it?"

"Ye beat an egg into milk," Ross answered,

"sweeten the mixture with sugar, and zest it with a drop of whisky."

In spite of disliking spirits, Blaze did not want to appear churlish. A drop of whisky would not kill her.

Blaze sipped the drink, smiled at her husband, and took another swig. "I like it," she said. "Put a couple of bannocks on my plate."

"Yer showin' yer Highland blood at last," Ross teased her. "I was beginnin' to think livin' in England had squelched it out of ye."

"Kyra and I want to go picnicking today," Blaze said, "and we need an escort."

"I was hopin' to take ye doup-dippin'."

"What's that?"

Ross grinned, his black eyes gleaming. "Swimmin' naked."

Blaze blushed like a virgin. "I never learned to swim."

"Doup-dippin' doesna require swimmin'," he said.

"Save your doup-dippin' for the tub," Blaze said. "Kyra and I prefer a picnic lunch."

The June day was a Highland rarity. The breeze was a gentle caress. A brilliant sun rode high in a clear blue sky. No clouds marred the day's perfection, and the air smelled clean.

Ross bundled them into the coach. Blaze held Kyra on her lap, and Puddles sat beside them for the ride a few miles along the loch's shoreline.

"Awe is the longest loch in the Highlands," he told them, "but it's also mostly shallow."

"Where's Inverary Castle?" Blaze asked.

"Ye climb up to the moors, walk through the forest

to the valley of Glen Array," Ross answered. "Then ye walk down the other side of the mountain."

Ross halted the carriage when Kilchurn House was out of sight. "The loch is shallow here," he said, "so we can wade if we want."

Blaze spread the blanket while Ross carried the food basket. Kyra giggled watching Puddles dashing around like a newly-freed felon.

Dropping on the blanket, Ross pulled his boots off and rolled the legs of his trousers up. Blaze removed her ankle boots and hose and then walked around on the grass.

"Tell Papa to take your shoes off," Blaze called to Kyra, "and let the grass tickle your feet."

When tickling their feet grew stale, Blaze and Kyra sat with Ross on the blanket. "Did ye know Loch Awe has a monster?"

Blaze smiled at that. The little girl inched closer to her father.

"The MacArthurs call the monster the Big Beast of Loch Awe," Ross told them. "The Big Beast is a great eel with twelve legs and slithers in the loch's deepest waters."

"Have you seen the Big Beast?" Blaze asked him.

"I've never had the pleasure," Ross answered, "but Donal has seen the beast. Ask him if ye dinna believe me."

The three wandered to the water's edge. Ross skimmed a stone across the sparkling water. "I havena done that in years," he said with a smile. "I'd wager our fathers stood together on this spot and skimmed stones across the loch."

"Considering their ages," Blaze said, "that must have happened in ancient times."

"I'd like to teach my girls to swim," Ross said.

"Who's yer girls, Papa?"

"Yer my little girl," Ross answered, "and Blaze is my big girl."

"Jeez, this is fun," Kyra said.

Blaze covered her mouth to keep from laughing. She shook her head at her husband, warning him not to laugh.

"I'll show ye how to tickle a fish." Ross waded into the loch's shallows.

"Ye must be quiet and still," he told them. "Ye bend over, slowly placin' yer hand in the water, and wait. Fish are curious creatures and will swim closer to investigate ye. Gently tickle his underside with a finger. When he's paralyzed with pleasure, flip him onto the shore."

"What happens then?" Blaze asked.

"Ye cook him up and eat him." Ross smiled at them. "It's great fun."

"I'd wager the fish isn't laughing." Blaze looked down at her stepdaughter. "Do you want to tickle a fish?"

Kyra wrinkled her nose and shook her head. She inched closer lest her father insist on her trying.

"Ye girls arena any fun."

"Only a barbarian would consider killing and eating an animal great fun," Blaze said.

Ross leaned down and splashed water at them. Blaze and Kyra laughed and ran toward the blanket.

"Let's splash your papa," Blaze whispered in the girl's ear.

Hand in hand, Kyra and Blaze ran back to the water's edge and splashed water at him. Ross splashed back, and Puddles joined them, barking and running in and out of the water.

"Enough." Ross walked toward them.

"Tell him to say uncle," Blaze whispered.

Kyra pointed a finger at her father. "Say uncle."

"Uncle." Ross threw his hands up in surrender and walked out of the water. "I'm goin' to teach ye swimmin' so ye'll need to undress."

"Someone will see us," Blaze said.

"Yer in the Highlands," Ross said, gesturing to the mountains and the loch. "We've more sheep than people. Besides, yer safe from pryin' eyes on MacArthur land."

Ross unbuttoned his shirt and dropped it on the blanket. He tossed his trousers aside next, leaving him standing in black silk underwear.

Blaze helped Kyra undress, leaving the girl standing in her chemise. Then she dropped her gown and, like her stepdaughter, wore only her chemise.

"Who wants to learn first?" Ross asked them.

"Her." Blaze and Kyra pointed at each other.

Ross laughed. "Kyra, fetch me a stick over there." When she returned, he said, "Watch, Puddles."

"Fetch it." Ross tossed the stick into the loch and the mastiff gave chase. Puddles swam to the stick and carried it in his mouth to shore.

"I'm goin' to teach ye the doggie paddle," Ross said. "Mama Blaze goes first."

When she waded into the loch, Ross led her out until the water reached her waist. Taking her hands in his, he said, "Let yer legs float behind ye off the loch's bottom. That's right. Now kick yer feet."

For a few minutes, Ross pulled Blaze back and forth in the water while she kicked her feet. Then, "I'll hold ye beneath yer belly while ye kick yer legs and paddle yer arms like Puddles."

Ross demonstrated the paddle for her. Then, with his hands under her belly, Blaze kicked her feet and paddled like a dog. She glided back and forth in the water and never noticed when his hands dropped away.

"I was swimming," she exclaimed.

"Come, Kyra," Ross called. He gave his daughter the same lesson, kicking her feet first and then paddling like a dog.

"Look, Mama," Kyra called. "I'm swimmin'."

Watching from the shoreline, Blaze applauded her stepdaughter's accomplishment. "Who wants to dry off and play pretend?" she asked.

"I do," Kyra called.

The three returned to the blanket. Ross turned his back, dropped his drawers, and pulled his trousers on while Blaze removed the girl's chemise and dressed her in the gown again. Then Blaze turned her back, dropped her chemise, and donned her gown.

"Listen, Kyra," Blaze said, crouching to eye-level with the girl. "Ye must never swim unless your papa is with you."

"Spoken like a true mother," Ross said, smiling. "Ye'll probably be worryin' for the next twenty years or so."

"Mothers worry about their children, no matter

their ages." Blaze looked at her stepdaughter. "Shall we play pretend?"

The girl's dark eyes, so much like her father's, gleamed with the day's excitement. Blaze felt an insistent tugging on her heartstrings. She'd wager her last penny that her husband had never taken the time to play with his own daughter.

"Let's pretend we're dancing with handsome gentlemen at a grand ball." Blaze looked at her husband. "We'll need your help with this."

"Stand on top of your father's feet," Blaze instructed Kyra. "Papa, you hold her like you are waltzing. I'll hum a tune."

"Who will ye dance with?" Kyra asked her.

"Lord Puddles," Blaze said, enticing giggles from the girl. "Puddles, up." The mastiff leaped up, placing his front paws on her shoulders, and balanced himself on his hind legs.

Blaze began humming a waltz. Holding his daughter on top of his feet, Ross waltzed her around on the grass. Puddles and Blaze swayed back and forth where they stood.

At the dance's end, Ross lifted his daughter into his arms and gave her cheek a smacking kiss. "I thank ye for the dance, Lady Kyra."

Two hours later, Ross packed the carriage. They had lunched on bread, cheese, cinnamon cookies, and lemon barley water. Afterwards, Blaze and Kyra rested on the blanket while Ross tossed stones into the loch, enticing Puddles to give chase.

A groom appeared when Ross halted the carriage in front of Kilchurn House. Puddles leaped down first and dashed for the door where Donal stood. Ross lifted his daughter down and then assisted Blaze.

"What's this?" Ross asked when they entered the foyer.

Blaze followed her husband's gaze. Several traveling bags had been set on one side of the foyer.

"Ye've a houseguest," Donal said, "sippin' yer father's vintage whisky in the dinin' room."

A silver-haired woman walked down the hallway to the foyer. Though advanced in age, the woman carried few wrinkles on her face, and her blue eyes gleamed with genuine pleasure.

"I'd recognize ye anywhere," the woman said, walking toward Blaze. She placed the palm of her hand on her cheek. "Yer lovelier than I ever was at yer age. Most likely, the babe yer carryin' gives ye more glow."

Blaze stared in surprise at the woman, who couldn't possibly know of her pregnancy. She narrowed her gaze on the woman.

"Who are you?"

"I'm yer aunt Bedelia Campbell."

"You're alive?" Blaze exclaimed.

Bedelia looked down at herself. "Apparently, I am livin'."

Standing nearby, Donal and Ina chuckled, and Ross joined them. Kyra giggled when her father laughed.

"Papa speaks about you as if you were dead," Blaze told her.

"So does my father," Ross interjected.

"My husband Colin and I had high times with Magnus and Jamie," Bedelia told them. "Those were the days. We could never anticipate their mischief-makin'.'" She looked at Blaze. "Yer father hasna visited me since marryin' that gossipin' magpie."

"Gossiping magpie?" Blaze had never heard her stepmother described in those words.

Bedelia nodded. "Och, the woman is a dimpled gossip. I'm surprised all of England doesna know the length of his pizzle."

Everyone chuckled at that.

"What's a pizzle?" Kyra asked.

The chuckles grew into laughter.

"Donal, have someone carry Bedelia's bags upstairs," Ross instructed his man.

"Dinna do that." Bedelia looked at Ross. "We willna be here long enough to unpack."

"Where are we goin'?" Ross asked, smiling.

"We'll be leavin' for Newmarket in the mornin'." Bedelia looped her arm through her niece's. "D'ye know I've never left the Highlands before." Bedelia held her hand out to the girl. "Come along, Kyra. Puddles, come."

"How did you know their names?" Blaze asked, stepping with her down the corridor.

Bedelia gave her an ambiguous smile. "I know because I know."

Blaze laughed. "You sound like my sister Raven."

"I've a gift for ye in the dinin' room," Bedelia said.

"We've arrived only yesterday," Ross said, following them down the hallway. "Why would we leave?"

"Bad news is comin'," Bedelia answered. "Come along, Ross, and we'll drink whisky together."

They sat at the dining room table. Bedelia and Ross had tumblers of whisky in front of them. Blaze sipped black tea and helped Kyra hold her glass of lemon barley water.

When Ina served them tea scones and ginger-bread cakes, Bedelia said, "Ye forgot the dog's cinnamon cookies."

The old woman's knowledge surprised Blaze. She looked at her husband. He appeared as surprised as she.

"What's that?" Kyra pointed toward the windows. A ball of white was climbing the draperies.

"That's Blaze's gift." Bedelia pried the kitten, claw by claw, off the draperies and gave Ross an apologetic look. "Sometimes they leave wee snags."

Bedelia set the white, blue-eyed kitten on Blaze's lap. "Sugar needs yer protection because she's deaf and canna meow."

Blaze cuddled the kitten for a moment and then called, "Here, Puddles." She looked into the mastiff's eyes. *Guard Sugar.*

Puddles lay down beside her chair. Blaze set the kitten on the floor, and the mastiff positioned his front legs to surround the kitten.

"Yer mothers were lovely women," Bedelia said, her gaze on the portrait of Ross's mother.

"Ye knew my mother?" Blaze asked her.

"Magnus worried for her health when she was carryin' yer oldest sister," Bedelia told her. "He sent Gabrielle and Smudge to me at Inverary where the air is clean."

"I never knew that," Blaze said.

"Ye werena born," Bedelia said. "I advised Magnus to do the deed wearin' his boots if he wanted sons"—

she smiled at Ross's chuckle—"but yer father never did take my advice on anythin'."

Donal walked into the dining room, followed by a courier. The man handed Ross a missive.

"It's from my father." Ross read the note and looked at them, his expression grim. "Hercules died on the way to Epsom Derby. We'll be leavin' for Newmarket in the mornin'."

Bedelia nodded. "Someone fed Hercules poisoned carrots."

"I dinna want ye to go," Kyra cried.

"I couldn't live without my little girl," Blaze told her. "You're coming with us."

Her husband looked irritated. "Blaze—"

"I can protect her."

"Let the girl come," Bedelia said. "My niece would protect her from Old Clootie himself."

Blaze looked at her. "Who's Old Clootie?"

"Satan."

Chapter Fourteen

"What do you think?" Blaze asked.

Aunt Bedelia peered out the coach's window at her nephew's estate. Manicured lawns, precisely clipped shrubs, neat rows of trees. In the near distance rose the mansion with its landscaped front courtyard.

"I think my nephew's estate is contrived," Bedelia answered her.

Blaze glanced at her husband holding his daughter on his lap. He was smiling at the old woman's criticism.

"What do you mean?" Blaze asked her.

"The Highlands is a fresh-faced maiden whose natural beauty is unequaled," Bedelia answered, "and this English estate is an artfully adorned matron tryin' to recapture her youthful beauty. No cosmetics or jewels can make a woman young and beautiful once her time has passed."

"Ye possess a poet's tongue," Ross told her.

"The Highlands affects people like that," Bedelia

replied, "which ye'd know if ye visited more than a week or two or three."

The coach halted in front of Inverary House. Ross passed Kyra to Blaze and climbed down first. Then he turned to assist the women.

The front door opened. Beneath Tinker's supervision, two footmen hurried toward them to assist Ross and carry the bags inside.

Holding Kyra with one hand and cuddling Sugar with the other, Blaze ushered Bedelia into the foyer. The mastiff followed behind them.

"Welcome home, Lady MacArthur," Tinker greeted them, his gaze shifting between the girl and the old woman. "We did not expect you in Newmarket for several weeks."

"My husband wants to investigate his horse's death."

"A sorry business," Tinker said, shaking his head. "And who are these lovely young women?"

"Kyra is my little girl, my husband's daughter," Blaze answered, "and this is Aunt Bedelia Campbell."

"You're alive?" the majordomo exclaimed.

"My heart was still beating the last time I checked," Bedelia answered.

"I said the same when we met." Blaze smiled at the man. "Where's my father?"

"Their Graces are taking tea in the drawing room."

"Bring a bottle of my nephew's best whisky to the drawing room," Bedelia told the majordomo.

"Yes, my lady." Tinker hurried down the hallway.

When Ross walked into the foyer, Blaze passed him Sugar. Taking her stepdaughter's hand, she looped her arm through her aunt's.

Together, the three climbed the stairs. Ross and Puddles walked behind them.

"Papa, look who I've brought," Blaze called, walking into the drawing room.

The Duke of Inverary's expression registered surprise, and then he came out of his chair. The duke hurried across the room to pull the old woman into a lingering hug, and she patted his back as if consoling a small boy.

"Come and meet my wife," the duke said, his arm around her.

Holding a bottle of whisky, Tinker rushed into the drawing room and passed it to his employer. Bedelia lifted it out of her nephew's hand, telling the majordomo, "Dinna bother with glasses."

"Tinker, fetch my daughters," the duke ordered, and the majordomo hurried out of the drawing room.

"Aunt, I present my wife," the duke introduced the women. "Roxie, meet Aunt Bedelia Campbell."

The Duchess of Inverary stared at the old woman. "You're alive?"

"What have ye been tellin' them?" Bedelia asked. "Everyone believes I've gone to meet my Maker."

Blaze laughed and sat on the settee with her husband. She pulled her stepdaughter onto her lap.

"Magnus speaks so highly of you in the past tense," the duchess said, "I thought you were a dead saint."

"Only his youth died," Bedelia said, sitting beside her nephew on the sofa. She opened the whisky bottle and sipped. "There's nothin' in the world like Highland whisky."

"What finally pried you out of the Highlands?" the duke asked her.

"I've come to catch a murderer."

The Duke of Inverary frowned at Blaze, but his words were for his aunt. "How do you know about that?"

Bedelia looked into his eyes, her expression deadpan. "I know because I know."

"Aunt Bedelia arrived at Kilchurn House to inform me bad news was comin'," Ross said, "and the bad news arrived soon afterwards."

"I'm sorry about Hercules," Duke Magnus said. "Your father feels responsible."

"What killed Hercules?"

"Someone fed him carrots dipped in poison, we think."

Ross slid his gaze to Bedelia, a surprised expression on his face. The old woman gave him an I-told-you-so look.

"Who is this?" the Duchess of Inverary asked, her gaze on the little girl.

"I present Kyra MacArthur, my stepdaughter," Blaze answered.

"Stepdaughter?" The duchess snapped her gaze to the marquis. "I didn't know—"

Ross held his hand up. "My first wife died shortly after deliverin' Kyra."

The Duchess of Inverary looked at her husband. "Did you know?" When he shook his head, she asked, "Are you lying to me?"

The Duke of Inverary smiled and shook his head.

"Are you lying about lying?" the duchess asked.

The Duke of Inverary laughed as did everyone else.

Kyra leaned close to Blaze, whispering, "Yer supposed to say my little girl."

"Oops, I made a big mistake." Then Blaze announced, "Kyra is my little girl."

The four unmarried Flambeau sisters appeared, hurrying across the drawing room. Their surprised expressions announced that Tinker had told them the silver-haired woman's identity.

"Aunt Bedelia, I present my daughters—"

"Dinna say another word," Bedelia interrupted him. "I know my own nieces." She paused to take a sip of whisky from the bottle and then gestured to the first sister. "Bliss will always keep her sisters in coin, and Sophia—beside her—loves painting and colors." She winked at her, adding, "I ken ye see people's colors."

"What are people's colors?" the duke asked.

"Ye wouldna understand," Bedelia said, patting his hand. She looked at the next sister. "Light and airy as a sprite, Serena sings and plays her flute. She can calm the waters or call down a tempest. Figuratively speakin', of course."

Bedelia sipped her whisky. "And this is Raven who sometimes knows what others do not."

Raven registered surprise. "How do you—?"

"I know because I know."

Everyone laughed. Raven had spoken those same words more times than anyone cared to remember.

"I'm an old woman close to death"—Bedelia took a healthy swig of whisky—"and God has shown me how yer problems are resolved."

"Sisters, meet my little girl," Blaze said, breaking the silence that followed the old woman's comment.

"Kyra is Ross's daughter. Aunt Bedelia gave me the white fur ball Ross is holding. Sugar is deaf."

"Kyra has your eyes," Raven told Ross, and the other sisters nodded.

"James will be thrilled to see you again," Magnus told his aunt.

"Invite James here alone first," Bedelia said, and then looked at the duchess. "Ye must then invite James and his wife to dinner on Saturday."

"Why do you want James to visit without his wife?" the duke asked.

"The reason is this," Bedelia said, annoyance tingeing her voice, "I want to see James but not his wife."

The Flambeau sisters laughed. Blaze knew they were laughing because no one had ever spoken in that tone to their father.

Magnus patted her hand. "We'll do things your way."

"Dinna patronize me." Bedelia sipped the whisky. "Yer denser than a brick and canna conceive what I know."

"I apologize," the Duke of Inverary said. "I meant no disrespect." He looked at Ross. "Constable Black is traveling from London, and we'll be meeting the day after tomorrow."

"I'll be here," Ross said, and then looked at his wife. "We need to leave now."

"Ross, take Kyra and give Blaze the cat," Bedelia ordered. "I need a private word with yer wife."

Ross lifted his yawning daughter into his arms and started toward the door, calling, "Come, Puddles."

Bedelia looped her arm through Blaze's and walked her to the door. "Leave Juno and Beau here until Sunday," the old woman whispered. "Bring me somethin' belongin' to Celeste."

Blaze stared at her a long moment and then nodded. "You can depend on me."

The ride to MacArthur House was short and silent. Kyra had fallen asleep on her father's lap, and traveling had wearied Blaze. Sugar snoozed on her lap, and Puddles sprawled on the coach's floor.

"Welcome home, my lord." Dodger stood in the open door and ushered them into the foyer. "I'm sorry about Hercules."

"Thank ye, Dodger."

"Sugar is my deaf kitten," Blaze told the major-domo, "and I require a box of sand in my chamber. Puddles is my dog."

"The mastiff is enormous." Dodger smiled, adding, "I feel safer knowing he lives here. Is Puddles gentle?"

"Your only danger from Puddles is being slobbered to death," Blaze answered, and then followed her husband upstairs.

The drawing room was formal, almost too formal for Newmarket. A black marble hearth was the room's focal point. Above the hearth, Celeste's portrait looked down on the room's occupants. Persian carpets in gold, cream, and shades of blue covered the hardwood floors. The furniture was a mixture of textiles in the same colors. Exquisite brocade draperies dressed the windows.

Blaze doubted her menagerie would please Celeste. She could almost hear the witch's shrieks when Sugar climbed those drapes.

"I need a list of anyone who had access to Hercules," Ross said without greeting or preamble.

"I knew ye'd come home," his father said. "I've listed the names already."

"What's she doing here?" Celeste asked, her gaze on the sleeping girl.

"Her name is Kyra," Blaze answered, "and she lives here."

Celeste glanced at her husband and amended herself. "I meant, Kyra is usually absent when I'm in residence."

Blaze gave the woman a serene smile. "Usually does not include this time."

"I wonder you didn't leave her in the Highlands," Celeste said to Ross.

"Her name is Kyra," Blaze repeated.

"My wife didna want to leave her little girl behind," Ross said.

"Kyra is the marquis's daughter," Blaze said, earning a frosty look from the woman. "She is also the duke's granddaughter."

"Old people canna remember everythin'," the Duke of Kilchurn teased his wife.

"Tomorrow I will embroider Kyra's name on the front of her clothing," Blaze told her father-in-law, making him chuckle. "We dropped Aunt Bedelia at Inverary House."

The duke grinned. "Bedelia Campbell?"

Celeste looked at him. "I thought she was dead."

"I never told ye that," James said. "I've got to ride over there."

"Wait until tomorrow," Celeste said. "The journey must have wearied her, and the dinner hour is approaching."

"I dinna care aboot dinner," the duke said, "but yer right aboot Bedelia. She isna gettin' any younger."

"My aunt is spry enough to sip whisky out of a bottle," Blaze told him.

"That sounds like Bedelia." The Duke of Kilchurn laughed. "When yer father and I were boys, Bedelia persuaded Uncle Colin she wanted to feel the thrill of raidin' like in the old days of clan feudin'. During the next full moon, Colin and Bedelia sneaked onto MacArthur land and lifted my father's sheep. Of course, they sent him a note the next day confessin' what they'd done and promised to return the livestock."

"Blaze dear, what are you holding?" Celeste asked.

"Bedelia gave me Sugar, a deaf kitten." Blaze stepped aside. "And here stands Puddles, my dog."

"I dislike children and animals underfoot."

"You'll get used to it," Blaze told her.

Celeste looked at her husband. "James?"

"Like she said, ye'll get used to it." The duke turned to his son, saying, "Put Kyra to bed, and yer wife looks like she needs a rest, too."

Ross and Blaze quit the drawing room, the mastiff following behind. Together, they climbed the stairs to the third floor, and Blaze could not help thinking that she and her husband would climb the stairs every night for the next forty years or so. When Kyra grew older, her husband would be carrying their children up the stairs.

"Considerin' the disruption to the household, Celeste seemed reasonable," Ross remarked.

"What disruption can a five-year-old, a dog, and a kitten make?" Blaze countered. "Celeste seems reasonable because she hasn't figured how to deal with me."

"When she does figure ye out," Ross said, "I wish she'd tell me."

Kyra's bedchamber had been decorated in pink and white with splashes of yellow here and there. Though the nannies shared the bedchamber next door, a cot had been set in the child's room. Taking turns, either Morag or Jean slept in the room with their charge.

"Dinna wake her for dinner," Ross instructed the nannies. "If she's hungry later, ye can fetch her somethin'."

"Send for me if she wakes and wants me," Blaze told them.

Ross and Blaze retraced their steps. Half-way down the corridor, he stopped and opened the bedchamber door. "Lady MacArthur, our boudoir."

"Thank you, my lord."

"Jeez, are we sleepin' with the animals?"

After setting Sugar in the box of sand, Blaze called Puddles across the room. "Lie down. Stay."

She looked at her husband. "We'll let them loose in a few days once they've learned the lay of the house, and the servants are comfortable."

"Puddles roamed Kilchurn House alone," Ross reminded her.

"We weren't living with the enemy," she said.

Her husband's bedchamber had been decorated with almost spartan masculinity, reminding her of her father's office. The four-poster bed, the highboy, and several other pieces had been crafted in dark mahogany. The upholstered pieces, the bedcurtains, the coverlet, and the carpets had been designed in muted shades of blue and a mixture of textiles.

The bedchamber needed feminine touches. She would take care of that this week. Perhaps she would visit Newmarket and take Kyra to the sweet shop.

"Ye can have a tray sent up if yer too tired for dinner," Ross said.

"I wouldn't miss dinner for all the whisky in Scotland," she said.

"When I danced with ye at yer sister's weddin'," Ross told her, "I thought ye were sweet, innocent, and feminine. Now I discover yer a bloodthirsty wench." He planted a kiss on her lips. "Ye relish arguin' with Celeste."

"I do not enjoy arguing with anyone," Blaze said, "but I dislike Celeste."

"Can ye coexist in peace?"

"I doubt it."

Ross smiled. "Could ye try?"

"I will give it my best effort," Blaze said, "but handling bullies means taking the offensive." She turned her back, asking, "Unbutton me, please."

Ross unfastened the row of buttons from the back of her neck to her waist. Parting the two sides, he slid a finger down the column of her back. His lips followed his finger, and then he nibbled on her neck.

Blaze purred with pleasure and let the gown slip off one shoulder. "Kiss me there," she whispered.

"Lady MacArthur, yer tryin' to seduce me."

Blaze heard the smile in his voice and leaned back

against his hard body. He slipped his arms around her and cupped her breasts through her gown.

"Sit on the bed," Blaze whispered, "and I'll seduce you."

Ross turned her around in his arms. "I'm game and easy."

Crossing the room, Ross sat on the edge of the bed. Blaze stood in front of him, a smile flirting with her lips, her gaze holding his captive. Inch by inch, Blaze let the bodice of her gown slide off her shoulders and drop to her waist. Then she let the garment pool at her feet. Stepping out of it, she pushed it away with her foot and then kicked her shoes off.

Blaze stood in her chemise and stockings. She lifted her right leg and rested it on the bed beside him.

"Roll my stocking down," she invited him.

Ross slid his hands up her leg and drew the garter off. Tossing it over his shoulder, he slid her stocking down her leg.

"Come to bed," he said, his voice husky. "I'm hard for ye."

Shaking her head, Blaze removed her right leg from the bed and set her left leg beside him. Ross rolled the garter down, tossed it over his shoulder, and then slid the stocking down her leg.

She fixed her gaze on his and slid the straps of her chemise down. The garment pooled at her feet, leaving her naked.

She dropped on her knees in front of him and tugged at his trousers. When he pushed them down, she dipped her head and kissed his manhood.

"Sit on my lap," Ross said.

Blaze straddled him, taking him deep inside her. They rocked back and forth, their bodies touching from groin to chest, their lips locked in a hungry kiss.

Blaze reached paradise first, waves of pleasure washing through her. He held her steady and thrust deep within her, shuddering his release.

"Ye've killed me." Ross fell back on the bed, taking her with him. "Jeez, I dinna have forty years left in me."

"Don't worry about dying and leaving me." Blaze lifted her head and smiled. "I'll remarry."

"The hell ye will." Ross rolled her over and gazed at her. "I'll come back to haunt ye."

Blaze pulled his head down and kissed him. She poured all her love into that single, stirring kiss. And he returned her kiss in kind.

Husband and wife descended the stairs later, more than a few minutes tardy for dinner. Walking down the hallway, Blaze steeled herself for what was to come. She regretted leaving the Highlands and wished her stepmother-in-law would disappear. The babe made her weary, cranky, and nauseous, which meant her patience was low.

"You've kept us waiting," Celeste said, when they walked into the dining room.

"Ye didna need to wait," Ross said.

"Your father decided we would dine together on"—Celeste glanced at Blaze—"on her first night in residence."

"My name is Lady MacArthur," Blaze told the woman, and heard muffled sounds of amusement. The Duke of Kilchurn was smiling, and Mairi

MacArthur had covered her mouth with her hand. Only Amanda Stanley appeared not to appreciate the humor. Her gaze had fixed on her mother, waiting for the woman's response. The daughter looked a bit nervous. Most likely, she had never witnessed anyone challenging the old witch.

"Lady MacArthur," Celeste said. "Please be seated."

"Thank you, Your Grace."

The Duke and Duchess of Kilchurn sat on either end of the table. Blaze and Ross sat opposite Mairi and Amanda.

Feeling the tension emanating from the duchess, Blaze placed her napkin on her lap and prepared to dine with her. She almost smiled with relief when a footman placed the bowl of cucumber soup on the table in front of her.

"My wife doesna drink spirits," Ross told a footman. "Serve her lemon barley water."

"This looks delicious." Blaze dipped her spoon into the soup and tasted it. When the footman delivered the lemon barley water, she said, "Tell Cook the soup is delicious."

The footman seemed surprised that she had spoken to him. "Yes, my lady."

"We do not converse with staff," Celeste told her.

Blaze kept her expression placid and her smile serene. "I converse with whomever I please."

The Duchess of Kilchurn developed a pinched expression. "Yes, of course."

Blaze had a bad moment when the calf's liver salad arrived. Taking her plate in hand, Ross transferred her slices of calf's liver onto his own plate.

"Dodger, tell Cook my wife doesna eat meat, fish, or poultry," Ross said.

"Yes, my lord."

"We do not cater to finicky eaters here," Celeste said.

"My pregnant wife will eat what she wants," Ross informed his stepmother. "She doesna need caterin' but willna be served those three foods."

"What's left to eat?" Mairi asked her brother.

"Everythin' else." Ross looked at his stepmother. "Servin' her calf's liver salad without the calf's liver isna any trouble."

"I understand." The duchess looked at her. "My footmen will not be used for your animals' needs."

"*My* footmen will do whatever she asks," the Duke of Kilchurn told his wife. "I pay their wages, not you."

Mairi MacArthur smiled at her. "Welcome to the family."

Blaze could not suppress her giggles. She glanced at her husband. He was smiling at his sister.

"I think yer brave for ridin' in the races," Mairi told her.

Amanda Stanley nodded in agreement. "The news of Pegasus's death saddened us."

"All of Newmarket wept when they heard the news," Celeste said. "I cannot understand fussing about a horse's death."

Silence fell like an axe. All movement ceased, the staff staring at the duchess.

Blaze glanced sidelong at her husband. Ross was looking at her, awaiting an emotional outburst.

Delaying any reaction, Blaze sipped her lemon barley water and then dabbed her mouth with the napkin. She knew the duchess wanted her to lose control, with either anger or tears.

At this moment, Blaze appreciated her own stepmother's teachings. Keep your face expressionless, never cut and run, always return an insult.

"Living means dying." Blaze looked at her stepmother-in-law. "Some sooner than others, I suppose." Then, "Oh, drat. I forgot to warn you that Puddles protects Kyra and Sugar and will inflict severe bodily harm on anyone who mistreats them."

Ross choked on his wine and gasped. "It went down the wrong pipe."

"James, I'm frightened of the dog," Celeste complained. "We should leave it outside."

"His name is Puddles, not *it*," Blaze corrected her.

"There's nothin' to fear," the duke said. "Her dog stays inside, not outside."

The main course arrived then. Carrying a platter, a footman walked into the dining room. Roasted potatoes circled a roasted goose.

"Jeez, I should've known goose would be served," Ross muttered.

"What did you say?" Celeste asked him.

"Nothin'."

"Ye've a fondness for animals?" Mairi asked.

"I adore animals." Blaze narrowed her gaze on her stepmother-in-law. "Whoever harms my animals will suffer the same fate."

"Are you threatening me?" Celeste asked her. "Ross, your wife is threatening me."

Ross didn't bother to look at either woman. He lifted his wine glass to his lips. After taking a sip, he said, "Dinna threaten Celeste, darlin'."

Blaze looked at him, her blue eyes wide, her face a mask of innocence. "Do you actually believe I would threaten your stepmother?"

She placed the palm of her hand on her chest and dropped the other hand to her belly, murmuring, "Eating and arguing gives my son heartburn."

"Celeste, do not upset Blaze," the Duke of Kilchurn ordered. "She carries the future of the MacArthurs inside her body, and I willna let her sicken because ye canna guard yer tongue."

Blaze gave Celeste a sidelong glance. The woman looked like she had a pin stuck in her unmentionables. Suppressed anger had reddened her complexion.

Catching the older woman's eye, Blaze arched a copper brow at her. A triumphant smile touched her lips.

Mairi MacArthur burst into laughter and then coughed to cover it. When her husband's sister gave her a wink, Blaze hoped she had found a friend.

Pleading weariness from travel, Ross escorted Blaze to their chamber after dinner. He closed and bolted the door and then rounded on his wife. "Roxie would have swooned at yer behavior tonight."

"I learned this behavior from Roxie," Blaze said, "but an observer would consider me rude."

"Rude? Ye were damn threatening."

"If Celeste feeds Puddles a poisoned cookie," Blaze said, "I will force a poisoned cookie down her throat. Isn't a warning kinder than a killing?"

"I see yer point." Ross pulled her into his embrace. "What makes ye think she'll poison Puddles?"

"Celeste poisoned Hercules."

* * *

Blaze managed to avoid her stepmother-in-law the next morning. She skipped breakfast in the dining room, taking her tea and dry toast in her own chamber, and then walked down the hallway to her daughter's chamber.

Accompanied by Puddles, Blaze and Kyra walked outside and meandered the formal garden. Blaze could not think of a reasonable excuse to avoid luncheon in the dining room. Only bleeding, convulsions, or unconsciousness could save her from another confrontation with the old witch.

"Let's sit on this bench." Blaze held a yellow flower she'd picked from the lawn. "When I hold this dandelion beneath your chin, it will tell me if you like butter."

Kyra looked confused. "The flower talks?"

"Flowers talk to my older sister," Blaze told her, "and animals talk to me. Shall I show you?"

"Yes." Kyra clapped her hands together.

"I will call Puddles to us," Blaze whispered in the girl's ear, "and then I will tell him to give you his paw. Are you ready?"

Kyra nodded.

Come Puddles. The mastiff dashed toward them and sat in front of his mistress. *Give Kyra paw.*

Cookie?

Later. Give Kyra paw. The mastiff lifted his paw.

"Puddles didna talk," Kyra said.

"Puddles talked to me."

"I didna hear him."

Blaze giggled and put her arm around the five-year-old. "You are my favorite little girl."

"Ah, jeez," Kyra said, sounding like her father. "Here comes Dodger."

"My lady, luncheon will soon be served," Dodger informed her. "Her Grace dislikes tardiness."

"Thank you, Dodger. Who will be lunching with us?"

"Her Grace."

"Where is everyone else?"

"His Grace has gone to Inverary House," Dodger answered. "His Lordship is investigating Hercules's misfortune. Miss Mairi and Miss Amanda are visiting friends."

"We'll take a tray in Kyra's chamber," Blaze said.

"Coward."

"Avoiding trouble is not cowardly," Blaze informed him.

"Indeed, my lady, it is not," the majordomo agreed. "However, Her Grace will believe you are a coward, and the battles will never cease."

"You don't like Her Grace, do you?"

"His Lordship's mother would have adored you," Dodger said, ignoring her question.

"Thank you for the compliment." Blaze smiled at the man. "Kyra and I will be taking the long way around and could arrive a bit tardy."

"Very good, my lady."

The duchess was already seated by the time Blaze and Kyra walked into the dining room. Puddles followed behind them.

"The dog does not enter my dining room," Celeste said, her voice brooking no disobedience.

"Puddles eats what falls on the floor," Kyra said, eliciting smothered chuckles from the staff.

Celeste turned her basilisk's stare on the five-year-old. "You be quiet."

Blaze crouched down beside her stepdaughter. The girl's bottom lip was trembling.

"Don't cry," Blaze soothed the girl. "The mean lady won't hurt you."

More smothered chuckles from the sideboard did not help the situation.

"I will defer to your wishes," Blaze told the duchess. "Puddles, sit outside the door." The mastiff obeyed instantly.

Blaze caught the footman's eye and gestured to her stepdaughter. "Can you find a thick book to boost Kyra at the table?"

Blaze sat down and drew her stepdaughter close while they waited. Within a few minutes, the footman appeared and set an unabridged Shakespeare on the chair. The majordomo lifted the girl up and pushed the chair closer to the table.

A footman served the duchess first and then delivered their plates. Apparently, her husband's message had been delivered to Cook who also had made allowances for a five-year-old.

Kyra's plate contained toasted cheese and chicken cut into tiny pieces. Blaze's plate had grilled mushrooms on toast and a small salad of greens. The duchess's plate held something Blaze preferred to ignore.

Blaze watched her stepdaughter spear a piece of chicken and plop it into her mouth. "Is it delicious?" she asked her.

Kyra nodded and glanced down the table at the duchess. "What's that?" she asked, pointing at the woman's plate.

"Her Grace is eating broiled *poussins* with mustard sauce," Blaze answered.

Kyra looked at her. "What is it?"

"Chicken babies."

The girl looked horrified, and Blaze heard more muffled laughter near the sideboard.

Kyra looked at her own plate and pointed at the chicken. "What is this?"

"Meat."

Her answer satisfied Kyra who began eating again. The five-year-old scooped a piece of chicken that promptly fell on the floor.

"Leave it there," Blaze said. Too late.

Kyra had already climbed off the chair and was searching beneath the table. She stood, chicken in hand, and said, "Jeez, we need Puddles." Outside the open door, the mastiff heard his name and began whining for the chicken.

Blaze heard not-so-smothered chuckles at the sideboard. She didn't think that would sit well with the old witch.

"Put the piece of meat on the table," Blaze said. Too late, again.

Kyra popped it into her mouth and held her empty hand up. "I ate it."

The duchess's silverware clattered to her plate. "The maid's daughter disgusts me. I refuse—"

Blaze pounded both fists on the table, silencing the duchess. Then she stood to look down on the woman. "You will respect Kyra and me, or you will regret it."

Surprised, the duchess stared at her and then rage contorted her expression. She opened her mouth to speak, but the unmistakable sound of growling coming from the doorway encouraged her to remain silent.

"I will speak to my husband about this."

"Please do," Blaze said, her expression placid again. "I'm certain His Grace would appreciate knowing how insulting you've been to his granddaughter."

Turning her back on the woman, Blaze lifted her stepdaughter off the chair and led her out of the dining room. "Come, Puddles."

Unused to rebellion, Celeste would never heed her warnings. Ross had been correct to remove his daughter from that woman's presence. They would need to move into Inverary House until the witch left Newmarket.

"Morag, pack a bag for Kyra and yourself," Blaze ordered the nanny. "Jean, pack a bag for me and yourself."

"Kyra, I want you to sit here for a few minutes while Morag packs our bags," Blaze said. "I need a word with Dodger, and then we're visiting my papa and stepmother and sisters. Won't that be fun?"

The girl nodded and sat on the stool in her chamber.

Blaze hurried down the stairs to the foyer. "Dodger, I want a coach brought around."

"Yes, my lady."

"Which chamber is the hag's?"

Dodger gave her a puzzled look. "Her Grace's chamber is the first door on the left."

"Keep her from coming upstairs."

"I will do my best, my lady."

Lifting her skirts, Blaze dashed up the stairs and entered the first door on the left. She needed something belonging to Celeste.

A pair of kid gloves lay on the bureau. Beside the gloves were an ivory comb and hairbrush. Which would be best?

Blaze snatched one of the gloves and the comb. Opening the door a crack, she peered outside and then sprinted down the hallway to her chamber. She stuffed the glove and the comb into a reticule and took a deep breath. Grabbing Sugar, Blaze walked down the hallway to her daughter's chamber.

Holding the kitten in one hand, Blaze held out her free hand to Kyra. "Come, Puddles."

With the mastiff leading the way, Blaze and Kyra descended to the foyer. Morag and Jean walked behind them, each carrying two bags.

Dodger looked at the traveling bags and frowned. "Are you leaving, my lady?"

"We'll be gone for a few days."

"What shall I tell His Lordship?"

"Tell my husband we've gone to Inverary House," Blaze answered, "and I'm keeping his daughter."

Chapter Fifteen

His wife had a sweet surprise coming her way.

Ross walked the length of High Street, his thoughts on his wife and a smile on his lips. He'd pulled a sneaky trick by leaving her and his daughter alone with Celeste.

His father had ridden to Inverary House before lunch. Mairi and Amanda were lunching with friends, not that those two would suit as a buffer against his stepmother's tongue. That left Blaze to fend for herself and his daughter.

He should have returned home in order to keep the peace, but his wife could defend herself and his daughter without his help. Buying nougats for Blaze and lollipops for Kyra would sweeten their moods.

Reaching the Birdcage Tavern, Ross ducked inside and paused to adjust his sight from brilliant sunshine to dimly-lit tavern. He scanned the room and spied his man sitting alone at a corner table.

Ross raised his hand in greeting and wended his way through the tables. He dropped into a chair and set his package on the table.

"Have you brought me a gift?" Alexander Blake asked.

"I'm hopin' nougats will keep my wife from lockin' me out of our bedchamber," Ross said.

"You are not in accord either?"

"What do ye mean by either?"

"Raven is furious but refuses to tell me the reason." Alexander poured whisky into two glasses and pushed one across the table.

"No wonder yer drinkin' at this hour," Ross said, and lifted the glass of whisky to his lips. "The ladies think we men are mind readers. Men dinna settle their differences by givin' each other the silent treatment. Though I do admit, Blaze doesna usually hold her tongue when she's irritated."

"Blaze is an Original."

Ross smiled. "I think so."

"Constable Black will be arriving late today," Alexander said. "Will you be attending the meeting at Inverary's tomorrow?"

Ross nodded and reached into his pocket for a parchment. He placed it on the table in front of Blake. "My father listed the names of anyone with access to Hercules."

Alexander perused the list. "Why are the Stanleys listed?"

"Dirk and Chad are my father's stepsons," Ross answered. "I suppose they figured there was safety in numbers along the road."

"Don't they own thoroughbreds?"

"Emperor raced at Epsom but finished second to Inverary's Thor."

"Let's review the chain of events," Alexander said.

"Someone murdered Inverary's jockey two weeks before The Craven."

"The Inverary stables had an intruder the night Pegasus won The Craven," Ross said, "and someone drugged Blaze before The First Spring."

"What about Pegasus's death?"

"Peg's death was an accident," Ross answered. "She broke two knees."

Alexander sipped his whisky. "Could anyone have done something to cause the filly's knees to break?"

"Bobby Bender is the best in the business," Ross said, shaking his head. "He examined Peg before we put her down and would have recognized foul play."

"Your father was transporting Hercules from Newmarket to Epsom Downs when the horse died."

"Someone fed Hercules carrots dipped in poison."

"Who placed at Epsom?" Alexander asked.

"Inverary's Thor won," Ross answered. "Stanley's Emperor was second and Wakefield's Ajax was third."

"Yours is the third list I've received," Alexander told him. "Raven believes the villain attended the Jockey Club Ball and your wedding. She gave me a list of guests and suggested I compare them."

"How does she know?" Ross asked him.

Alexander rolled his eyes. "Raven knows because she knows."

"What d'ye mean?"

"The betrothal ring I gave Raven is a rare star ruby," Alexander answered. "Legend says the star ruby will darken blood red if its owner is endangered. Apparently, the ruby darkened at the Jockey Club Ball and your wedding."

"Jeez, the sister's as daft as my wife," Ross said. "No offense meant. Do ye believe in such thin's?"

Alexander Blake shrugged. "I've learned not to discount anything."

"Where'd ye learn that?"

"Constable Black believes in anything that helps solve a crime," Alexander told him. "He does not scoff at Raven's hocus-pocus."

"I apologize for stealin' yer weddin' arrangements," Ross said. "Ye'd be married today if Blaze and I hadna taken them."

"Your need was greater," Alexander said, "but Raven annoyed me when she offered it before she'd consulted me. I refused her offer to set another date, and now she's making me pay."

"Whoever labeled women the weaker sex had his head stuck up his arse," Ross said.

Alexander laughed. "Truer words have never been spoken." He pocketed the list, saying, "The constable and I will compare the three lists tonight and bring them to Inverary's tomorrow."

Ross stood and shook his hand. "I'll see ye tomorrow then."

Thirty minutes later, Ross climbed out of his coach in front of MacArthur House. He hoped his wife had not suffered too badly either from his stepmother or boredom. Blaze wasn't the needlework type. She preferred activity, though her condition demanded she take life easier.

Nougats and lollipops should smooth the way for him. How fortunate his wife wasn't a fur-and-jewel woman like her stepmother.

"Welcome home, my lord," Dodger greeted him.

"Thank ye, Dodger." With package in hand, Ross crossed the foyer to the stairs.

"Lady MacArthur isn't home," Dodger said, "if you were hoping to find her upstairs."

Apparently, he'd been worrying without reason. His wife had been taking care of herself.

Ross retraced his steps across the foyer. "Did Lady MacArthur mention her destination?"

"Lady MacArthur said she was going to Inverary House," Dodger answered, "and she was keeping your daughter."

Ross snapped his brows together. The message sounded like his wife had left him. She'd been in high spirits this morning.

"Did somethin' happen today?"

Dodger nodded. "At lunch, Lady MacArthur and Her Grace exchanged unpleasant words."

"Did ye happen to hear the unpleasant words?"

"Her Grace called Miss Kyra the maid's daughter," Dodger told him, "and Lady MacArthur threatened Her Grace. Afterwards, Lady MacArthur packed their bags and went to Inverary House."

"Thank ye, Dodger."

Ross didn't trust himself to speak to Celeste. He walked out the door and stood in the courtyard until he could dampen his anger.

His father should never have married the social-climbing witch. He knew his father had been lonely after his mother's accident but—

Ross knew he shouldered most of the blame. He should have insisted Celeste show respect for his daughter and his late wife.

Removing Kyra from the witch's presence had

been easier than confrontation and turmoil in the family. He would take care of Celeste now, and then he would collect his wife and daughter.

Ross walked into the foyer and looked at Dodger. "Is Her Grace home?"

"Yes, my lord."

"Is His Grace home?"

"Yes, my lord."

Setting his package on the foyer table, Ross climbed the stairs to the second floor and walked down the hallway to the drawing room. He paused a moment before entering, hoping his father would not defend the witch. The last thing he wanted was an argument with his father.

Ross walked into the drawing room and advanced on his stepmother who sat near a window overlooking the garden. His father was working at the writing desk across the room.

"How dare you show such disrespect to Blaze and Kyra," Ross said without preamble.

"Your wife was disrespectful to *me*," Celeste defended herself. "She threatened me with that monster dog."

"Blaze would never threaten anyone without provocation," Ross said, and noted his father approaching them. "You called Kyra the maid's daughter."

"She *is* the maid's daughter."

"And you are the vicar's daughter," Ross countered. "My wife and my daughter carry the blood of aristocrats while you, madam, carry none."

"What has happened, son?"

"Celeste browbeat Janet into a grave," Ross

answered, looking at his father. "Since then, she has treated Kyra unkindly. I protected my daughter by removing her from your wife's presence when I should have removed your wife from my daughter's presence."

"Why did ye never tell me before?" his father asked him.

"James, you cannot believe that I—"

"Be quiet, Celeste."

"But—"

"Shut yer lips or I'll shut them for ye."

"I never mentioned this because I didna want to create turmoil in the family," Ross told him. "At lunch today, yer wife referred to Kyra as the maid's daughter. Blaze packed their bags and moved to Inverary House to protect my daughter. *Yer granddaughter.*"

"That solves the problem," Celeste said, looking at her husband. "They can stay there until we leave Newmarket."

"Blaze and Kyra have more right to live here than ye," the duke told her.

"I'm your wife—"

"Kyra carries my blood," he interrupted, "and Blaze carries the heir."

"Everything was peaceful until you married the Flambeau bastard," Celeste told Ross.

"Dinna tempt me to send ye to the Rowley Lodge and sue for divorce," the duke warned her.

"Divorces are impossible to obtain," Celeste said, "and you don't have grounds for it."

"Yer stupid if ye believe that," the Duke of Kilchurn told her. "A wealthy man can purchase grounds for divorce, and Magnus Campbell will use his influence to make certain the judges grant a divorce."

"Ross should have married Amanda," Celeste said. "All would be well if he had."

"I married the woman I love," Ross said, turning to leave. "I'm bringin' my family home, and ye'll treat them with respect."

"Celeste, yer cruelty to a five-year-old sickens me," the duke said. "I regret marryin' ye."

Father and son walked out of the drawing room, leaving her sitting alone. When they reached the staircase, Ross asked, "Why *did* ye marry her?"

"I was lonely for yer mother and Celeste was handy," his father answered. "I'll send her to London and give her a pension."

"Dinna do anythin' rash," Ross advised him. "Use the racin' season to mull the situation in yer mind."

Ross walked downstairs to the foyer. "Send someone for my coach," he ordered the majordomo. Retrieving his candy package from the table, he headed outside to wait.

Less than a half hour later, Ross leaped out of his coach in front of Inverary House. He would insist Blaze and Kyra return home with him.

After what happened with his father, Ross doubted Celeste would persist insulting his wife and daughter. His stepmother was no fool about money or social status. She didn't know his father very well if she considered his threats idle.

"Good afternoon, my lord," Tinker greeted him, opening the front door. "We've been expecting you."

"Where is my wife?" Ross asked, heading for the stairs.

Tinker rushed across the foyer and blocked his path up the stairs. "I apologize, my lord, but Her Ladyship gave me orders."

"I want my wife." His voice brooked no disobedience.

Tinker nodded. "I will tell Her Ladyship you have arrived."

"Thank ye, Tinker." Folding his arms across his chest, Ross leaned against the foyer table.

"Dodger delivered my message?"

Ross looked at his wife. She'd descended those stairs quieter than Sugar the kitten.

"Ye left me," Ross accused her, "and ye stole my daughter."

"I rescued your daughter from that evil witch."

"Dodger told me aboot the trouble at lunch." Ross ran a hand through his hair. "I should've left Kyra in the Highlands."

Blaze touched his arm. "Your daughter belongs with you."

"Then what's she doin' here?"

"Kyra and I are visiting Aunt Bedelia for a few days," Blaze told him, "and Kyra is enjoying herself with my sisters. Sophia is drawing her portrait while Serena entertains her with flute playing. My sister Belle will be visiting us later. Her stepdaughter is Kyra's age. Making friends will be good for our daughter."

"Ye really are a sneaky witch," Ross said, placing the palm of his hand on her cheek. "I can see that makin' friends will be good for our daughter, and I doubt Kyra has ever had this much attention."

"Why don't you stay here, too?"

"I canna insult my father by movin' to Inverary House."

"You moved to Rowley Lodge whenever they were in residence," Blaze argued. "What is different now?"

"I dinna want my father alone," Ross told her. "He knows now what's been happenin' and was talkin' aboot divorcin' Celeste. Ye know, darlin', I miss ye when ye arena around."

"You miss me?"

"That surprises ye?" Ross asked. "A man misses the woman he loves."

His wife looked flabbergasted. "You love me?"

"I married ye."

"You married me because you loved me?"

"Well, I didna marry ye to make ye miserable," Ross answered.

"I thought you married me because I was pregnant," she told him.

"Darlin', I loved ye before we fell into bed." Ross passed her the candy package and winked at her. "A man only buys nougats and lollipops for a woman he loves."

His wife's smile was pure sunshine. "I love you, too."

"I knew ye loved me."

"How did you—"

"I'm wealthy, titled, and handsome." Ross pulled her into his arms. "The woman who could resist me hasna been born."

"You're also arrogant, stubborn, and conceited."

"Nobody's perfect."

Ross dipped his head and claimed her lips in a

passionate kiss. That melted into another. And another.

"Now we've settled this love business," Ross said, drawing back. "Fetch Kyra and we'll go home."

"Aunt Bedelia insists I stay until Sunday," Blaze said. "That's only three days from today. She wants you to bring your father and stepmother to dinner Saturday evening."

"I dinna understand."

"Neither do I," Blaze agreed, "but Bedelia said you should humor an old lady."

"I suppose I can do without ye for three days," Ross said. "I'm meetin' with yer father tomorrow so I'll see ye then."

"Thank you for the nougats." Blaze ran a finger down his cheek. "You're welcome to stay for dinner."

"I dinna want to leave my father alone tonight."

"The spying produced no clues?"

Alexander Blake shifted his gaze from the passing scenery to Constable Black. "Spying only produced trouble between Raven and me."

"You'll settle your differences," the constable said, "and we'll dance at your wedding."

"I can't settle our differences," Alexander replied, "if I don't know what they are."

"Raven will tell you when she's ready."

"I made Crazy Eddie a child minder," Alexander said, smiling. "You should have seen the look on his face."

Constable Black chuckled, a sound few people heard. "That could prove dangerous to our witness."

"Inverary is protecting the boy," Alexander said. "Eddie escorts Jack around town during the day trying to find the man who drugged Blaze."

"The gossip about Inverary's daughter jockeying a thoroughbred reached London," Constable Black said. "I gather she's safely married and settled now?"

"Blaze is married," Alexander said, "but the jury hasn't decided on settled yet."

Their coach halted in Inverary House courtyard. The two climbed down and headed for the front door.

"Good afternoon, my lord," Tinker greeted them. "Good to see you again, Constable Black."

"His Grace is expecting us," Alexander said.

"The MacArthurs have already arrived."

"Thank you, Tinker. We know the way."

The Duke of Inverary was sitting behind his desk. Four leather chairs had been positioned in a semi-circle around the front of the desk.

After the introductions, the four sat in the leather chairs. The Duke of Inverary poured a measure of whisky into five tumblers, and they were ready to discuss the problem.

"Nothing we say leaves this room," Constable Black said, glancing at each man in turn. "Whatever we plan must be kept secret."

"We discussed possible suspects," Alexander spoke up. "Obviously, the guilty party would benefit financially by rigging the Triple Crown."

"The Duke of Inverary would benefit," Constable Black said, "but His Grace would not hire a ruffian to murder his own jockey."

"The Marquis of Awe would benefit," Alexander said, "but Ross would not poison his own horse."

"A horse need not win the Triple Crown to make good money," the Duke of Inverary said. "A thoroughbred can make a fortune from stud service. A horse that showed or placed in the Classic Races can make almost as much money as the Big Three winner."

"That's true," Ross MacArthur agreed. "On any given day, a number of factors can interfere with the best horse not winnin' the race."

"The constable decided the villain need not be a horse owner," Alexander said. "He could be a gambler."

"Or he could be a she." Ross sipped his whisky while the others chuckled at his statement. He held the tumbler up and looked at his father-in-law. "Speyside?"

The Duke of Inverary nodded. "Thor will be targeted because of his Derby win."

"We must protect Thor," the Duke of Kilchurn said, "but we must also catch the murderer. Killin' a horse is one thin', but killin' a jockey is another."

"Catchin' him will be easy if we know which night he plans to move," Ross said.

"Good thinking, my lord." Constable Black lifted his whisky glass to toast the marquis. "We'll force him into action on the night of our choosing."

"How do ye propose to do that?" the Duke of Kilchurn asked.

"We need to catch him in the act," the Duke of Inverary added. "If not, we can only prove trespassing."

"Any ideas?" the constable asked.

"We'll place a loose, visible line of guards around the Inverary estate," Alexander said. "The villain will see the guards and postpone action. The night before the 2000 Guineas Race, we'll remove a few guards. They'll be waiting inside Thor's stable."

"Why dinna we do that tonight?" Ross asked.

Constable Black looked at Alexander. "Well?"

"If we do it tonight, he'll be warned if something goes wrong," Alexander said. "Waiting for the night before the race means he'll be desperate, and desperate men make mistakes."

"Did ye compare those lists?" Ross asked.

"What lists are those?" the Duke of Inverary asked.

"I listed anyone who had access to Hercules," the Duke of Kilchurn said.

"Raven slipped me the guests lists from the Jockey Club Ball and the wedding," Alexander said. "She's convinced the murderer attended those events."

"If you still have the glass used to drug your daughter," Constable Black said, turning to Inverary, "I would like Raven to do another reading."

"My aunt Bedelia is visiting," the duke said. "If she does the reading, we may learn something different."

Constable Black nodded. "We'll ask your aunt to read the jockey's ring, too."

"Tinker," the duke called.

The door opened instantly, and the majordomo appeared. "I was walking down the hallway—"

"Fetch Aunt Bedelia," the duke said, "and do not repeat anything you heard."

"Yes, Your Grace."

Several doors down the hallway from the duke's office, Aunt Bedelia and Raven sat together in the drawing room. On the wall near them was Gabrielle Flambeau's portrait.

"I thank a merciful God," Aunt Bedelia said, "the duchess is visiting Lady Althorpe."

Raven smiled at the old woman. Her stepmother was definitely an acquired taste.

"Yer mother was exquisitely beautiful," Bedelia said. "I can see the reason Magnus gave her his heart. Too bad they werena able to marry."

"Did Papa truly love her?" Raven asked. "Or was she a lovely convenience?"

"Magnus has never stopped lovin' Gabrielle," Bedelia said, patting her hand. "I always believed yer father's first marriage was a mistake, his third marriage is pleasant companionship, and yer mother was the wife of his heart. I'm hopin' they find peace together in the afterlife."

Raven fell silent. Her aunt's words heartened her. All children wanted their parents to love each other. Raven wondered if Alex and she would ever share that grand love. His behavior at the wedding cast a shadow over that possibility.

"Lady Bedelia," Tinker called, hurrying into the room. "His Grace—"

"Tell my nephew I will be there directly."

"Yes, my lady." Chuckling, Tinker left the drawing room.

"The gentlemen want a readin'," Bedelia said, rising from the settee. "Are you comin' along?"

Raven smiled. "I would never miss an opportunity to torment Alexander."

Arm in arm, Aunt Bedelia and Raven walked down the hallway. Raven tapped on the office door and then opened it without waiting for permission. She followed her aunt inside, her gaze slamming into Alexander's.

"Hello, Brat." Giving her a warm smile, Alexander crossed the office.

"Hello, Alex." Her smile was more polite than warm.

"I stopped by yesterday," he said, "but you weren't home."

"Prince Lykos escorted me and my sisters to Newmarket." His dismayed expression heartened Raven.

"I would have taken you if you'd sent me a note."

"I didn't want to bother you," she told him. "I know you're busy with the investigation and other things."

"I would have taken time out of my schedule," he said.

"I'll consider your offer next time."

Alexander gave Bedelia his attention. "Come and sit in front of the desk," he said, taking her arm.

Bedelia glanced at his hand on her arm. "I'm old, not crippled."

Raven giggled, and the men chuckled. Even Alexander smiled.

Bedelia sat in a leather chair in front of her nephew's desk and lifted someone's tumbler of whisky. She sipped the amber liquid.

"Speyside whisky." Bedelia looked at her nephew. "Give me Highland whisky, and dinna bother with a glass."

The duke opened a bottle and passed it to her. Bedelia sipped the whisky and then nodded. "That's better."

"Aunt Bedelia, I want you to meet Constable Amadeus Black and, of course, you've met Alexander Blake, Raven's young man."

Bedelia looked at the constable. "Ye must come to dinner on Saturday."

Amadeus Black smiled. "Is there a particular reason?"

"Yer sharp for an Englishman," Bedelia said. "Trust me, constable. You shouldna miss Saturday." She flicked a glance at Alexander, adding, "Bring the boy with ye, too."

Raven could not contain her laughter, earning an irritated look from the boy. She had a feeling Alexander was no match for Bedelia, and she would do well to watch her aunt's strategy.

"Magnus, everyone in this room must attend our dinner on Saturday," Bedelia said. "Roxie and Celeste must come, too."

"That's easy to arrange, Aunt."

"May I call you Bedelia?" Constable Black asked her. When she inclined her silver head, he said, "I would appreciate—"

"Give me the ring first," Bedelia said.

Constable Black, Alexander Blake, and Ross MacArthur dropped their mouths open in surprise. The Dukes of Inverary and Kilchurn smiled, as did Raven.

Bedelia was dazzling the gentlemen, which made them take her seriously. Raven tucked that idea away for future use.

"Do you need privacy?" the constable was asking her aunt.

"No." Bedelia held her hand out, and Constable Black passed her the boar's head ring.

Holding the ring in the palm of her left hand, Bedelia covered it with her right hand. "I see a night sky with hundreds of glittering stars and a perfect crescent moon. A MacArthur plaid is draped across the moon, and a dirk rests on top of the plaid."

"Did you tell her?"

Raven looked at Alexander. "I beg your pardon?"

"You told your aunt what you saw," Alexander accused her.

"Not everyone is a cheat like you."

"What do you mean by that?"

Raven gave him an ambiguous smile. "Ask my aunt for a reading."

Bedelia sipped the Highland whisky. "Young man, there's more in this world than yer logic can explain." She looked at the constable. "Give me the glass."

Bedelia held the glass in her left hand and covered it with her right. "I see a candle with a prominent wick which becomes a man handin' this glass to a scrawny boy."

"Can you describe the man?" Constable Black asked her.

"The man is blond, his face a candlewick." Setting the glass on the desk, Bedelia rose from the chair and glanced at each man in turn. "Do not forget Saturday dinner, or ye'll regret it. Raven, take the whisky."

Chapter Sixteen

She missed him.

Dressed for dinner, Blaze crossed her bedchamber to inspect her reflection in the cheval mirror. She looked at herself without really seeing, her thoughts on her husband.

Aunt Bedelia had promised she would sleep beside her husband that night. Ross had professed his love, and she could hardly wait to begin the rest of their lives together.

Even the prospect of seeing her stepmother-in-law could not dampen her mood. Besides, Aunt Bedelia had promised Celeste MacArthur would never bother her again. She didn't know how that was possible, but she had faith in her great-aunt.

"Enter," she called, hearing a knock on the door.

Raven walked into the bedchamber. "Aunt Bedelia wants to see us privately before dinner."

"Does my belly look bigger?" Blaze asked, turning sideways.

"No." Raven rolled her eyes and turned away, saying, "Aunt Bedelia is waiting for us."

Dressed for dinner guests, Aunt Bedelia sat on the chaise in front of the hearth in her bedchamber. Puddles snoozed at her feet, Sugar cuddled in her lap, and a large reticule lay beside her on the chaise.

"We make our move tonight," Bedelia told them.

"What move is that?" Blaze asked, glancing at her sister.

"We're goin' to catch a murderer," Bedelia said. "All ye need to do is follow my instructions."

"Isn't that the constable's job?" Raven asked her.

"The gentlemen willna catch the villain," Aunt Bedelia answered. "I saw the resolution in my vision."

"Which vision was that?" Blaze asked her.

"The vision sent me to Kilchurn House to accompany ye to England," Bedelia said. "The villain is comin' tonight because he knows stablehands drink on Saturday nights. The gents are plannin' to catch him the night before the race."

"Why don't we tell the constable?" Raven asked her.

"They willna believe an old lady," Bedelia answered. "If they guard the stables, the villain willna move. We need to catch him, not merely prevent him from harmin' Thor."

Blaze placed a hand over her belly. "Was anyone hurt in your vision?"

"Follow my instructions and all will be well," Bedelia assured her. "Sneak into Thor's stable. Bring Puddles, Sugar, and Beau with ye."

"Beau is housed in Thor's stable," Blaze said.

"Let Beau out of his stall," Bedelia instructed her. "Let yer animals wander wherever they want inside the stable."

"What should I do?" Raven asked her.

"Yer wearin' the star ruby," Bedelia said. "Stand near a window openin' so ye can see the ring in the moonlight. When the ruby darkens, the villain is near, and signal Blaze."

"What do we do when the murderer enters the stable?" Blaze asked.

Bedelia passed her the reticule. "Use my pistol."

"Pistol?" Blaze exclaimed. "I don't know how to use a pistol."

"Ye take the pistol out of the reticule and point it at the intruder," Bedelia told her.

"How do I fire it?"

"Let me show ye." Bedelia removed the pistol from the reticule and chuckled when the sisters backed away. "Hold it like this"—she demonstrated—"and put yer finger on the trigger here."

"And then I pull the trigger?"

"Dinna pull the trigger," Bedelia ordered. "The pistol isna loaded."

"What good is an unloaded pistol?" Raven asked her.

"We want to frighten, not kill him," Bedelia said. "I'll send yer men to the rescue at the appropriate moment."

"How do you know the appropriate moment?" Raven asked. "If you make a mistake—"

"I know"—Bedelia interrupted—"because I know."

Blaze laughed at that. Raven smiled and nodded at her aunt.

"Here's the reticule and Sugar," Bedelia said. "Take the servants' stairs. Ye willna need to wait long."

"How will you excuse our absence from dinner?" Blaze asked.

"I'll tell them the truth," Bedelia answered. "Yer doin' somethin' for me, and they'll see ye soon."

Blaze and Raven hurried down the hallway to the rear stairs, the mastiff following behind. Reaching ground level, they met the majordomo.

"You never saw us," Blaze said.

Tinker smiled. "I haven't seen you all day."

The sisters scooted out the garden door. Dusk had fallen and was rapidly fading into night. One by one, the stars appeared in the night sky like torches being lit. The full moon had risen in the east, beginning its journey westward.

"Are you frightened?" Raven asked, walking down the dark path to the stables.

"There's nothing to fear," Blaze answered. "An unloaded pistol and a slobbering mastiff are protecting us."

Raven giggled. "Do not forget a deaf kitten and a donkey."

"I doubt the villain will be carrying a weapon," Blaze said. "He poisoned Hercules and will probably try the same on Thor."

The stableyard was deserted. Men's voices and laughter wafted through the yard.

"Bedelia was correct," Blaze whispered. "The stablehands are drinking."

"Papa will have their heads if we can't save Thor."

Raven opened the stable's door. Blaze slipped inside, followed by Puddles, and then the door closed behind them.

Blaze smelled the familiar scents of musky horses

and hay. She heard the familiar sounds of horse-
shoes clomping on the floorboards and snorting
horses. The darkness felt unfamiliar, almost expec-
tant.

"Stand by the window opening in the stall opposite Thor's," Blaze said, releasing the donkey from
his stall. "When I level the pistol, you light the
torch." Then she set Sugar on the floor.

The sisters stood together in the stall. Raven
fixed her gaze on the star ruby ring, and Blaze removed the pistol from her aunt's reticule.

Blaze watched Beau meander from the rear of
the stable to the front and then meander back
toward the rear. Puddles had disappeared into an
empty stall, probably relaxing on top of a bale of
hay. Sugar dug her claws into the wood beam and
inched her way up to the loft.

Feeling her sister's touch on her arm, Blaze knew
the moment had arrived. She heard the creak of
the door opening and broke into a sweat. The
sound of boots on the floorboards came closer and
closer.

Blaze saw a dark figure stop at Thor's stall. She
stepped forward on silent feet.

"Put your hands in the air," Blaze ordered, level-
ing the pistol on the figure.

Raven lit the torch and gasped. "Chadwick Simmons?"

The squire smiled and stepped toward them.

"Don't move," Blaze ordered, cocking the trigger,
"or your head and your body will part company."

The squire stopped in an instant.

"The wick man," Raven murmured. "Chad*wick* Simmons."

"I was attending your parents' dinner," Chadwick said, smiling. "Your father asked me to check on Thor's safety."

Blaze flicked a glance at his hands. "Are you holding carrots?"

"I thought Thor deserved a treat."

"How kind of you. Eat one."

The squire lost his smile. "I beg your pardon?"

"Eat a carrot."

And then the sound of men's voices in the stable-yard distracted Blaze. Chadwick tossed the carrots, grabbing her pistol and her.

The stable door crashed open. Ross rushed inside, followed by Alexander and the constable. All three stopped short.

"Stay where you are," Chadwick said, pointing the pistol at her head, "or I'll kill her."

"The pistol's not loaded," Raven shouted.

Chadwick threw the pistol at Ross and grabbed Blaze's neck. "Take a step and I'll snap it."

And then pandemonium erupted.

Sugar leaped off the loft onto the squire's shoulder, digging her claws into him. Chadwick screamed and lost his grip on Blaze.

Beau emerged from a stall behind the squire and kicked him, sending him flying toward the men. Before Ross could grab him, Puddles attacked, his enormous mastiff's mouth attached to the squire's leg.

"Puddles, let go," Ross ordered. The dog released the squire and ran to Blaze's side.

Ross and Alexander rolled the squire onto his stomach. Grabbing a rope, Constable Black tied his hands behind his back.

"Are ye all right?" Ross asked Blaze.

"Yes."

"Are you all right?" Alexander asked Raven.

"Yes."

"Take the squire to the house," Constable Black told them. "We'll send a footman to fetch the local authorities."

Without another word, Ross and Alexander dragged Chadwick out of the stable. Blaze put Beau into his stall and lifted Sugar into her arms.

"Raven, grab those tainted carrots," Blaze said. "Come, Puddles."

Cookie?

Cookie for Puddles.

Blaze and Raven followed the men down the path to the mansion. "Look at them," Blaze said. "You'd think they caught the culprit instead of us."

Raven nodded. "And they don't seem too concerned about our health."

Blaze and Raven entered the house through the rear door and climbed the servants' stairs. The sisters could hear the Duchess of Kilchurn before they reached the second-floor drawing room.

"My son would never murder anyone or hurt an animal," Celeste MacArthur was insisting.

Blaze and Raven paused in the drawing room's doorway. Their sisters were there as well as Dirk and Amanda Stanley and Mairi MacArthur.

"Do you think all the Stanleys are involved?" Blaze whispered.

"No."

"How do you—?" Catching her sister's look, Blaze shut her mouth.

"I cannot believe Chad is involved," Dirk Stanley defended his brother, his sister nodding in agreement.

Chadwick Simmons looked at the Duchess of Kilchurn. "Tell them, Mother."

"What do you mean?" Celeste asked.

"I'll not hang alone," Chadwick told her, and looked at the constable. "I did my mother's bidding."

"That's a lie," Celeste exclaimed. "Unnatural son—"

"You're the unnatural one, Mother." Chadwick looked at Dirk. "I should have held the title since I was the earl's oldest son."

"Stop lying," Celeste cried.

"While she was married to Simmons, Mother engaged in an affair with the Earl of Boston," Chadwick told his siblings. "I am a product of that union as are you. She poisoned Simmons and married the earl.

"That wasn't enough for her, though. She wanted to be a duchess. Mother dispatched our father"—Chadwick looked at the Duke of Kilchurn—"and arranged an accident for your wife."

"That's a lie," Celeste screamed. "James, he's lying."

When Ross took a step toward her, the Duke of Kilchurn put his arm in front of his son. "Let it play out."

"Mother wanted you to marry Amanda so she could live in luxury when your father passed," Chadwick told Ross. "Your first wife stood in her way and sickened when my mother visited the Highlands that October."

"What did Celeste gain by murdering a jockey and poisoning my son's horse?" the Duke of Kilchurn asked.

"Mother did that for Dirk," Chadwick answered, looking at his brother. "You could never measure up when compared to Ross. She considered you a loser and wanted you to best Ross one time."

Tinker interrupted, escorting the local authorities into the drawing room. Constable Black forced Celeste off the sofa and tied her hands behind her back.

"These two are facing charges for multiple murders," the constable said. "We may need to transport them to London."

"James, I'm your wife," Celeste shrieked.

The Duke of Kilchurn turned his back on her.

Constable Black looked at Alexander, who said, "I'll follow you in a few minutes."

Blaze could not believe how many lives had been ruined by the witch's malicious greed. Dirk Stanley was white with shock. Amanda Stanley was weeping while Mairi MacArthur tried to comfort her. Ross had lost his mother and Kyra's mother. The Duke of Kilchurn had lost a beloved wife.

"Amanda, ye arena responsible for yer mother," the Duke of Kilchurn said. "I consider ye my own and want ye to live with us."

"I'll take Amanda home with me," Dirk Stanley said. "My sister can decide what she wants in a few days."

"Dirk, ye suffered a bad shock, too," Ross said,

surprising Blaze, "and I dinna think ye should be alone. Pass the night at MacArthur House."

Dirk Stanley looked surprised by the offer. "I don't want to impose on your own sorrow. After all, my mother caused—"

"Family isna an imposition," Ross said, "and we consider ye our family. Mairi, take them home now."

"Someone send for my hartshorn," the Duchess of Inverary said, fanning herself.

Aunt Bedelia passed her the whisky. "Take a swig."

Surprising everyone, the Duchess of Inverary gulped whisky out of the bottle. And then she took another swig.

The Duke of Inverary put his arm around his friend's shoulder. "Come with me, Jamie," he said, ushering his friend out of the room. "We'll sit in my office and share a drink or two."

"If the candle was Chadwick," Raven asked her aunt, "where did Celeste fit?"

"Ye canna take visions at face value," Bedelia answered. "Ye need to ponder the meaning of the symbols. What's another word for heavenly?"

"Celestial."

Blaze crossed the drawing room to her husband's side. "I'm sorry about your mother and your wife."

Ross put his arms around her, holding her close. He dropped a kiss on the crown of her head. "Ye gave me a fright when I saw that pistol pointed at yer head."

Alexander advanced on Raven. "I want to know the reason you've been cold to me."

"I saw you kissing Amanda Stanley at my sister's wedding," she told him.

"I wasn't kissing Amanda Stanley," Alexander said. "She was kissing me."

"Oops," Blaze whispered to her husband. "He should have apologized and begged for forgiveness."

Raven narrowed her gaze on him. She held her left hand out and pulled the betrothal ring off her finger.

"Don't do this," Alexander warned her. "You'll regret it."

Raven looked from the ring to his face and the ring again. She caught her stepmother's horrified expression.

Then Raven slipped the betrothal ring onto the third finger of her right hand. She lifted her nose into the air and walked out of the drawing room.

"What does that mean?" Alexander followed her out of the room. "Are we betrothed or not?"

Ross smiled. "Yer sister is an expert tormentor."

"Our stepmother schooled us on tormenting men," Blaze told him. "Raven was her star pupil."

"Let's sleep in your bedchamber tonight," Ross suggested, "and we'll take Kyra home in the mornin'."

"Is there any dinner left?" Blaze asked. "My baby wants food."

"Tinker," Ross called. When the majordomo appeared in an instant, he said, "Fetch my wife somethin' to eat. We'll meet ye in the dinin' room."

"What shall I serve you, Lady MacArthur?"

"No meat, no fish, no poultry."

Eleven Months Later

"Here we are," Blaze said. "Clean, fed, awake, and smiling."

Holding her stepdaughter's hand, Blaze led a small parade into the drawing room. Kyra's nannies, Morag and Jean, carried the twins. Dodger followed behind, carrying a tray of refreshment.

"Kyra, you sit here with Papa MacArthur," Blaze said, and the six-year-old climbed on her grandfather's lap.

Blaze lifted one of the twins out of Nanny Morag's arms. "Papa, you hold Baby Colin."

"Jamie, our grandson resembles you more and more each passing day," the Duke of Inverary said. "Look at those black eyes and hair."

"Aunt Bedelia, you hold Baby Bedelia." Blaze lifted the other twin out of Nanny Jean's arms and passed her to her aunt.

"Baby Bedelia inherited your red hair," the Duchess of Inverary said.

"I'm old, Roxie, not blind," Aunt Bedelia said. Then, "Dodger, ye forgot the whisky and Puddles's cookies."

"Come on, wife." Ross walked into the drawing room. "Juno is waitin' to show ye her foal."

Blaze rolled her eyes. "How do you know?"

Ross winked at her. "She told me."

"Colt or filly?"

"A chestnut red colt."

Ross and Blaze left the drawing room and walked downstairs. Leaving the mansion, they headed down the path to the stables and paddocks. The nearest paddock to the stables had Juno and her son, the MacArthur stables' newest addition.

"You have a handsome son," Blaze praised Juno, standing at the fence. The colt veered between wobbly legs, spurts of energy, and the security of leaning against its mother.

"I want ye to name him," Ross said.

"A champion needs a special name that commands respect," Blaze said. "Give me a couple of days to consider it."

Blaze stroked Juno's face and then turned to her husband. "Our company is waiting."

"Family isna company, darlin'." Ross put his arm around her shoulders and steered her away from the paddock. "I'm glad we named the twins Colin and Bedelia."

Me love.

Blaze stopped short. When her husband looked at her, she placed a finger across her lips for silence. Had she imagined those two words?

Me love.

Turning around, Blaze walked back to the paddock. The colt stood at the fence beside his mother. Blaze stared into its eyes.

Love Peg.

Me love.

Blaze laughed, even as tears streamed down her cheeks. *Love Peg.*

Me love.

"What is it, darlin'?"

"Pegasus has returned to me."

"Huh?"

"Pegasus is here." Blaze gestured to the colt. "Juno's son is Pegasus. He told me."

"The twins keepin' ye up at night isna good for mental alertness," Ross said, managing to get her away from the paddock. "Company is waitin' for us."

"Family isn't company," Blaze said, glancing over her shoulder at the colt. "We'll need Bender and Rooney. I wouldn't trust anyone else."

"Jeez, I'm livin' with a madwoman." Ross rolled his eyes. "Horses canna come back from the dead."

"I'd know Peg anywhere," Blaze insisted.

"Even if a horse could come back," Ross said, "Pegasus was female and the colt's male. Females canna be males."

"Jeez, I'm living with a spiritual brick."

Ross yanked her into his arms and kissed her. "I might be a brick, but ye love me as much as I love ye."

"I do love you," Blaze said, "but the colt is Pegasus."

"If ye say so."

"I *do* say so."

Ross put his arms around her shoulders and ushered her down the path toward the mansion. "Did I ever confess aboot lyin' to ye?"

Blaze stopped walking. "You lied to me?"

"I didna save Beau from a beatin'," Ross told her. "I bought the donkey and concocted the fairy tale to impress ye."

"Your rescuing Beau did impress me." She gave him a seductive smile, an invitation in her eyes. "I was more impressed the first time you dropped your breeches."

"The old folks can care for the twins," Ross said.

"Let's sneak up the servants' stairs and hide in our chamber for a while."

"I'm game," Blaze said, and started walking down the path again. "Do you think Baby Pegasus will balk at holes?"

"Men dinna balk, darlin'."

She smiled. "If you say so."

Ross pulled her into his arms, his lips hovering above hers. "I *do* say so."

And then he kissed her.

More by Bestselling Author
Hannah Howell

Romantic Suspense from
Lisa Jackson

See How She Dies	0-8217-7605-3	$6.99US/$9.99CAN
Final Scream	0-8217-7712-2	$7.99US/$10.99CAN
Wishes	0-8217-6309-1	$5.99US/$7.99CAN
Whispers	0-8217-7603-7	$6.99US/$9.99CAN
Twice Kissed	0-8217-6038-6	$5.99US/$7.99CAN
Unspoken	0-8217-6402-0	$6.50US/$8.50CAN
If She Only Knew	0-8217-6708-9	$6.50US/$8.50CAN
Hot Blooded	0-8217-6841-7	$6.99US/$9.99CAN
Cold Blooded	0-8217-6934-0	$6.99US/$9.99CAN
The Night Before	0-8217-6936-7	$6.99US/$9.99CAN
The Morning After	0-8217-7295-3	$6.99US/$9.99CAN
Deep Freeze	0-8217-7296-1	$7.99US/$10.99CAN
Fatal Burn	0-8217-7577-4	$7.99US/$10.99CAN
Shiver	0-8217-7578-2	$7.99US/$10.99CAN
Most Likely to Die	0-8217-7576-6	$7.99US/$10.99CAN
Absolute Fear	0-8217-7936-2	$7.99US/$9.49CAN
Almost Dead	0-8217-7579-0	$7.99US/$10.99CAN
Lost Souls	0-8217-7938-9	$7.99US/$10.99CAN
Left to Die	1-4201-0276-1	$7.99US/$10.99CAN
Wicked Game	1-4201-0338-5	$7.99US/$9.99CAN
Malice	0-8217-7940-0	$7.99US/$9.49CAN

Available Wherever Books Are Sold!
Visit our website at **www.kensingtonbooks.com**

Thrilling Suspense from
Beverly Barton